Marvin James grew up in West Africa and England before emigrating to Canada, British Columbia. He is a professional engineer doing various projects around the world. His hobbies are reading, car collecting, fishing, painting and cooking for friends and family.

Avid reader of James Mitchener and Wilber Smith who inspired me to write about beautiful British Colombia, its natural beauty and fascinating history.

Marvin James

THE BIG FIR

AUSTIN MACAULEY PUBLISHERS™

LONDON • CAMBRIDGE • NEW YORK • SHARJAH

Ordering Information
Quantity sales: Special discounts are available on quantity purchases by corporations, associations, and others. For details, contact the publisher at the address below.

Publisher's Cataloging-in-Publication data
James, Marvin
The Big Fir

ISBN 9798886939644 (Paperback)
ISBN 9798886939651 (ePub e-book)

Library of Congress Control Number: 2023918109

www.austinmacauley.com/us

First Published 2024
Austin Macauley Publishers LLC
40 Wall Street, 33rd Floor, Suite 3302
New York, NY 10005
USA

mail-usa@austinmacauley.com
+1 (646) 5125767

Table of Contents

Chapter One
The Big Fir

In 1066 AD, on a beach in England, a bowman's barbed arrow changed the course of history forevermore. An army of conquerors ran up the beach as King Harold tried to pluck it from his eye.

At the same moment, in a dark forest, over four thousand miles to the west, a similarly important event occurred. A tiny fir cone, no bigger than a robin's egg, fell over four hundred feet to land with a muffled thud on the forest floor. A deer browsing nearby was the only witness. She pricked up her ears and looked around. But, seeing no danger, she continued to graze by the creek's edge.

The lands people, whose ancestors were wanderers from eastern Asia, called this place of serenity *Damelahamid*. In eight hundred years, it would be called British Columbia.

A young man, Wolf Salmon, tensed at the same time the deer did. He met its big, brown eyes through the early-morning mist and waited motionless.

The deer looked away and continued to graze.

Wolf Salmon's supple leather moccasins pushed the fir cone into the soft earth as he silently crept on. The sun shone on the doe's velvety skin, and the mist clung to cobwebs on the damp grass. Wolf Salmon slowly drew a polished arrow of arbutus wood and picked the soft spot behind the doe's shoulder blade. He took a deep breath, held his aim, and then gently released his fingers.

The doe looked over her shoulder when she heard the soft whistle. All she saw was a black speck before she felt the arrow plunge through her flesh and deep into her heart. Her eyes rolled as her legs buckled. She was dead before her head hit the grass.

Wolf Salmon ran lightly over the forest clearing and bent down at the doe's side. He was pleased. His aim had been perfect. He withdrew the bone-tipped arrow, which steamed lightly in the morning's chill. He touched the bloodied tip, and thanked his Creator for his good fortune today.

He grunted at the strain of carrying the doe across his shoulders: one hand clasping its feet around his neck, the other holding his bow and arrows. He placed the deer in his cedar dugout canoe and pushed off into the rippling current.

The creek carried him swiftly back down the way he had come, past the glade where he had shot the deer. He ducked under the sweeping bough of a huge, moss-laden red cedar, its sweet aroma filling the morning air. Wolf Salmon paddled down the large creek and turned into the main current of the Stikeen River, which was broad and deep at this point. Just downstream lay his village. They would eat well tonight.

Behind him, reaching over four hundred feet into the sky, rose a magnificent Douglas fir. The soil's minerals and its hungry quest for sunlight had allowed it to reach mammoth proportions. None on earth surpassed its grandeur and stature.

The tiny seeds of the Douglas fir, *Pseudotsuga menziesii*, were each less than a quarter of the size of a newborn baby's thumbnail, nestled as they were in the cone that had dropped. But each had the potential to increase in volume by at least twenty million times.

Long summer days dragged out a small, white tendril of life from one of the seeds, which quickly burrowed into the soft earth. Birds and small animals had already eaten some seeds. Others had cracked open in the hot sun to dry out, die, and be blown away by morning breezes.

By summer's end, a tiny green tip pushed up through the earth. The first light snowfall cocooned it in a cold grip. Soon it was buried under three feet of snow, and there it lay all winter.

The next spring and summer saw much growth. The young fir grew to over six inches, with small, even branches covered in minute needles, just like a baby's soft down. A shaft of strong sunlight fed it most of the day. Its giant parent had lost a large limb in the last storm, which now let the life-giving light reach the forest floor.

One afternoon in the late fall, a black tail deer and its fawn came down to the glade to feed on the succulent grass at the creek's edge. A thin covering of snow lay all around. The baby fir poked out, frozen in a shaft of sunlight, its lime-green foliage juicy and tender.

The deer ate constantly now that fall had arrived, and their muscles were coated with a fine layer of fat. The mother looked over and snorted eagerly when she spied the grass poking out of the snow. She gently nuzzled her baby forward to tread with high, little steps up the gentle, snow-covered slope. Her large eyes continually probed left and right, and remained alert for the sound of a stealthy cougar or pack of wolves.

She snuffled a small sound of encouragement to her fawn, which had now also seen the green delicacies. The fawn buried his glistening nose into the fresh snow and sheared some grass stems off with his sharp front incisors.

The mother, now sure of safety for the present, also began to nip at the fine tips showing. From the corner of her eye, she saw the fir and its promise of a good mouthful beneath the snow.

With a furtive glance, over her shoulder to the fawn, she slowly tiptoed to the baby fir. She craned her head forward and her finely-haired lips curled back to expose her chiseled teeth.

As her front lip tickled the delicate fir, a soft, muffled 'whoosh' filled the air. Her head shot up, eyes darting to pinpoint the sound. Her whole world went crazy white as thick snow cascaded around her.

A breeze had stirred the valley just before she had bent down, breaking the fine equilibrium of a snow-laden branch high above her head.

The deer hopped sideways, her back arched, eyes wide in shock. She shook the wet, clinging snow from her body in jerky movements.

After the initial shock was over, she calmed down and reassured her fawn with a lick to his flank. The fawn resumed foraging and the mother turned back to finish her rudely-interrupted delicacy.

Where the succulent shoot had been was now just another white, featureless, blanket of snow. She pawed the snow around the mound, but soon lost interest when nothing else was to be found.

Slowly, the deer and fawn wandered deeper into the semi-gloom of the forest, until they were like shadows lost in the half-light.

The baby fir was now enveloped in a soft case of fluffy snow. Luckily the doe's body had protected it from the deadly impact of the snow. Such an impact could have snapped off its delicate tip, leaving a sore wound that would be open to the cold without enough sunlight left to repair it before the harsh winter set in.

Millions of other seedlings of fir, spruce, balsam, and cedar had already succumbed to the valley's healthy population of deer. Only a tiny fraction had survived the summer. They now lay safely buried from hungry eyes in the cold, but insulating, embrace of snow, which would not melt until next spring.

Over the next ten years, the fir survived other close calls. Now it stood over six feet tall, with a sturdy, wrinkled skin of bark to protect it from the elements and beasts of the forest.

Its parent, the old Douglas fir, had begun to lose more of its higher branches. The fiber of her being had become too weak to hold the tons of snow that yearly assaulted its lofty heights. In addition, a few fierce windstorms had broken some of its limbs, which snapped with age instead of giving and swaying to the relentless gusts.

In 1096 AD, the first crusaders stood at the walls of Constantinople. The fir stood a mighty thirty feet at this time, thirty years old itself.

The summer was an unusually hot one, and a grizzly stood panting by the creek's edge. Fishing had been good, and a dozen half-eaten carcasses of sockeye salmon lay at his feet. This was his favorite fishing spot; by standing in the shallows, he could chase and scoop out the salmon with his huge paws.

He abruptly stopped in his efforts. The faint breeze wafted an unfamiliar scent across his nose. He stood erect, trying to see the other grizzly he smelled. He dropped to four paws and followed the scent into the woods.

At the base of the young fir, he smelled the powerful odor of urine: another bear's urine. He rubbed his fur against the tree and it trembled from his massive bulk. Then he sprayed his own marking scent against the young tree.

He rose to his ten-foot height and put his paws against the trunk. His curved claws dug into the bark. The grizzly bunched his shoulders and raked downward, tearing the bark down to its inner wood. The young fir trembled to its roots, and it bent under the grizzly's thousand-pound weight. Its roots started to give under the strain as the grizzly dug deeper.

Just then there was a roar behind him, and the intruding grizzly charged. Both met head-on, claw matching claw in a desperate battle.

The fight lasted over fifteen minutes. The two grizzlies were very evenly matched in size. The interloper, however, was quite a bit younger, and the older grizzly began to tire. Blood streaked his sides. The older grizzly backed down and fled. The valley had a new king to rule it.

Over the next hundred years, the Crusades continued and the fir grew quickly. The only sign of the grizzly encounter were deep scars in its thickening bark.

As the years passed, the old, parent fir began to show signs of its increasing age. In the fork of one of its higher branches, a pair of bald eagles had made their aerie. The aerie had grown to over twelve feet across and weighed over three tons. From their lofty perch, the eagles feasted well on the salmon that returned to the creek by the millions year after year. The salmons' myriad bones lay intertwined in the branches.

In the early 1200s, Genghis Khan swept the plains of Asia and crossed the snow-laden passes into China. In the same winter, the valley had a particularly heavy snowfall; five feet lay balanced on the aerie.

The weather warmed slightly, and the heavy snow turned to freezing rain, adding more tons. It was too much stress for the brittle branches. That night, the wind blew and the aerie swayed like a pendulum, until the fatigued fibers reached their tired limit. The whole aerie came crashing down to the forest floor, stripping more branches off the old fir on its way down.

The old fir had now lost most of its sun-catching needles, and was looking tired and tattered. For a full fifty feet at its base, the core was a pulpy sponge of decayed wood, slowly being eaten away by the countless bacterial spores and fungi.

In Europe, a continent and the Atlantic away, it was the days of The Papal Inquisition. In 1231 AD, heretics were tortured and burned at the stake. The teenaged fir was now one hundred and eighty-five years old. It had a diameter of four feet and towered over one hundred and fifty feet into the blue sky. It had outpaced the slower-growing cedars around it, and now only a few of the older giants stood above it. Still, enough sunshine shone through the broken branches of its parent to give it continued growth.

The grand old fir was in its last throes of life. Only a few tattered branches supported its pitifully small numbers of sun-catching needles.

The afternoon was hot and oppressive, and thick nimbus clouds gathered in the turbulent sky. A few drops of rain fell and the sky rumbled to the sound of thunder.

Suddenly, a white flash lit the sky and hit the old fir on its upper tip. Twenty million volts ignited the top. A hundred feet down, a fork in the trunk cracked and burned, until it overbalanced and tumbled down to earth. The old wood exploded into fragments. The rain put out the still-smoldering wood.

Some of the grand old fir's brothers and sisters had already succumbed to old age. These lay scattered around the small grove. Their moss-covered trunks slowly gave back their goodness to the soil.

Some of them were nursery logs, supporting cedars and firs whose young roots encircled their fallen trunks, reaching for the forest floor. The years brought further decay, and the young trees grew steadily. Eventually, all that would remain would be a large hole at the base of a sprawling trunk, looking for all the world as though a giant mole had passed that way.

When the young adult fir, passed its four hundred and twenty-sixth birthday, far away across the continent a ship called *La Santa María* discovered the Americas, its commander a man called Columbus. It marked the first touch of great change.

The four hundred-year-old fir now surpassed its parent's broken top. However, the life-giving creek began to pose a serious threat. In the last few years, the creek had moved nearer the grove because of heavy rainfall and had started to undercut the bank. Up to this point, its passage had been turned aside by the presence of some large boulders, but even these were now being slowly loosened by the loss of supporting pebbles.

After six continuous days of torrential rain, the creek was now a raging torrent. Fine silt and clay had colored the waters to a dark brown. Standing waves six feet in height boiled over large submerged boulders. The valley roared as smaller boulders were swept up into the current and sent crashing into the banks. Shattered trunks and whole, uprooted trees were swirled and tossed around like matchsticks on the creek's headlong path down the valley. In some places, the creek had broken its banks and cut across corners, tearing up everything in its path.

The rain stopped but the creek still rose. The valley had not yet given up all of its waters. A large root ball of black spruce sideswiped the bank that supported the old fir. The overhang broke off with the impact, to be swallowed by the creek. Even some large boulders were ripped loose, exposing unprotected loose gravel and earth. The creek seemed determined to go straight ahead instead of veering to the left around the grove. It was winning and the bank began to crumble at an alarming rate.

The roots of the old fir now lay exposed to the icy waters. Behind it, its progeny felt the tremor of the scouring creek in its own roots.

The creek now engulfed the old fir's large, knotty roots and soon most lay exposed and vulnerable. Some of the weaker ones were torn off and swept away by the current. Imperceptibly, the grand old fir began to tremble and lean toward the creek. Its timbers creaked in stress as its angle increased.

In the next rainy season, another attack by the creek scoured between its roots. Not fifteen feet away, the young fir trembled and shuddered.

From the grand fir's topmost reaches, a coal-black raven flapped in alarm. With a lurch, the tree beneath it began to topple. The fir's vast, three-hundred-ton bulk accelerated, and the whip action of its fall broke its back.

Its fifteen-foot diameter trunk hit the water with a roar, scattering a couple of grumbling black bears just downstream. A wall of water twelve feet tall careened across the swollen creek and crashed into the far bank. The wave broke a large portion of the far bank down and the creek attacked it immediately.

The very fast current swung the huge trunk around until it thundered into the bank. Its remaining roots bore the full force of the creek now, but one very large root still burrowed into the bank, entwined in a twisted embrace with its progeny's nearby roots.

The young fir trembled and a shower of pine needles fell to the ground. Its guts were being stretched to their breaking point.

The creek crested to its full height. Round the bend a tangled web of young cedars that had been ripped from their banks came swirling downstream. They bore across the bend and speared into the roots of the old fir. Some broke off under the tremendous water pressure, but a large mass stayed firmly stuck. The old fir's body protected the bank downstream from further undercutting, and the weakened bank on the far side took on the increase in pressure.

The balance swung as the creek found a weaker opening, and slowly its force shifted in that direction. More floating debris entangled in the roots, and a small log jam began to form. The creek's pressure helped to pack and squeeze, adding more material to the growing obstruction. The creek receded from the young fir.

More trees became entangled, and the spiked growth of entwined debris piled higher and ever deeper. The old fallen fir, born at the birth of Christ, was entombed in wood.

The young fir's trembling finally ceased. Now over five hundred years old, it had lost the feel of its parent's decayed root. It rose majestically to over three hundred feet. Four men could not clasp hands in a final link around its trunk.

It was the sixteenth century, and Ivan the Terrible of Russia reigned supreme. His land trembled at his cruelty. Europe was in a state of flux as it came out of the Middle Ages, and its exploring ships started to sail the seven seas. From that time, Europeans flooded the country. The North American continent would never be the same.

***

Wolf Salmon, like his father and the fathers that bore his name before him, came to the valley often. This part of the Stikeen Valley had been handed down to his house clan since time began, and only he and his clan could hunt here. Today, he brought his new bride, Wind Walker, to visit his family's domain.

At the creek bend, he helped her from the canoe onto the warm, soft, silty sand, which sparkled with the fine flakes of mica that were common in the valley. They walked toward the grove of giant firs.

Wolf Salmon waded toward where a fir had fallen and left a big hole from its roots. He peered down the hole. "Aye! Look, Wind Walker. The mother of all trees lies buried here."

Wind Walker came over to look and peered into the dark hole. Not four feet below lay the trunk of the grand old fir.

"Look, the canoe would not fit across its middle, and still it disappears in the earth. It truly must have been the mother of all trees," Wolf Salmon said.

He could see the line of the tree and followed it with his eyes. At the far end, he saw a large root ball at the base of the Big Fir, the tallest tree in the grove.

Only recently had the connection between parent and child been severed. The old fir had acted as one huge nursery log for many years, and the Big Fir drank in the decayed nutrients of one of the last untouched giants of its time.

After exploring around for a while more, the two young lovers went back to the creek. The sun was hot and both looked at each other somewhat shyly.

Wolf Salmon led the way into the rippling creek. It was icy cold, but refreshing after their long paddle upstream.

"Come on, my wife," he taunted Wind Walker. "The water is nice."

She gingerly entered the shallows and shrieked as he splashed her with the icy water.

"I'm sorry. I won't do it again," he promised as she retreated.

She slowly entered until her knees were covered. She only came up to Wolf Salmon's chest. His fine-muscled body shone with a bronze color in the sun.

"You know, Wind Walker?" he said. "You are Mother Nature's finest creation."

Wind Walker blushed and splashed him to hide her embarrassment.

He shrieked aloud and splashed back.

A couple of minutes later both were soaked to the skin and breathless. Wind Walker's soft doe-skin tunic had slipped off one shoulder, and Wolf Salmon feasted his eyes on her firm breast. Her nipple poked out tight and hard. He reached out to her as he felt his heat rise.

She blushed again when she saw his member push the front flap of his tunic aside to meet the afternoon air. They held each other lightly, and his hardness pressed against her flat belly. He brushed her long, fine, black hair aside, and they kissed long and hard in the warm sun.

Wolf Salmon tore his lips away, bent down, and lifted her effortlessly in his arms. They kept kissing as he crossed the sand to a grassy knoll growing atop the grand old submerged fir.

They knelt down while still holding each other, and he slipped her tunic over her head. He stared into her big brown eyes as he traced a line from one firm nipple to the other.

Wind Walker reached down and gripped his now very hard, erect member. He shuddered a little as she stroked him gently. His fingers probed for her softness, and she parted her thighs for him. He watched in delight as his hand brushed her fine pubic hair.

She lifted one knee up, and he sank in her wet softness. She arched her back as his probing went deeper. He leaned forward and gently nipped at her nipple. She watched an eagle soaring in the invisible airs above them as her first gentle wave of orgasm rose.

Wind Walker reluctantly freed herself, then lay down on her back, opening her legs to him. Wolf Salmon dropped his tunic and came to her. The tip of his swollen member gently opened her lips.

Wind Walker yelled out, "Now, my husband, now; deeper please," at which he drove in his full length. She grabbed his back and raked it slightly, making him arch his back further.

Both moaned and nuzzled each other. She felt him grow and pulse. With a final deep drive, he impaled himself in her, releasing a million Wolf Salmons in her depths.

They lay still for a while. Wolf Salmon loved the warm sun on his back. He never lost his hardness as Wind Walker squirmed and rubbed against him. This time they played long and slow in their lovemaking.

The eagle soaring above caught a wave of air and spiraled higher, looking down at the couple by the big trees.

Reluctantly they left in the late afternoon. After bathing once more in the creek, they paddled downstream back to their village. It was one of those long summer days when dusk lasted late into the early morning of the next day.

An older couple taking a stroll by the river welcomed them at their village. Waves of hunger swept both of them as they smelled the faint aroma of boiled salmon from the communal cooking fires.

Some of the older women poked fun at the young couple; only Wolf Salmon was close enough to Wind Walker to see her deep blush in the near-darkness.

Wolf Salmon slapped Golden Eagle hard on the back. "You were right, my friend: marriage is good, and soon I will fill the valley with sons who can play with yours."

"Hey, I have proved that I shoot live salmon: you haven't yet, so u go away with your idle threats." Golden Eagle laughed hard and long.

Wolf Salmon took a huge draft of tepid salmon egg oil and smeared the back of his hand over his full lips. One of his aunts passed him a whole sockeye salmon on a cedar platter and he tore into it hungrily.

Wind Walker brought him a bowl of bubbling salmon eggs. They were delicious; some dribbled down his chin in his eagerness. As he scooped another handful up, Wind Walker licked one off his chin.

Golden Eagle laughed. "Wolf Salmon. You may be right in filling this valley quicker than you think."

Life was good in the valley. There had not been a raid or skirmish with another people for years, although tonight they planned for one on the following moon. A lot of young men were desperate to prove themselves in battle, and they could not be restrained any longer.

Wolf Salmon and Golden Eagle, being the two most battle-seasoned warriors, would each lead a party of forty men on a sweep around the inlet to the next valley, the Kildala. On the valley peninsula lay, the village of the Kildala people; since time began, the two tribes had raided each other, usually every five years or so. When they got really lucky, in addition to valuables a few captives would be taken to be kept as slaves.

Wolf Salmon called his own such slave over and told him to bring another salmon and some more roe. His belly was slightly distended, but he still had more room. At an important feast, such as this, the tribe would eat and drink but sleep little for three days in an orgy of excess.

After two more fish, some whale oil, and eggs, Wolf Salmon vomited. He swilled his mouth out with water and went back for more, but at a slower pace. The raccoons and the occasional bear took advantage of the feast and scavenged the woods for the remains of half-digested fish and oily roe.

Now that Wolf Salmon had a wife, and thus more responsibilities, he decided he would try to get two female slaves on the raid to help out with the chores. His present male slave, Wolverine, was lazy and quite often had to be beaten to be reminded of his duties. Wolf Salmon also decided to make himself some new weapons for the raid. There was a good store of sharp ribs for hatchets and arrowheads, left over from the last whale the people had killed.

In the morning, only a few hungry babies broke the stillness. A thin wisp of smoke curled up into the clear sky. Most had slept where they had fallen, but Wind Walker and Wolf Salmon lay under their beaver blanket in his family's longhouse.

His father was still chief, and they had a splendid longhouse made of cedar logs and split planks nearly fifty feet long. Eight families of aunts, uncles, nephews, and grandparents shared the warm, dry dwelling.

Just offset from the building, facing west, was a hundred-foot totem pole of the Wolf Salmon clan. It was carved from a single cedar log and colored lightly with a dozen hues of various berry extracts. The highly-stylized carvings showed semblances of a wolf and a salmon.

Wolf Salmon had the only piece of iron in the village, which he had found on one of the windswept islands beyond their inlet. It had come from a lost Japanese fishing junk that had been blown off-course. He had made a very crude knifelike from it. It was far longer lasting than the half-moon shaped ones they made from large flakes of flint.

Over the next week the men made their preparations. Wolf Salmon and Golden Eagle grilled their respective warriors nearly to the point of exhaustion. Many of the younger ones had never been in battle before and started to strut around in front of the unmarried women in their fighting regalia.

The women repainted the two huge war canoes. Each was made from a single cedar log by burning the wood out. Wolf Salmon's looked splendid in its white and red colors.

The night before the raid, the village's medicine man made incantations in a secret ceremony to help guard all the men against evil spirits. They fired them up with tales of great raids and battles.

Not many slept that night, and early the next morning the whole village saw them off with great ceremony. Some, though, looked upon the event with sadness, as some warriors may never return.

The chief gave his son, Wolf Salmon, a new fighting knife and an otter pelt of the finest quality. There were tears of pride in his eyes as the two great war canoes, each with forty men, swung into the current and headed downstream.

Their first challenge was negotiating the canyon rapids, but the river was low and the paddlers strong and skilled. In the later morning, they left the coolness of the canyon and swept into the wide estuary. The air filled with their whoops of youth and fervor for battle.

By day's end, they had covered the long fifty miles to the entrance of their inlet, Eagle Channel. The blue sea before them was calm, and under a starlit sky they made their war plans. They would stop short of the enemy village tomorrow to swoop down at first light.

The next mid-morning, they entered the wide inlet leading to the Kildala river valley. They kept close to the dense cedars lining the shore. No talk was allowed.

A smaller river flowed in from the south, the Kwinimass, which was home to the great grizzly. Here, at the confluence of the river and inlet, they would hide their canoes from prying eyes.

By nightfall, they made their camp behind a small hill on the south side of the village. No fires were kept; they ate dried salmon and fetid roe stored in the bladders of deer. The plan was for one party to attack from the south and the other from the east in a pincer movement. They would do their damage and steal the villagers' canoes in order to quickly return to their own hidden in the inlet. If the raid was successful, the additional canoes would be needed to carry the slaves and booty they hoped to acquire.

Wolf Salmon woke his men before first light, and each man quickly gathered his weapons of war: great gnarled clubs, bows, arrows, and short stabbing spears. Each man now felt nervous; they hoped their attack would be a complete surprise. If they were lucky, they may take the whole village before the defenders could regroup and repel them.

The two parties split up in the dark, each one like a sinuous snake, creeping through the forest's dense undergrowth. They lay deathly still just outside the village, waiting for the first rays of dawn to come.

Wolf Salmon's ears pricked up as the brush moved to his left. They had hidden next to the villager's toilet area, empty at this time of morning.

Wolf Salmon drew his eight-inch long knife, and crept silently forward until he saw the outline of a woman squatting in the bushes. He smelled the acrid, sweet smell of urine. She finished, yawned, and, still half asleep, went back to the village.

He watched the first orange glow of dawn through the trees. When it turned yellow, he whistled the call of a bald eagle twice. Each man rose to his feet, following him toward the sleeping village.

Wolf Salmon's mouth was dry and his heart pounded as he led his men toward the southernmost longhouses. Around the corner of the first house he broke into a jog, and nearly ran headlong into a young man.

Before the man could react, he lay on the ground with a slashed throat. His life's blood sprayed the legs of the following warriors as they ran past.

Wolf Salmon swung open the doors of the longhouse and stormed in with a blood-curdling yell. In the dim light, he lunged at the nearest sleeping figure and found yielding flesh and terrified eyes.

All hell broke loose as twenty warriors hacked, stabbed, and bludgeoned the longhouse's occupants, including women and children. They had attacked four longhouses simultaneously, but that left four more, from which half-asleep warriors were already swarming out into the early morning.

A few of the village warriors were starting to form a defense. Hand-to-hand fighting started. Wolf Salmon saw a big warrior fell some of his men, and he charged into the fray.

He came with his bludgeoning club held high, but the other warrior met his eye, and Wolf Salmon missed on his first blow. He felt the sting of his opponent's stabbing spear.

Wolf Salmon twirled around and struck to his left. His blow was deflected by his challenger's spear, and he felt the sting of another cut. The man was good, so he slowed his savage attack to take stock.

The man was very big, and grinned when he saw the fresh blood on Wolf Salmon's arm. When Wolf Salmon feigned pain and made as if to swap hands with his club, the warrior sensed weakness and attacked.

At the last instant, Wolf Salmon kept his original grip and swung with a backhanded swipe. The vicious club split open the warrior's cheek; the white of his teeth protruded momentarily before being lost in a welter of bright blood.

Still, he stood up and they circled each other, just like the many other combatants around them.

Wolf Salmon drew his knife for a two-pronged attack. He swung the club, forcing his adversary to raise his arm to protect himself. Wolf Salmon's arm jarred in its socket as the heavy bone shaft broke over his opponent's arm.

At the same time, he swept up with his knife and felt it sink into the warrior's lower abdomen. The man's eyes flew open at the pain.

Wolf Salmon flicked his wrist and pulled up hard. The sharp whale bone knife easily cut through muscle and sinew. The man's intestines spilled onto the ground, steaming in the cold morning air. Wolf Salmon slashed his throat, and the warrior sank to the ground, seconds from death.

The tide of the skirmish turned, and small knots of the defenders fled for the safety of the nearby woods. It was very dangerous to chase them in the dense forest, so Wolf Salmon's warriors let them run. They whooped in joy at their victory and rounded up some stragglers to take as captives. The wounded and dying all had their throats cut; the village compound ran red with rivulets of blood.

Time was precious, so Wolf Salmon directed his men to the beach before the village could direct a concerted counterattack. On the way, a few warriors were dispatched to ransack the longhouses for valuable furs and weapons before they, too, retreated to the beach.

A few of the villagers' canoes were quickly loaded with the booty, while a few warriors smashed the remainder. They had been lucky; only two of their own men were left behind with the dead. The others had only sustained minor injuries, later to be showed off back at the village. Better yet, they had captured over twenty slaves of both sexes and various ages.

They paddled away in four large canoes taken from the village. A few arrows splashed the water around them harmlessly.

The warriors soon relaxed when they realized that pursuit was impossible. They sang their tribe's victory song to the swish and dip of their paddles. Their poor captives mostly cried as they realized their dire future: at best hard work; at worst, beatings or indescribable tortures.

The successful warriors pulled their canoes through the rapids by ropes of cedar bark. The whole village was on hand to help; it was a joyous occasion.

Wolf Salmon hugged Wind Walker nearly breathless. Her eyes rolled when she saw his wounded forearm. He brushed her administrations off, but in a quiet moment, when no other warriors were around, he let her bathe and bandage the wound in fresh leaves and soft doeskin.

The twenty captives were bound up and then paraded around the village. The chief had the first pick, followed by the more senior leaders and their warriors. Wolf Salmon picked a beautiful young maiden just past puberty, with which Wind Walker was none too keen about. Then he picked a middle-aged fellow for the manual chores.

Twenty young warriors could now choose wives, and tonight their favors were highly sought after. Before long, sounds of pleasure could be heard from the nearby woods.

Two of the slightly wounded captives, a man and a woman, were separated from the rest and given to the old women of the tribe, who were instructed in the fine art of torture. The tribe had lost two of its members, and a punishment had to be extracted. It would serve as a deterrent to other nearby tribes who considered challenging their might.

The prisoners were taken to a knoll behind the village. The stoic tolerance of pain was expected, so it wasn't unusual that it took a whole day for them to give in to screams. The male's penis was skinned and his testicles ripped out. Next, one tooth was removed at a time. The flesh on his legs was rubbed away bit by bit with coarse sand, which mingled with his raw flesh until he fainted in pain.

The poor girl fared no better. Her nipples were torn off by two huge Dungeness crabs, themselves taunted to distraction. Between her legs, dried blood caked her inner thighs as her insides were stuffed with earwigs and biting ants.

Each time one of the captives cried in agony, the village let out a collective groan of glee and some sorrow. Wind Walker shut her ears to it and was morose the whole week. Even Wolf Salmon turned away, sick at the sight of the two, and offered to kill them quickly. He was shooed away by the old crones.

The whole village admired the captives for their bravery and after seven days threw them, or what was left of them, into the river to be swept downstream and battered by the rapids.

A large potlatch took place, and the entire village helped in its preparation. Wolf Salmon gave many furs away; if it had not been for Wind Walker, the man slave would have been given away as well. The more prosperous and powerful a family became, the more presents were given away, and his place in the village hierarchy rose. In return, his family received many favors; it was a good balance and distributed the total wealth.

Their society was a highly-stratified system based on chiefs, nobles, workers, and slaves. Only chiefs and their family nobles held the best fishing, hunting, and berry sites; they controlled the whole village's wealth with a firm grip. Only if they died in battle or produced no daughters did the rights get passed to another family. Although the men held all the titles, the bloodlines passed through the women.

At the potlatch, which lasted for three days, the storytellers told of the tribe's beginnings. It was their belief that a man emerged from a clamshell on the beach, and after twenty moons the Great Spirit felt sorry for the man and gave him woman to keep him company and have children. All the animals had revered places in their religion, and one was never killed without the animal's spirit being blessed with the proper ceremonies.

Village life resumed its normal course, and the years passed on slowly with hardly any change. Wolf Salmon became chief and the line was passed on down to his children. Another two hundred years of life, birth, death, raids, fishing, and berry-picking passed in its normal course.

***

In 1778, four hundred miles to the south and west, on Vancouver Island's rugged west coast, a group of Nootka people were out halibut fishing. It was a misty, hazy day, with only a slight ripple on the sea. Two twenty-pound halibuts lay in the bottom of the canoe.

One of the fishermen heard an eerie sound out on the water.

"By the fore, sand she is and ten fathoms."

"Listen," the fisherman said, and again very faintly heard the sounds repeated. The men all looked at each other and pulled in their fishing lines.

One peered toward the sound. Through the mist he saw a darker mass in the distance.

"Look, Tayelic. Do you see anything?" He pointed into the mist.

All looked. A bulbous, whale-like shape with a long, pointed nose parted the mist. Trees grew from its high back where huge white cloths hung, flapping in the breeze. Threads festooned the trees, and skulls stared at them with their empty sockets.

"Aye," they all cried as the apparition approached. They threw their fishing lines inboard and paddled quickly for shore. Their bodies glistened with sweat as they ran up the pebbly beach back at the village.

"There is a supernatural being coming with men's skulls hanging in huge trees growing from its back." The man sucked in a breath before he carried on. "It also talks in a strange tongue. I think it is heading toward the inlet, so let us arm ourselves in preparation for the spirit."

The whole village went down to the beach to see what the commotion was. The chief, called Maquinna, listened with interest, and he immediately summoned ten war canoes to be manned.

In the afternoon, they set off down the inlet and out of the cove. The early morning mists had burned off, and the sun shone brightly as they rounded the cove's point.

"Listen to the sound it makes, and look at all the white ghosts swarming on its back. Quick, my chief, let us turn back while we can."

"Oh, keep quiet." Maquinna replied. "This is no spirit, but a white man's ship. I have been told about them by the tribes down the coast."

The war canoe approached with the others close behind it. All the men, as was their nature, were now very curious, but were also wary of the ship lying in the bay. Maquinna picked up his war club and many followed suit. Now only twenty yards separated them from the ship.

A pale-skinned man stood at the edge of the ship, holding some items high over his head. He threw them out at the lead canoe. The red-cloaked warrior in the front urged his canoe forward to the items and picked them up. He passed them to Maquinna, who inspected the fine cloth of two blankets and an otter skin.

He thought for a moment. He nodded for his paddlers to continue, which they did at a very slow pace. The war canoe glided to a stop and rubbed against the wooden ship's sides. Maquinna climbed the net to the waiting friendly faces. His heart beat in a staccato rhythm. He was not sure he was at all wise, but he could not lose face in front of his warriors.

He nimbly stepped aboard and said in a booming voice, "I am Chief Maquinna, chief of all the Nootka people, valley, rivers, and creeks. Welcome to my land." He smiled his best smile.

The smile was the universal language.

The man who had thrown the blankets stepped forward and said, "Welcome aboard His Majesty's ship, *Discovery*. I am Captain Cook. Cook," he said again as he pointed to his chest.

Maquinna, although he did not understand the words, understood the gesture and did the same to himself. "Maquinna, Maquinna."

For the first time in history, Europeans had contact with the native people of British Columbia, but unfortunately it would have dire consequences for the natives with relatively little long-term gain.

***

In the late 1790s, the new Wolf Salmon led the shaman above Emerald Creek to the berry patches along its steep slopes. In the valley, far below the Big Fir grew loftier. Little did Wolf Salmon know that one of his ancestors had pressed the tiny fir cone into the soft earth seven hundred and thirty years before. A bald eagle, resplendent in its white head, looked up with its luminous yellow eyes at the humans high on the grassy slopes and took off to investigate.

The shaman held a gleaming sockeye salmon up to the heavens and offered it to the berry patch's supernatural being in thanks. The villagers chanted a rhythmic greeting of thanks for its bounty. Soon all spread out to pick the succulent wild salmonberries. They looked very similar to gobs of salmon roe, including the same orange glow.

Higher up the valley, an emerald-colored lake shimmered in the summer sun. The peaks of the mountains still had traces of snow hidden in the gullies and clefts, and a few mountain goats traversed their craggy slopes. A snoozing cougar, over eight feet long, waved its sinewy tail in pleasure on a high, rocky ledge overlooking his tree-cloaked domain.

All was peaceful in the valley. Time had been good to them, and the wealth of the village was unsurpassed, its people many and healthy. The salmon had returned in their millions, and the berry patches had produced well.

Wolf Salmon had heard of strange white men the last time he had come to trade with the interior peoples and he was very curious. He'd heard that they traded fabulous goods for furs. So, Wolf Salmon took some pelts with him and set off with ten strong warriors over the mountain pass to the next village. Here he met his first white man. He was short, but very stocky, and had a most strange name which Wolf Salmon had difficulty with: John Dickenson.

Dickenson, a North West Company man, had come overland on a grueling, three-month trip over the high mountains from Alberta. Through sign language, he expressed his wish for Wolf Salmon to take him over the pass to see the sea.

Wolf Salmon was at first reluctant, but when offered a stunning metal knife, he quickly agreed. They set off the next morning back to his village over Raven Pass.

Dickenson virtually ran up the pass, so eager was he to see the distant Pacific. At the summit, he saw a long winding valley, which disappeared between ragged, snow-clad peaks. In the hazy distance, he could spot a winding fjord.

Two days later, they passed the valley of the Big Fir. Dickenson pointed out the towering trees and Wolf Salmon smiled.

He pointed to his chest and said, "It is all mine: good fishing, hunting, and big trees." He used a crude sign language to help express himself.

Dickenson took note and thought of the wooden ships of England and all those fine ships needing tall, straight masts. It would go in his next report.

The whole village, except for a few who peered from within their longhouses, greeted the stocky stranger. Dickenson even ate a few raw salmon eggs, but he nearly choked on their incredibly strong odor and mushy texture. Bravely, he swallowed.

Dickenson pointed out the fine furs and soon was buried in them; each family brought out their best to show off. He couldn't believe his eyes. Hundreds of fine sea otter pelts of various sizes were strewn across the floor of Wolf Salmon's longhouse. Dickenson soon ran out of the few beads he had left, which the villagers seemed very eager to get. Soon he had a dozen fine furs to take back with him.

The next morning Wolf Salmon promised to take Dickenson to the sea. On the way down, they stopped to fish at the rapids.

Just before the rapids, the main Stikeen River fanned out in a broad tail. At the mouth of the deep gorge, a large boulder broke its course. The fishing ledges were on the north side of the narrowest portion of the river. The prime ledge, of course, belonged to Wolf Salmon, and this is where he took Dickenson.

The water was eight feet deep and its surface like clear glass. As Dickenson looked down into the depths, he spied long, dark shadows powering upstream on their migratory journey to the spawning grounds.

Many other people were on ledges up and downstream, with their spears raised ready to strike. The harpoons were about six feet long and tipped with sharp antler that pointed up and in.

Wolf Salmon's body was tense, every muscle sharply defined as he waited. One, two, three fish passed and still he hung poised; they were not the ones he was looking for. Slightly downstream he saw a bigger shadow emerge from the greenish depths.

The four-foot long Chinook had fed well on its way down from Alaska. Herring, shrimp, and prawn had filled her flanks thick with fat, and her stomach bulged tight with creamy roe. She arched her foot-deep tail and surged forward. Suddenly, she felt a sharp pain on her back, forcing her downward, and her instincts made her shoot forward with tremendous power and speed.

Aided by the forward momentum of the fish, Wolf Salmon leaned down, grasped the spear like a hay rake, and with every muscle in his powerful body surged up and around. The shining silver salmon cleared the water and gracefully flew in an arc to land with a thud on the rock ledge behind him.

"Yahee, Tanakee," Wolf Salmon screamed as he leaped on the struggling salmon. With a polished fist-sized rock, he hit her once between the eyes. Her tail flicked and every scale shivered; she lay stone dead, her eyes glazing over to black spots. The salmon, a big one for her species, weighed around half that of a man and could feed a whole clan at one sitting.

Wolf Salmon slit her belly cleanly and pulled out a six-inch thick skein of orange roe. Blood still dripped from it as he thrust it toward Dickenson, who humbly declined. Eggs ran down Wolf Salmon's chin as he eagerly gulped a large mouthful of the sticky roe.

Dickenson pointed to the spear, expressing his wish to have a go. Wolf Salmon smiled and removed the forks of the spear from the salmon's back.

Dickenson stood on the ledge, but missed on his first three attempts. He grew frustrated as the salmon swam upstream just to the side or below his thrusting spear. Wolf Salmon came to give advice and laughed at Dickenson's attempts.

Another very large shadow came into view, and Dickenson struck hard. The spear was torn from his grasp before he could even start to swing. The thin leather wrist thong broke and drew blood.

Wolf Salmon nearly fell down laughing; in fact, several others did as they saw Dickenson hobbling upstream over the rocks after the quickly-disappearing tip of the spear. At the tail-out, he caught up with it and leaped into the three feet of cold water. He grabbed the spear and hung on for dear life as it writhed in his hands. Even with his strong grasp it headed upstream, and he stumbled after it getting soaked in the process.

Wolf Salmon joined him and both held on tight. Wolf Salmon felt the power beneath them and realized that this was no salmon.

The 'fish'" broke surface. The whiskered head left the water, its flashing teeth bared. The seal lunged at its attackers and both fell backward. Wolf Salmon grabbed its tail flippers while Dickenson bravely jumped on it in a bear hug.

Slowly they stumbled and fell toward shore, where more help arrived. Two hundred pounds of very angry seal thrashed on the rocks. It hung onto the arm of one man, who let out a howl of pain.

Wolf Salmon grabbed a large rock and struck it over the head. Its skull cracked open, and blood and brains flew in all directions. Congratulations were given all around, and the women attended to the poor fellow who had not been quick enough to miss its sharp teeth.

A shaman was summoned from the village. Serious incantations ensued, and high respect was awarded to the dead seal and Dickenson.

A couple women sliced up the seal into thick slices of yellow blubber. Over two fires they lightly cooked the succulent meat, and more people from the village joined them as the delicious aroma wafted on the morning's breeze. Wolf Salmon told Golden Eagle about the fight and everyone laughed hard and long.

Dickenson strutted about showing off his kill. The tribe decided to rename him "Tak a lat Mulat," which translated to "he who chases the seals."

Dickenson bowed deeply when a beaming Wolf Salmon presented him with a bloodied incisor threaded on a leather thong.

Both men were warm and their bellies full, so they decided to carry on to the sea. Golden Eagle accompanied them as they set off down the gorge.

A few days later, Dickenson reluctantly left the valley and headed back to the interior. He would never return, but news of his newfound riches would reach the clubs of London within the year, where it would start off a flurry of activity.

In the next two years, two ships visited the inlet, and trade was so profitable for both parties that Wolf Salmon made a permanent trading-village at the sea. Tribes from the interior came to the village, but Wolf Salmon never let them trade directly with the white men. He charged a healthy percentage for anyone who wanted to trade with the strangers. The village was now full of beads, iron pots, knives, hundreds of blankets, and a dozen guns of disputable age, which were more dangerous to the user than any adversary or game.

All the young men scoured the inlets for sea otter pelts and the creek valleys for beaver. Skirmishes became quite common between hunting parties, and the death toll increased due to the widespread use of firearms. The chiefs became richer, but the supply could not keep up with the demand.

Wolf Salmon realized the pelts' latent wealth, and now each trading ship, much to their dismay, had to pay a higher price. In fact, in one of the native villages in the Nass Valley, a ship from Boston used its cannons on the village when it found the price to be way over that of the previous years. The native people complied once many dead and wounded littered their village.

Leisure activity for the native people of status grew, as they were able to own many more slaves. The wood carvers were blessed with sharp steel axes and adzes, and had more time to carve intricate totem poles and ceremonial masks.

Wolf Salmon's tribe became very wealthy and powerful. Some ships were turned away when the tribe did not have enough furs or they did not require anything else.

Wolf Salmon had his first taste of alcohol when one of the Boston ships arrived in port. After a couple of generous rums, Wolf Salmon felt like dancing. The ship's crew laughed at the strange dance and its incantations, but Wolf Salmon did not understand their goading and danced until he was sick. Some furs were exchanged for the strange brew.

One sailor offered Golden Eagle a seat where he had placed a lot of gunpowder. Golden Eagle sat down and took another gulp of rum from the smiling sailor. The small trail of gunpowder sizzled closer, and although he smelled its acrid scent, he suspected nothing and remained seated.

Wolf Salmon smelled it also and pointed to the chair with a scowl on his face. Too late, Golden Eagle saw the smoke. He was thrown a good ten feet into the air to land on the deck in an ungainly heap.

Wolf Salmon immediately sobered. He drew his knife, and the sailors tensely pointed their guns in retaliation. Wolf Salmon put his knife back and helped his friend to his feet. They left the ship with the other native men and trading stopped for two whole days as Golden Eagle had his wound tended to by the medicine man.

To make matters worse, the Boston ship fired a broadside into the village when Wolf Salmon refused to trade further. It then left, leaving a bitter memory in the villagers' minds: two of their men had been killed on shore. One of them was Wolf Salmon's young three-year-old niece, and the whole village went into mourning at their loss. Revenge was deeply rooted in the native peoples' psyche, and the insults and deaths would be avenged as soon as the opportunity arose.

Four more ships came and went the next season, and trading was brisk. But the crews were always on guard for any trickery, since they had heard the Boston ship had fired upon the village.

In the summer of 1803, the sea otter was hard to come by, and a beaver had not swum past the Big Fir for two seasons. In all the inlets and valleys, the sea otter and beaver were basically extinct, and hunting forays now had far to go. More battles with other neighboring tribes took place over hunting grounds.

The First Nations, always warlike, were now even more so, as alcohol fueled the old feuds and weapons were plentiful. Tribes in the Nass Valley constantly warred with each other over hunting and fishing areas, and the death toll increased year by year.

At the end of September, another ship from Boston entered the inlet. It was new to the coast, and all were eager to trade. It was a small ship, with an all-American crew except for one, a John R. Jewitt from England. He was the ship's armorer and was out to make his fortune.

The ship dropped anchor, and Wolf Salmon went on board with a party of men. The ship held a crew of twenty-six, and they seemed friendly and trusting.

Later that night, under a starlit sky, the war council made their final plans.

The next morning, Wolf Salmon led Golden Eagle and six canoes to the ship. The captain had mentioned earlier his need of salmon and fresh meat. Wolf Salmon suggested that the captain send a longboat with three of his people's canoes to a bay up the coast where salmon and deer were plentiful. Wolf Salmon's eyes lit up when the captain agreed and the long boat left with ten men.

Only sixteen remained on board the ship. None of them commented on the bright red face decorations the natives wore, passing it off as just the normal attire for these people when visiting foreigners. In fact, the night before, the shaman had painted their faces during numerous dances and prayers to the spirits, and every warrior felt immortal.

Wolf Salmon had the first of his men bring the furs and skins on board, and trading began between the Boston men and thirty of his people. John Jewitt retired below deck to repair some of the blocks and tackle damaged in the last storm.

The captain held out a particularly fine sea otter pelt, and Wolf Salmon let out a low, but audible, whistle. The captain looked up. At the look on Wolf Salmon's face, he dropped the pelt and reached for his pistol.

Before his hand touched it, he felt the sharp sting of steel slash across his throat. He dropped to a heap on the deck.

All the warriors pounced at the same moment. A couple of sailors had managed to draw their cutlasses and cut down their attackers. Blood flowed everywhere, and the last two frightened defenders, now with some open wounds, backed up the bridge steps. One of them drew his pistol and fired it, point-blank, in one native's face, which disappeared in a tangled mess of tissue and brains.

Wolf Salmon picked up a fallen cutlass and leaped over the bridge rail, quickly followed by twenty screaming men. The two poor sailors looked upon the blood-spattered warriors. One let his bowels go in rush as the warriors advanced with their clubs and knives.

Wolf Salmon struck one, throwing all his weight behind the swing. The cutlass jarred his arm as the sharp edge embedded deep into the man's arm. It made a sickening grating sound as he pulled it free.

A large war club crashed into the sailor's skull from behind, and Wolf Salmon wiped the brains off his face as the man crashed to the deck, dead.

The last wounded sailor looked around in terror and felt his legs buckle from blood loss. A blow to his already-damaged leg caused him to scream.

Wolf Salmon saw his chance and drove the point of a cutlass into his gaping mouth. The sailor's two front teeth broke beneath it as it drove deep into the soft brain and through the back of his skull. His body spasmed, and Wolf Salmon held on tight as the sailor jerked on his feet. Another warrior took his skinning knife and gutted him from sternum to navel as Wolf Salmon held the man up. His guts writhed out onto the deck.

On the deck below, the other warriors were busy hacking the heads off their fallen enemies. Blood ran over the ship's sides. When the ship's hatch opened, revealing the frightened face of John Jewitt peering out at all the commotion, a warrior cracked him on the head with a war club before returning to his grisly work. There was a thump as Jewitt crumpled backward to the deck below.

Golden Eagle and his men returned in their canoes. All of them were blood splattered. He held up a sailor's head by the pigtail; an artery still dripped blood as it waved in the gentle breeze.

Once they were all aboard, all the severed heads were lined up on the gunwale, turning the water around the ship a pinkish red.

"Golden Eagle, you and our tribe have been avenged, Aye," Wolf Salmon shouted, and Golden Eagle bent down and kissed Wolf Salmon's bloodied feet.

Wolf Salmon was reminded of the sailor below in the hold and sent two men to bring him up. They lifted the half-unconscious John Jewitt out from the hold and up the ladder. Horror crossed his bloodied face as he saw all his shipmates lining the rail. Some had their eyes hanging out, and severed tongues were strewn about the deck. He threw up. He could hardly stand because of his own wound and went in and out of consciousness. A group of warriors surrounded him and jabbed him with their spears and knives.

"Stop, I say."

"We have to kill him, Chief, or else the others will not trade with us anymore," one argued.

"No, look, he is the maker of iron," Wolf Salmon countered. "He will arm our hands with steel so that we may be strong and invincible. Enough, I say; he is mine. Stand back and let him be."

Wolf Salmon glared until none stood in his way.

John Jewitt and another sailor, later found hiding in the chain locker, were kept as Wolf Salmon's slaves for over two years. John Jewitt kept a diary of their time, and when they made their escape, Jewitt returned to England. He made his fortune in the publishing of his account and holding talks at various lecture halls.

The West Coast was now known as a wild coast of blood-killing devils, rich in furs, fish, and wood of the finest quality. Ships heard of the massacre and for years avoided the inlet; the Stikeen people were forced to trade with the peoples further north at a lower price.

Eventually ships came back, but they were extremely wary and let only two natives on the ship at a time. The ship's crew was always aware of the handsome chief who stood at a distance in the lead war canoe. Wolf Salmon's fame as the 'Avenging Indian' traveled far and wide along the coast. No more tricks were played on the West Coast until the fur trade finally died and the economy on which the First Nations had come to depend vanished forever.

In 1804, twenty-three ships visited the coast, and many returned with empty holds. The next year, only two ships visited, and even these bypassed the village. The men could not find sea otter or beaver, no matter how far they traveled.

After one ship visited, one of the native men developed a fever, and even the medicine man could not help. The man sweated and sweated. After five days, his lungs choked with fluid and he died an agonizing death.

In the meantime, the pneumonia spread throughout the village. Soon, there were over one hundred people sick. Wolf Salmon's aging wife helped nurse the sick, and on the tenth day, she also contracted a fever. Wolf Salmon watched the life slowly leave her eyes.

Her last choked words were, "I leave now, my dear husband; be not long in joining me."

The next scourge that hit the village was smallpox, and those lucky enough to live bore the scars of the deadly disease. Over the next ten years, the village was depleted to only half its original number; decay settled in as apathy took hold of the tribe.

Then came another deadly epidemic from the east: missionaries. They invaded the inlets up and down the coast, systematically destroying the First Nations' traditions, and thus their souls. Together with alcohol, this loss sapped them of their will to live the natural life. Many villages disappeared forever. Only moss-covered totem poles and a few longhouses were evidence of the vitality that had once been in every major inlet and valley along the coast.

With just under thirty years of European contact, the First Nations in British Columbia had lost half of their number, nearly fifty thousand souls, and almost as many sea otters. The sea otters had extracted a life for a life: its whiskered face was not seen for many years along the British Columbia coast.

Meanwhile, the grove of big firs in the Stikeen Valley had only grown thicker. Their trunks were unsurpassed in girth. The last time Wolf Salmon visited it, one of his sons had taken him. Tears streamed down his face as he sat under the Big Fir and remembered sunny afternoons with his now-deceased wife.

Shortly after, a huge balsam fell down in a windstorm, and its trunk diverted the creek. The silt revitalized the soil for miles around. The aerie a bald eagle had built in the Big Fir's branches had grown, and the eagles had an unsurpassed view of the valley. Alas, in this last year only a solitary pair of beavers had passed by, hidden away in a forgotten tributary. The wolves howled in hunger; the deer and moose populations had been decimated to feed over a hundred ships.

The Hudson's Bay Company expanded westward over the land as Wolf Salmon lay on his deathbed. The Kildala people, whom they had attacked all those years before, had retaliated the previous year, and half the people of the village tribe had been killed. The village was in a sorry state; it did not have its self-esteem of earlier years, nor its wealth. Many had left for the missionary posts up the coast, and mostly only the old and very young were left.

The mighty Fraser River to the south had been navigated from east to west. In 1827, a fort was founded by the Hudson's Bay Company at the mighty river's mouth. Salmon had found a steady market, and much of it was salted, smoked, and shipped to the lucrative new colony in Hawaii.

As the fur trade died the salmon trade bloomed, and the First Nations were very adept at catching large quantities.

In 1858, gold was found in the northern interior and the gold rush started. Twenty thousand miners boarded anything that floated from San Francisco. The First Nations were swept aside in the wave of mass migration; if they got in the way, they were shot like vermin.

In the 1880s, white men outnumbered the First Nations for the first time. The end was near. The potlatch and secret societies were outlawed, and many First Nations women became miners' wives and prostitutes in order to feed their families back in the villages. Many such villages starved in the cold winters. The missionaries did their best, but they were, in the end, only another nail in the coffin. Reserves were defined, and the tribe of the Stikeen was allotted a meager piece of land near the original village site on the river.

Around them, valleys of pristine forests were cut down in a tangled mess by logging companies run by interests in England. Only the prime timber was taken: the rest was left to rot, and young trees had trouble poking through the debris. Some of the largest trees in the world were cut down to make way for new docks, ships, railway trestles, and buildings.

In the Great War of 1914–1918, the First Nations joined His Majesty's service in the war. Subsequently, they lost their Indian Status and native rights forever. They were not allowed to vote in their own country, and their numbers dwindled even further as the onslaught continued.

The Stikeen River's once huge salmon runs had been decimated, and it was now very difficult to spear a salmon at the ledges. Only a few dozen fish now spawned at the creek where the big trees grew, and the aerie lay empty; the eagles had starved the year before. Only the trees continued to grow, but now no humans stood in their shadow to fish and hunt.

Houses in the village fell into further disrepair, and many left for the big city of Vancouver, where they died in the gutters because of alcohol and drugs. Their language was nearly dead, with only the old people still speaking it. The old crafts were forgotten in their malaise.

Since white men had first arrived, over eighty thousand First Nations people had perished, leaving a nearly-genocidal number of just over twenty thousand souls. No war had ever been declared, and no war could have been so effective.

One of the last Wolf Salmons had a village riddled with broken families and alcohol. He tried to regroup the village: they started to rebuild the totem poles and a large longhouse for ceremonial purposes, but the government money was not enough, and they were left half-built.

However, the remnants of the tribe hung on, and the salmon returned in greater numbers as the years passed; enough that the men could sell the fish commercially. More importantly, though, pride was injected into the village.

One summer, government helicopters flew up and down the valley, and government men visited the forest and village. The whole valley and its entire watershed were mapped out and called Tree Forest License 41. At 340,000 hectares, it was the last and largest of all the tree forest licenses in British Columbia.

The latest Wolf Salmon was afraid for his people. It was the mid-1960s and he had seen the effects of clear-cut logging up north and did not want it here. Without the forest, there would be no reason to live in the valley; he saw the end approaching. He hired a small-time lawyer, and they claimed title to the land. However, the British Columbia government had a policy of not recognizing any native claims, and the claim gathered dust in the courthouse under a pile of others.

Life dragged on. Wolf Salmon had no living sons, but one beautiful daughter called Wind Walker. He cried at night as he thought of her future: the few younger men left in the village, usually drunk, kept hounding her. They had little respect for Wolf Salmon and his policies. Wolf Salmon feared for his tribe and tried desperately to hold on to what little power he had left.

Pulp mills and sawmills grew to the north in Terrace and Prince Rupert. The trees dwindled in direct proportion to the number of jobs, and whole valleys were stripped of their timber. Landslides occurred in every valley. The creeks became clogged with debris, and the salmon beds choked on the waterborne silt. The pulp mills were hungry for chips, and every day ten acres of land were cleared to feed them.

The growling lumber trucks traveled further and further afield, and now trees above the four thousand feet level were eyed hungrily by loggers.

The wind rustled through the upper branches of the Big Fir as timber companies began to make their moves.

Chapter Two
The Hockey Game

It was in the early 1970s on an ice rink on Vancouver Island, British Columbia that the talented right winger, Steve Thorpe, weaved right past the bewildered defender, closing in fast on the far side of the rink. He glanced up and saw the squat white-masked goaltender firmly entrenched in the small-netted goal. He picked his spot over the goalie's right shoulder, above his flat brown leather blocker, and raised his hockey stick for the slap-shot that would send the puck hurtling toward the goal at over eighty miles an hour.

Paul Whorton was not far behind his best friend, and only the big opposition player, number seven, lay between them.

The moment Steve lowered his eyes, the burly number seven made his move. Realizing he wasn't going to reach Steve in time, he swung his hockey stick one-handed in a sideways chopping motion.

Paul tried to shout a warning, but by the time he opened his mouth, the curved edge of the stick drove into Steve's unprotected face. It sliced through his upper cheekbone till it tore flesh, and with its continued momentum cut right down to his chin.

Paul saw Steve drop his stick and reach up to his face with his free hand. Blood spattered, leaving bright red streaks on the ice.

In his pain, Steve had forgotten the fast-approaching goal post. With a crack, the whole audience heard his unprotected shoulder hit the steel post at an awkward angle, scraping just past his ear. His collarbone cracked in half like a crisp carrot. His momentum spun him like a top, and he hit the boards head-first. His body slumped to the ice in an untidy heap.

Players and audience alike were momentarily silenced as the sprawled player twitched once, and then lay still.

The referee had already raised his arm and blown the whistle for the infraction. The Island Roamers' trainer was already halfway across the ice, bag in hand, to tend his injured star.

Paul reached Steve first and was shocked to see the gaping, four-inch wound on his face. Blood oozed in a spreading circle about Steve's head.

"Steve, Steve; it's me, Paul. Just lie still and you'll be okay, I promise," he whispered. His vision blurred with tears of concern. Bob, the Island Roamers' trainer and first-aid man, reached his side, and began to staunch the flow of blood with a wad of gauze.

"Help me keep him still and check his pulse while I hold his head, Paul."

Paul quickly checked for a pulse, breathed a sigh of relief at its strength, and smiled down at Steve. After a moment, Steve's eyes fluttered open, but they were glazed and unfocused.

"You're okay Steve; everything is all right. Just lie still a minute," Bob said.

Number seven nonchalantly leaned on his stick as he watched them gently lift Steve off the ice.

Paul watched Steve disappear toward the dressing room on a stretcher. Rage built in his guts. He looked over his shoulder at the opposition's number seven, Nick Barrett, still leaning on his stick. He shook his padded gloves off, clenched his fists into hard knotty balls, and started across the ice.

One of the linesmen started to intercept, knowing his intentions after such a dirty foul, but missed him.

"Kill the bastard," someone in the audience yelled, and the crowd growled its agreement. Nick raised his eyes and a look of doubt briefly flickered across his face.

The two players had met many times before in games but had yet to fight because of their respect for each other's strength. Both eighteen, they were within a few pounds of each other and were in prime physical condition. Nick was a few inches shorter, but more heavily muscled.

Nick dropped his stick and slowly skated backward, away from Paul. His eyes looked toward the ref appealingly, who promptly bent down to tighten his laces. The tension in the arena grew to a fever pitch as the two big combatants eyed each other up. Only feet separated them now.

"Drop the gloves, you bastard," Paul said in a controlled voice.

"Fuck off, pretty boy." Nick slowly backed off, weaving from side to side. Without warning, he swung his right arm up, and his empty, heavy leather glove caught Paul a stinging blow right in his mouth. Before Paul's shocked eyes had time to open, a hard fist jarred into his face.

Paul staggered backward, nearly losing his balance, and spat the salty taste of fresh blood onto the ice. His tongue probed his lower incisor. He felt it move and winced at the gash in his lower lip. He looked up in time to see the fast-approaching Nick bearing down on him, a hammer blow poised for his unprotected head.

However, his father's early boxing lessons gave Paul the controlled reaction he needed. He ducked swiftly to the right and earned only a glancing punch. At the same time, he drove his right arm into Nick's now unprotected stomach.

Nick gasped as the breath whooshed out of him, and he bent forward in pain. However, he was a veteran fighter and reacted accordingly. He whirled to his left, but still was not quite quick enough to avoid Paul's wicked left hook, which caught him just above his right eye. He blinked as blood flowed into the corner of his eye.

The crowd was now on its feet, hungry for revenge. They roared their approval as blood splattered the ice.

Fear crossed Nick's features when he spied the cold fury in Paul's eyes. Nick bent into a crouch and, fast as lightning, drove his head up.

Paul was taken by surprise by this new form of attack. Nick was one of the few players on the ice wearing a helmet, and Paul's head snapped back as the hard plastic struck under his jaw. His vision blurred, and he felt the world spin. Before he could recover, hard fists rained down on his bruised face. His unprotected head whipped left, then right, under the heavy onslaught. He tried to recover, ducking and weaving unsteadily on his skates.

The crowd was silenced by this vicious onslaught, and winced as they saw Paul's bruised and battered face, now covered in blood. Hope grew as he countered with a left, then a right jab, which slowed the avalanche to a trickle as Paul's counter shots took their toll on Nick.

The seesaw battle started to swing in Paul's favor as his honed boxing skills overtook Nick's more powerful, but clumsy, swings. Nick tried to protect his face with his forearms. Not all of Paul's punches found their target; some crashed painfully into the unexpected presence of Nick's hard helmet, and his knuckles started to split and feel tender.

In desperation, Nick crouched low and drove into Paul's lower body, trying to grapple him to the ice. Paul staggered back. At the last moment, before his sharp skates lost their fine grip in the ice, he twirled left, bent forward, and pushed Nick down hard onto the ice. Nick's helmet flew off and his nose crashed into the ice, bending it sideways as the cartilage broke. He covered his head against Paul's raining blows.

The two linesmen, always in easy circling range, pounced as both players fell heavily to the ice. The crowd cheered when they saw Paul land on top, as this was the symbol of victory, no matter what had happened before.

Both linesmen grabbed the flailing arms of Paul. The rage went out of him, and he went limp. He rose to his feet, and his whole body started to hurt. He took deep sucking breaths to fill his starved lungs. Nick rose slowly to his feet and tried to staunch the freely-flowing blood from his bent nose.

"You bastard," he spluttered, "I'll get you, just wait."

Paul turned away to the players' box, anxious to get news of his friend's condition.

***

Nick was escorted off the ice to the tunnel. His shame grew on hearing the boos as he left the ice. It burned in the pit of his stomach, and filled him when he looked in the mirror to see his ravaged nose and the cut above his right eye.

His frustration grew deeper at the hospital when he learned that the Island Roamers had scored the winning goal on a penalty shot due to his infraction, and worse still, Paul had scored it. The Island Roamers won the 1970 Island Cup, and his teammates never let him forget his disastrous blunder. They shunned him for the rest of the season, till he could take it no longer and left the team in shame.

Even the local paper had a write-up in the sports section, calling out his 'injurious foul' and demanding the player and club responsible be penalized. In the same article, Paul had been praised for the way he 'defended his teammate's honor' and conducted himself 'cleanly' in play.

Nick crumpled the paper up and hurled it across his room. That's only what it was called when the winner instigated the fight. He gingerly probed his nose and winced at its tenderness. The white bandage that crossed his nose partly obscured his vision. Smart tears burned his eyes, more out of self-pity than pain.

"The bastard," he shouted to the four walls around him. He picked up the model he had made of a 1955 Gullwing Mercedes and hurled it across the room, where it exploded into bits.

"Aaagh," he cried. The sudden movement had jarred his nose, causing it to bleed again.

If he was being honest, he wasn't all that angry about the article. It was that, on top of everything else, he had received a phone call from Michelle that morning. He'd gotten her tickets to see that game, and had asked her out. He thought things were going well.

But all she said was, "Sorry Nick, but I don't want to go out to that party next week. Bye."

She had hung up before he could reply. He had been trying for a date with her for months and dreamed of her constantly, especially her firm breasts and super legs. He rang back, but there was no answer. So, he fumed alone in his room.

His actions on the hockey rink hadn't been that bad, really—just unlucky that Steve had been hurt so much. It wasn't as if he had meant to slash Steve's face, only his arms, but they had both been moving too fast. It was an accident. The thought only made his self-pity even worse.

"Fuck it," he cursed as he left the room to go downstairs. After all, his old man was heading out and would not be back for hours.

***

Nick's father, Rand Barrett, Chairman and President of West Skeena Timber Products, had hit the roof when he saw the game, and promptly grounded Nick to the house for two months. In addition, he had taken the keys from the Mustang he had given Nick for his sixteenth birthday and locked it in the garage.

Rand Barrett was a giant in the industry. He himself was a hard man in business, but always fair. He didn't know where Nick had gotten the vicious streak in him, especially since he had everything he wanted and more.

Maybe that was the problem, he mused. He recalled all the other little incidents involving Nick, which he had dismissed as over-eagerness. Things were going to change, he vowed. He just hoped he hadn't left it too late.

The growing cancer, which was spreading through Rand Barrett's veins, had begun to sap his tireless energy. Typical of his nature, he had not told anyone yet; it was times like these he wished his late dear wife, Ruth, was still alive for him to confide in.

He had, however, started to prepare his affairs. An action plan on how his vast lumber sawmills, pulp mills, and other subsidiaries were to be controlled was well underway. The doctor had given it to him straight: two years, three at the most, before the cancer would finally kill him.

He had to get Nick into university before then, so that he could obtain his Forestry Degree. But so far only sports and girls ruled Nick's life; his son's scholastic career seemed doomed. He would have to ensure that Nick worked every holiday in the mills, so at least he would learn something he may find useful later on. After all, Rand had built up his empire without any schooling: just common sense, good luck, and lots of hard work.

He deliberated about whether he should tell Nick about the cancer, but thought he'd delay it for a year—or at least until his health deteriorated.

Rand Barrett braced himself for this afternoon's meeting with his competitor, Gordon Whorton. Gordon had started in the woods with him over twenty-five, maybe thirty years ago, up on the inside passage of British Columbia. Rand admired the man even though they were in competition with each other. Gordon Whorton owned a decent-sized sawmill on Vancouver Island and was satisfied with that. He had nurtured it into one of the best-run and most profitable in the business.

Rand, however, was always more ambitious, and had borrowed money left, right, and center. He bought tree licenses on spec, before a mill was even there. After the wood market depression, the wood prices rose sharply, and he sold at huge profits to offshore companies. After twenty years of wheeling and dealing, his company, West Skeena Timber Products, had become one of the top three in BC.

Both parties had benefited from an old mutual arrangement between them, which involved West Skeena buying wood chips off Whorton's mill for a fair price. Gordon Whorton increased his production by 30 percent while saving his own modest holdings, and Rand received good chips, which his pulp mills devoured at an alarming rate. It freed up a whole sector of his labor force to concentrate more on the pulp mills and their increasing complexity and cost.

A knock interrupted Rand's thoughts. He opened the door.

"Sir, the helicopter is ready," said the young, leather-jacketed aviator.

"Thank you, I'll be there in a minute," he replied. He swung the heavy strap of his F-1 camera over his neck to catch the wonderful scenery on the way. It was very rare for him to go on these little jaunts now, yet he still hungered for the wilderness, especially now he felt his life ebbing away.

***

Across the Georgia Strait, in a hospital on Vancouver Island, Paul had just finished talking to Steve's doctor. The news was not good, and Paul cringed at his next task.

Paul walked into Steve's room, trying to seem cheery. "Hey Steve, how're you doing?"

"Oh, not bad." Steve gave him a smile from where he was propped up on the bed. "There are some nice nurses at least," he said.

"Ah, ah, so you're on the mend already, I see." Paul took a deep breath and carried on. "Steve, I'm really sorry to tell you this, but I had a word with the doctor. He said your hockey days are over for a while." Paul looked down at his hands, thrust into his pockets. "In fact, more than that, he strongly recommends you give up the game."

Steve just stared at him.

Paul hurried on. "You see, he reckons one of the vertebrae in your neck was damaged, and he's afraid of it getting knocked again, which could be serious."

"Don't yank my chain, Paul, my neck feels fine; it's my shoulder that's the problem. The guy's blind," Steve said.

"No, I'm serious, Steve; anyway, it's not that bad." Paul tried and failed to give him a self-deprecating smile. "Hockey's only for over-muscled morons anyway."

"Yeah, but Paul, I love the speed: the dodging and weaving. I could run circles around most of those 'morons', and you know it."

Paul frowned. He didn't want to remind Steve that one of those same morons had caught him good.

"Look, it could have been worse; if that blade had been one inch higher, the bastard could have had your eye out, and then you really would have been in deep shit."

Steve smiled slightly.

"Yeah, I suppose you're right: I should count my lucky stars. I've a scar a mile long, a smashed collarbone, and a fucked neck, which that dildo of a doctor reckons is good for nothing better than tiddlywinks. Yeah, I'm lucky all right."

Paul looked away as the tears welled up in Steve's eyes. He knew how much Steve loved the game; hell, he was good enough to be future NHL material.

"Hey Paul, I'm sorry," Steve said as he placed his hand on Paul's arm. "It's not *your* fault. You did your bit. I wish I could have seen you smash that jerk."

Paul looked up. He knew his face did not look like that of a winner, all bruised and puffed as it was.

"Well Steve, I can sure tell you that the bastard can hit mighty hard. At one point, I thought a tree had fallen on me. Apparently, he's been suspended for a year, and to boot, that last dive on the ice broke his nose, so at least I got him to suffer a little."

Even so, it was small solace to the two friends, and neither took much enjoyment from the circumstances.

"Hey, never mind. I have some stellar news for you, Steve."

"What? Come on, give it to me."

"Well, guess who I ran into the other night after the game?"

"Judy?"

"No, keep trying."

"Carol—no, I know, I bet it was Beverly, wasn't it? No? Okay, I give up—who?"

"Well, remember those two cracking ten-out-of-tenner's who were in the front row, cheering on the opposition?"

"The pair beside the penalty box? You bet I do; I've never seen such a bombing pair of tits and eyes in all my life," Steve said.

"Yes, well, apparently the one called Tanya is just dying to massage your broken bones back to health, you lucky dog you. So, I made a date for the first week of summer vacation. And the best part? I get to chaperone you with her friend, Michelle."

"Hold it, how does that help us—they're in Vancouver?"

"Well, apparently Michelle's dad has a place on Saltspring Island and we're invited for the weekend. I talked to Dad, and he says we can have the Bayliner for a week in the summer. You know, go on a fishing trip."

Steve sat up a little higher in the bed. "What, on our own?"

"Yup. Dad says we've been out on it often enough, we should know our way around, just you and me. I figured we could use that time to visit the girls on Saltspring. Any good eh?"

"No shit, you mean we get to use that killer boat all week—and get a date with two gorgeous gals…Wow, I feel better already."

Steve gave him a sly grin.

"By the way, have you seen that sexy nurse with the green eyes on this ward?"

Paul smiled as he listened to Steve's vivid description of her. He was glad their favorite topic had quickly cast away their earlier gloom. *Yes*, he thought, *Steve's going to be all right.*

They chatted away for another hour until the sexy nurse chased Paul away, telling him visiting hours were over.

"See you later, dillweed," Paul said as he walked out the door.

"Hey, Paul."

"Yes?" Paul smiled. He knew what was coming.

"Up yours, and break a leg, eh."

They both chortled as the door closed behind Paul.

Chapter Three
Michelle and University

Over the spring, Steve's injuries healed well, and he was back to school for the last two months before graduation. Paul had planned the week's fishing trip on his father's boat in the Gulf Islands and had all the charts and boat ready. He had rung Michelle and confirmed the weekend they were to be there.

Steve was really excited when Paul reminded him of the trip.

"Wow, I can't wait. I'm just dying to get out again and fish," he said.

"Yes, and from what I can remember of Michelle and her friend, the scenery should be good as well," Paul replied.

They spent the weekend before the trip on a frenzied shopping spree. They bought every fishing lure imaginable, plenty of beans, canned food, and a liberal supply of Coca-Cola. They even sneaked in a case of beer and two bottles of wine for those special occasions. Like all good boy scouts, they also each bought a packet of condoms, just in case.

The twenty-four-foot Bayliner cruiser looked splendid nestled in its cream and navy-blue colors in the cluster of other boats in the marina. She was called *Tai Pan*, and had every amenity on board. A powerful engine could boot her along at over thirty knots when needed.

After hundreds of pieces of advice and ominous warnings of retribution, if she came back with as much as a scratch, the two young men set off as their parents waved from the dock. The morning was a crisp sunny one, which promised to turn hot later in the day.

"Yahoo, we're off. Let's hit her, baby," Steve yelled as they left the harbor mouth.

Paul opened the throttles of the Mercury engines, and the bubbling chatter quickly rose to a throaty roar. The *Tai Pan*'s bow sent up a sparkling spray of green saltwater as they sped on at over twenty knots.

"Well, where do we stop first? We have five days before we have to meet the girls," Paul shouted over the throaty roar of the twin exhausts.

Steve shook his bangs out of his eyes in the whipping wind. "Shit, give her hell till we reach Nanaimo, then we'll drop a few lines and try and hit a big salmon."

An hour later Paul eased up on the throttles. The *Tai Pan* settled into the water. "I reckon right over there by the drop off should do it. What's your take?" Paul said.

Steve leaned back on the rail with a cocky grin. "Sounds good to me; I can smell those salmon cooking on the grill now, can't you? I'll give you a go once I catch my limit," he said.

"Bullshit, five dollars says my rod hits first."

"Okay, but those bait-fish you kept catching last year don't count. They have to be over ten pounds for the bet, right?"

"You're on. Better get your money out." Paul flipped the engines to idle. "Come on fishy, fishy, come to see Paul."

Both virtually jumped down from the flying bridge to reach the open rear cockpit first and raced each other in assembling their rods. They only slowed to make the agonizing decision of what would be the killer lure. Paul chose his favorite: a pink hot shot lure. It was a piece of bent plastic a bit like a banana, which when trolled, bobbed, ducked, and weaved in a most enticing manner. Steve put on an imitation squid called a hoochie.

Paul bounded up the ladder to the flying bridge. While he slowly guided the boat toward the rocky shoal, Steve let out both lines behind them. They used a downrigger, a big lead ball attached to a wire, to which they attached a quick release. This allowed the bait to go deep, but once a fish was hooked there was no other weight: just the fish and fisherman.

Steve sat beside Paul and intently watched the depth sounder.

"There you go—we've got one at a hundred and twenty feet," he said in a feverish pitch. The small blip crossed the screen before disappearing off the side, where the bottom of the shoal came up into shallower water.

The warm sun felt good on their faces and Paul enjoyed the close silence for a while, soaking it up. A few seals sprawled on the rocks, and a bald eagle lazily circled above the approaching island.

It sure is good to be alive, Paul thought as the gentle bobbing eased away all the tension from his body.

The peace was only briefly interrupted, but each time they had to release the small, immature salmon they reeled in.

"What the hell," Paul said, "let's just keep heading south and follow the drop off."

The small group of islands became just specks as the afternoon wore on. The smooth sea hardly rippled in the faint breeze.

"I've got one, stop the engines," yelled Steve as he bounded down the ladder. His rod tip rose in the air as soon as it was released from the weight of the downrigger. Steve pulled the eleven-foot rod from the holder. He leaned back and put his hand on the rim of the reel.

"It's a keeper," he shouted up to Paul as the rod bent double. The fish had felt the sharp hook and taken off in the opposite direction. The reel's handles blurred and the ratchet screamed as the salmon swiftly peeled off fifty, then a hundred yards of line.

Paul quickly pulled his line and both downriggers in out of harm's way. "You lucky bastard, I hate you," he said and slapped Steve encouragingly on the back.

Steve grinned from ear to ear as he fought the fish.

"Do me a solid and get that five bucks ready for me," he taunted. "Aha, he's heading back this way." Steve frantically wound like mad, trying to keep the line taut as the salmon reversed its escape path.

Both saw a flash of silver twenty feet away as the salmon twisted and writhed to free itself from the sharp hooks. The line started to rise, and out of the port quarter the salmon leaped. It shook its head in midair and whipped its broad tail before landing with a splash.

"Wow, it's a beauty. Must be well over twenty by the looks of it," Paul said. "Keep a tight line, buddy, and don't rush it."

The silver-sided Chinook salmon made another powerful run as the line whistled piano-taut. Its ocean-going life and healthy diet of herring, prawn, and shrimp had given it plenty of lasting energy, used to strong tides and nimble prey as it was. Not many fish rivaled it pound-for-pound for endurance and aquabatics.

"Come on, you're babying it now," Paul chided fifteen minutes into the battle.

"No, I'm not; the prick just won't come near. Look at the rod: it's bent double." Steve adjusted his stance yet again to keep steady pressure on the rod.

Eventually, the salmon's runs became shorter and shorter, until it lay sulking directly beneath the boat.

"Come on, my sweet," Steve breathed as he slowly pumped the fish up to the surface.

Paul grabbed the net and anxiously peered over the side. "He's coming— keep it up. Yes, yes, a bit more." Paul laid the big landing net under the surface. The salmon feebly waved its tail as Steve slowly drew it in.

Paul quickly thrust downward with the net, but it dove away just in time and Paul missed.

Steve pulled hard again and the line sang in the breeze. This time the fish came up and rolled on its side. Paul gently slid the net under its white belly and, with a deft twist and pull, enveloped its two and a half feet in the green mesh. Spray dropped off his hair as the fish writhed madly in one last explosion of energy.

"Dude, that's one nice fish," Paul said admiringly, "and what a fight."

"Get the bonker, Paul, I'm keeping this. Salmon steaks for supper, eh?"

"I'm down with that." Paul cracked the fish over the head. The salmon rolled its indigo eyes, shivered once, then lay still.

After laying it in the fish holder, at the back of the boat, the two boys put the rods out again.

Paul dug into his pocket. "My turn. Here's your five bucks you lucky bastard," he said with a smile on his face.

As they neared the beautiful, tree-clad Gulf Islands further south, Paul had his chance. He released a terrific fighter of about twelve pounds, which had given him a short but heart-stopping fight. Both boys felt at their best, and praised each other's handling of the fish.

By early evening, they tied *Tai Pan* up at the government dock at Ganges, the biggest village on the island of Saltspring. Over a half-dozen hidden beers, they gorged themselves on succulent salmon, fried mushrooms, and slabs of thickly-buttered bread.

"Ah, this is the life," Paul said at the end of a magnificent burp, bringing with it the rich aftertaste of salmon and butter.

"You got that right. I'll tell you what, though: that sucker sure made my shoulder ache," Steve said slowly rubbing his right shoulder.

"Yeah, you got to watch that for a while. In fact, you better let me take in the next big one."

"Bullshit you will; it's feeling better already." Steve countered.

They chatted another half-hour before their eyelids began to droop and both decided to call it a day and retire below.

Sleep came instantly to Paul. The last thought he remembered was that Steve was going to be okay. He really was glad that Steve had caught the first fish, even though it had cost him some bread. It must have been the shits for Steve to be laid up for a month. With that thought, he fell into a deep sleep.

***

"Paul, Paul, wake up, you lazy dick," Steve yelled, "It's past nine o'clock and the day's gone."

Paul groaned, then threw a pillow at Steve's bunk when he tried to resume shouting again.

"If you're so perky," he growled, "then why isn't the table set and the bacon on? You just woke up yourself, so sit on it."

Paul rolled over, turning his back to his friend.

"Now earn your keep: two eggs, sunny side up, and half a dozen rashes of bacon—and be quick about it."

Steve only stretched with a yawn. "Yeah, I slept like a log."

Paul grabbed his rock-hard penis and inwardly groaned at the delicious feeling it gave him.

"You get up first and I'll cook tomorrow," he said.

"No, my shoulder still hurts, I'll swap you."

The jerk, Paul thought. *I could have had a crafty one while he was cooking.* He remained curled up in the bow's little berth, his hand still holding his throbbing old fella. A thought struck him. "Aha, I've got it. It's got nothing to do with your shoulder, you dillweed. I bet you've a hard on and don't want to get out of bed. I know you."

"No." Steve laughed back. "But I bet you have, you horny bastard. You shouldn't have described Michelle and Tanya so well last night—it's all your fault."

Shit, Paul thought, *my little counter-attack didn't work.*

"Hey, put on the cassette by your head. Yeah, that one—Neil Young. And don't rock the boat too much."

Neither wanted to start first, but Steve turned up the music a notch. Paul stiffened as he drew his foreskin back hard and the throb of the music washed over him.

"You finished yet, you randy asshole?" Steve's voice interrupted Paul's imaginings of his hand creeping under Michelle's tight panties as she lifted her bum to give him more room. *Damn it*, he thought.

"Fuck off and get that breakfast going."

While Steve rocked the boat a bit, Paul's hand became a blur. He felt the shower of tingling sensations wave over his body as semen spurted up his chest. *Man, that was killer*, he thought, and just in time, too.

"Come on, no need to have two," Steve yelled over the music.

"Hey, it isn't my fault you shoot your duff off early. Anyway, I'm up." Paul cleaned himself up and swung his legs over the side, pulling his jeans over his softening member.

Over platefuls of bacon and eggs they discussed the day's plans. "Well, I think we should go and see Chuck Stoneman. My dad practically gave me an order to do so, and I want to get it out of the way," Paul said.

"I assume this guy's a logger then? What's so special about him?" Steve sat back from his plate.

"Apparently he's been logging the same fifteen hundred acres for ages and employing two men as well. Dad was saying that our mill goes through an average of fifteen hundred acres in *one* year with three men. It should be interesting to see how he does it."

As Steve did the dishes, Paul looked on the chart and soon found the place. Chuck was at the south end of the island, near a place called Fulford Harbor.

An hour later, the boat nosed along the rocky shore opposite Chuck's property, which lay nestled in a small bay.

"Nice place he's got," Paul commented as they admired the small rancher, which overlooked the bay in front of an impressive backdrop of Douglas firs and cedars.

"Right, the anchor's held; let's go see if he's in." Steve unleashed the small Avon inflatable dinghy.

Nobody was at the house, so they followed a well-worn path through the towering trees. They welcomed the pleasant change of the cool shade, as it let their slight sunburns from the day before cool down.

A tall, wiry man in faded jeans and checkered shirt was closely peering at the ends of a substantial log pile. They walked up to him.

"Hi, I'm Paul Whorton, and this is Steve Thorpe. Could you please tell us where we may find Chuck Stoneman?"

"Look no further, young man," he replied and stuck his hand out. His blue eyes sparkled merrily as he pumped Paul's hand.

Damn, this old bird sure has a hard handshake, Paul thought as he felt the sinewy power in the hand that pumped his vigorously.

"And pleased to see you as well, son," the man said as he turned to Steve and gave him the same finger-crunching greeting. "Your dad told me you would be popping by. Say, how is the old logger baron anyway? It's been ages since I've seen him."

"He's good, sir—"

"Forget the 'sir', it's just Chuck. Now come on; I've something to show you lads. Follow me."

Steve gave Paul an inquiring glance before following Chuck and his lively pace.

"Now here I do things a mite different to your dad, as you'll see. Last year along this bit, I took out a hundred thousand board feet of prime lumber."

"What do you mean? Over the hill there?"

"No, right by your darn feet, lad. Really look carefully now; you'll see it if you keep your eyes open."

Both examined the trees on either side of them more closely.

"Ah, I see one." Paul pointed. "Over there, just behind that cedar: there's a stump. And another one over there."

"You see," Chuck answered, "unlike the clear-cutters, I take out only the mature trees here and there. That way, the ones remaining get far lighter and grow quicker. It's what I call selective logging."

Chuck leaned back, tugging on the suspenders of his bib overalls. "Once I've been through an area, all the trees left grow handsomely; in fact, I reckon twice as quick as an untouched stand. So instead of an eighty to one hundred year growing cycle, I can get it down to between sixty and eighty years, tops."

Chuck waved a hand at the trees surrounding them. "Better yet, I don't have a goddamn mess to clean up. I reckon I live here and want to see my beautiful trees. It's a bit like having a vegetable patch and watching my next year's harvest."

Paul thought about it for a moment. True, the harvested forest before them did not look much different from a natural, uncut forest, other than it being a little less dense. And to his untrained eye the younger, thinner trees seemed higher than they would be normally: he supposed because they got more sunlight.

He countered Chuck's method from what he had learned. "Yes, but my dad's always said how it's not cost effective to selectively log—plus more dangerous. Anyhow, we clear-cut, burn the brush, and then replant the next year. What's wrong with that?"

"I know your dad has done a fine job, and it's a shame the big boys don't follow his practice, but they don't. Even he secretly admits that there must be a better way in the long run. That's why you're here, isn't it?"

"Well, you have a point there," Paul conceded.

Chuck rolled his shoulders in a shrug.

"As to the danger, well. If you're a careful logger, you can lay a tree down to within a couple feet and not be a danger to yourself or other trees on the way down." He bounded forward over a patch of ferns.

"Lookee here: last year I dropped a two hundred-footer right over there, and not another tree was damaged."

"Wow," Steve said, "that must have been a tight squeeze. But how do you get them out once they're down?"

"Good insight, that's how. I gauge the longest length we can pull through with the skidder and chop her up to size. I have to optimize what I want of the last length, true. We may lose a little of the optimum cut, but by my reckoning what I lose, I gain in future growth."

Chuck clapped a hand on a trunk. "My fifteen hundred acres is all I've got. I can't cut too much, or else in the end I'll just be cutting pecker poles."

"Yes, but how do you make enough money this way?" Paul probed.

Chuck smiled at his forthright question.

"Now, I'm not after being a millionaire, but I make enough and hire two men full time every year. These fifteen hundred acres support the three of us year round forever. Whereas your dad has to move on in a little under one year. So, if you wait for an eighty-year cycle you would need…"

Paul quickly calculated in his head. "One hundred and twenty thousand acres."

Chuck raised his eyebrows.

"Yeah, sounds about right. And how many acres does your dad have?"

"Just over seventy thousand," Paul said. "At least, in our current license."

"Exactly my point, young fella. That means by simple math it won't last, and you can't cut down a forty-year-old tree—it's as simple as that."

Chuck patted the coarse trunk of a growing cedar. "I'm glad your dad sent you down here. Yes, my pestering must have sunk in a bit. In our younger days, there were millions of acres unclaimed. We really thought it was limitless."

Steve scoffed. "That didn't last."

Chuck shook his head sadly. "No. More and more companies got into the business, and now mill licenses border each other. Soon, there won't be any more pie to divide. Especially those damn pulp mills, gobbling up fine timber by the truckload; it just can't carry on."

Chuck clapped Paul on the shoulder, which sent the younger man stumbling a step. "Your dad's thinking about your future, son. He won't admit it to me, but he's worried about what he's left you in the years to come." He gave himself a shake, his voice brightening. "Anyhow, enough of the theory, let's carry on." And with that, Chuck strode off into the woods.

For the rest of the way to the top of the bluff, a stump here and a clearing there were the only signs of an active logging area. There were no ravaged areas, eroded slopes, or choked creeks. Only an experienced eye could tell that it was not quite natural.

The forest floor still had the old fall-downs and broken branches, but that helped enrich the soil as it always had. Seedlings sprouted in profusion. Chuck admitted that after a year these were thinned to leave only a couple of the stronger ones, which rocketed up into the strong sunlight.

Paul's admiration grew. The merits of the system far outweighed any disadvantages—at least, from what he could see at first glance.

"Look over here, lads: you can see the whole acreage from here. It goes from that far point to the next and then a mile inland." Chuck swept his long arms over his domain.

Yes, Paul thought, *you can hardly tell the difference. It's just not as dense as untouched old growth.* So often in clear-cutting the fallen trees were allowed to rot slowly on the ground. Paul used to think that a clear cut gave the new seedlings the best light for which to grow, but this year he'd learned that the fast-growers like alder quickly overgrew the others and smothered them. When they cleared a big area, it took an army to replant and thin each year. This way a man could use his time and men more efficiently.

Paul continued asking questions like a six shooter.

Eventually, Chuck held up his hands in surrender. "Okay, enough; an old-timer like me needs a breather. You sure know a lot about the forest, my boy. How about you, Steve?"

"Oh, I'm not in the business. My father is an accountant, so I never really took much notice." Steve stuffed his hands in his pockets. "Anyway, I want to go to sea. I'll let Paul here chop the trees down with his dad."

"Sensible thing, young man. Wished I'd seen more of the world when I was your age; but still, I've seen most of British Columbia, and this will do me for the rest of the few years I have left."

Chuck's eyes misted over as he surveyed his domain. "Come on, can't be gabbing all day; there's work to be done around here." At that, he quickly outpaced the younger men as he sprightly covered the forest floor in a smooth gait.

"Bloody hell, he's a fit old bastard," Steve wheezed as they neared the small logging camp.

"Thanks a lot, Mr. Stoneman—I mean, Chuck. You've certainly given me a lot to think about. I'll pass your regards to my old man. Maybe we can come again sometime?" Paul asked as they caught up with him.

"Yes, anytime boys; next time I'll show you around the old mill I have 'round the back'," Chuck replied.

"Oh, is it possible to see it now?" Paul asked in a pleading tone. Steve gave out a soft groan.

"Now hold on, fella, I've a pile of work to do. You come back later in the week and I'll show you."

"Okay, Chuck, it's a deal."

With that, they said goodbye and walked back along the fir-clad path to the boat.

The two friends had a lazy few day of fishing, swimming, and exploring the dotted islands. In the middle of the week, they visited Chuck again and saw the small mill. Paul was thoroughly absorbed in it. It was a high production season, and it was a pleasant thing to watch him carefully cut each piece with loving care. The machinery he used was from remnants of older mills, but it was all in fine working order, especially the basic saw: the backbone of any mill.

Paul was increasingly impressed by Chuck's love of his product and the craftsmanship he awarded the wood. It was a breath of fresh air compared to the other mills he had visited, including their own.

On Friday, they scouted the inlet on Saltspring Island where they were to meet the girls. Arbutus lined the shore, behind which small, weekend cottages of every description were scattered. All were empty, awaiting the weekend rush of city dwellers to come swarming onto the island.

Steve looked a lot healthier and his broad shoulders had begun to fill out again. His black, unruly hair shone in the sun.

"Come on, Paul, let's go to Ganges for the night; I need to buy some aftershave and stuff. We should also hit the swimming pool. It'll be good to have a nice soak after all this sea air—plus you're beginning to smell a bit, to say the least."

"Sit on it," Paul replied with a smile. He turned the *Tai Pan* around the headland toward Ganges. "Dude, I can't believe it, but I'm getting nervous. It seems so long ago that they asked us over," Paul said.

"Ah, just you wait: once they see my handsome features and fine physique, they'll be all over me."

"Bullshit, you ugly slug, they won't even look at you once they see me. There's no competition," Paul retorted.

Steve crossed his arms. "All right then—you want to lose another five dollars? I bet you I'll be the first one to get any."

Paul considered the challenge, but for some reason was reluctant, but couldn't put his finger on why. Instead, he diverted the conversation to safer ground as they approached the harbor.

Paul winked at the girl in the liquor store and with his tanned smile let her knowingly sell them a bottle of white California Chablis. At the local grocery store, they filled their cart with all the delicacies they could think of, including some smoked oysters.

"You can't cook, you pig, so I don't know what you're buying all this food for," Steve chided.

"Can so—wait and see. Salmon à la crème sauce, followed by wine, and bingo: down go the defenses and off with the panties, my man. Besides I cook, you wash—so up yours."

Steve was no longer paying attention to him. "Wow, look at that, will you?" he said. "Her legs go right up to her armpits." Both gawked unashamedly as a local beauty passed down the other aisle.

In the morning, they spent hours fussing over the boat: cleaning up the grease on the stove, stuffing their unlaundered clothes in the ice box, hiding the Playboy magazines, and, finally, filling up with gas.

"Dude, you smell like a pansy," Paul said.

"Hey, don't smell what you can't afford. It's Mystique for Men, but you've probably never heard of it," Steve replied.

"Hey, I put on my trusty Old Spice—and I didn't shower in it, you bugger." It was hard to miss the smell in the confines of the cabin.

Steve tossed an old shirt his way. "Just wrap up and get this rusty old tub on the move—the morning's a-wasting."

Tai Pan crept into the inlet by mid-morning. After dropping anchor, they headed for the cottage.

"Which one is it, Paul?" Steve asked.

"What're you whispering for? I think it's that cottage over there. The one with the porch and cedar roof."

"Right. Lead the way," Steve said.

They climbed the winding path through the arbutus. Paul stopped at one and ran his hand over the smooth, reddish-brown trunk, brushing aside a sliver of the paper-thin bark. Arbutus was one of his favorite trees. The wood was so smooth to the touch and the color was fabulous.

"Come on, keep going, Paul."

"No, it's your turn to go first; I've brought us this far, now go." He pushed Steve up front. They stopped behind a large Douglas fir and staked out the cottage before carrying on.

"I don't see anyone. You sure this is the right one, Paul?"

Paul inspected a crumpled-up piece of paper and nodded. "Go on, I'm right behind you."

"Bullshit, you spoke to them, not me."

"Oh, okay." Paul took a deep breath, squared his shoulders, and broke cover with Steve close behind.

They both winced as the porch steps creaked and peered for faces in the windows, but saw no one. Paul knocked once, not very hard, and jumped back a foot as it immediately opened. A strange man blocked the door.

"Hi, you two must be Paul and Steve, right?"

"Yes sir, I'm Paul and this is Steve. Pleased to meet you. Are Michelle and Tanya in?"

"Yes, you had better come in. You know what women are like: they've been in Michelle's bedroom for the last hour or two, but I bet they're still not ready."

"Thanks," Steve said.

They entered the homely cottage. The walls were lined in cedar planks, and the aromatic smell hung in the air. Paul admired the wooden model of a four-masted Barque over the fireplace. Sunlight flooded through a skylight, and flowers stood on the table. Little knickknacks were placed along the shelves, and the cottage smelled of baked bread.

"You guys take a look around, and I'll tell them you're here."

Steve reached out to pick up a piece of driftwood on display, but his hand shot back when they heard a voice behind them.

"Hi, I'm Mrs. Simpson. You must be the boys Michelle has told me about." The woman who smiled at them was shorter than Michelle, but had her same black, shiny hair.

"Paul."

"Steve, how do you do, Mrs. Simpson?"

"Good, thank you. Would you boys like a Coke or anything?"

Paul rolled his tongue around his dry mouth before replying. "That would be great, thank you very much."

The conspirators smiled at each other as she went down the corridor to the small kitchen at the back.

Mr. Simpson came back and explained that the girls would be out in a minute. The boys felt more at ease as he showed them the model ship and its fine workings in more detail.

Paul turned his head when he heard a muffled snicker behind his back. Michelle and Tanya were radiant in faded jeans and tight T-shirts. Paul gulped and tore his eyes away from Michelle's stretched top and coughed nervously.

Michelle and Tanya properly introduced themselves to Steve, who smiled at the attention. There was a pregnant silence until Mrs. Simpson came back with a tray of ice-cold drinks. Everyone took a glass eagerly.

"Why don't you guys go out to the porch to have your drinks? Donald, please come and give me a hand with the water pump: it's playing up again," she said to her husband, who was hovering.

"Come on, let's go outside," Michelle said. The young men followed, neither able to take their eyes off the two pert bums in the faded jeans.

Once outside, their tension eased, and soon they were all fighting for a chance to speak. *I think this is going to be all right*, Paul thought as his friendly, gray-blue eyes met Michelle's sparkling green ones. He noticed they were also speckled with a few dots of gray, and he loved the way her raven-black hair cascaded over her shoulders.

Steve was soon having to discuss his injuries and Paul deflected the talk away to more pleasant subjects.

"Anyway, you certainly look fit now."

Tanya blushed a little, and Michelle laughed.

"Well, what do you two lovely young ladies want to do this afternoon? Our boat, *Tai Pan*, is at your command." Paul couldn't help the romantic flair; he was beginning to really like Michelle and Tanya.

"I'd sure like to go over to Secret Cove and look for driftwood for my mom's flower arranging. When the tide goes out, the sun heats the sand up, making it really warm for swimming," Michelle suggested.

"Okay, let's go," Paul said.

"You guys go down, and we'll follow you after we get our swimsuits," Tanya said.

The boys sauntered down the path and kept close. "Mm, that Tanya—what a brick house. I'm already in love." Steve virtually hopped from one leg to the other.

Both Paul and Steve had their fair share of female admirers due to their good looks and better humor, but they were still excited by these two beautiful girls in the prime of their life.

"Here, help us with these, please," Michelle shouted.

The boys ran back to relieve her of two bulging beach bags.

"Hey, what's in here?" Steve mimicked weakness as he hefted the bags.

"Oh, my mom's a fusspot, just some food and some things," Michelle replied.

Paul took Michelle's hand as they walked along the wobbly dock toward the boat.

"Nice boat," Tanya said.

"Thank you. My dad's never let me have it by myself before. He must be slipping in his old age." Paul chuckled to himself as he helped Michelle on board. Both girls vied for the opportunity to climb the steps to the flying bridge first.

Paul and Steve quickly untied *Tai Pan* and jumped on board. Both were very conscious of the girls as they squeezed onto the flying bridge and gingerly sat between them. The soft, cream leather seats barely allowed four at a push. They laughed excitedly, and Michelle let out a squeal of delight, as the engines roared to life.

Soon, they were all chatting at once over the whistling wind as the sea was cleaved into a spreading 'V'.

"Better drop anchor here," Michelle advised when they got close. "The tide's going out, I think, and it goes out a long way on this shelving beach." Paul agreed, noting on the depth sounder that they had only fifteen feet under the keel.

"What kind of driftwood you after, Michelle?" Paul asked while the two of them walked the sand on shore. He mouthed her name again, savoring the romantic French pronunciation.

"Oh, unusual, gnarled and bleached stuff: the older the better." She showed Paul a lovely curled piece of alder root as an example.

"Yeah, that one's spiffy-looking." He admired the bleached, broken root and stroked its smooth surface.

Steve and Tanya were sitting on a scarred old cedar log, one of many that lay on top of each other along the curving beach. Paul carried their precious cargo of driftwood and followed Michelle's swaying behind back to where Steve and Tanya were seated.

"Tanya, let's dig in to that picnic, I'm starving," Michelle said.

"As usual." Tanya rolled her eyes with a giggle.

"Ha ha. I think it's all in the orange bag."

The pile of sandwiches, oranges, melon, soft drinks, and napkins grew and grew.

"Boy, there's enough to feed an army here." Steve passed a shrimp-and-rye sandwich to Tanya.

The sun soon warmed the four young friends, and Paul felt a bead of sweat drip past his ear. He and Steve ate heartily, as did the girls. After they had finished, they all agreed to try a swim if it was warm enough.

"Shoot, forgot my trunks on the boat," Steve said, and Paul volunteered to help him paddle back and get them. They fairly raced back to the boat, got their trunks on, and booked it back breathlessly.

The girls just lifted their tops and dropped their jeans as the boys scrambled out of the dinghy. Tanya had a jet-black bikini, while Michelle's was a fluorescent orange that highlighted her tan beautifully.

"This is one time where the men go first: so, hop to it and test the water," Michelle challenged.

Paul involuntarily drew his toe back from the ocean's icy grip and Steve did the same.

"Go on then, what are you waiting for? It's great once you get in."

"We know, just testing first," Paul called back. He grabbed hold of Steve's hand. Steve looked at him, winked, and yelled as they both ran splashing in the shallows before diving in head-first.

They heard the girls shriek with delight upon entering the refreshing inlet. After their mad dash to show off, Paul and Steve slowed to a leisurely breaststroke, their wake rippling the rocky shoreline.

Michelle and Tanya swam slowly but strongly, and met the boys halfway. There were pockets of really warm water where the sand had heated the sea up, and they met in one of these.

"Wow, you were right, this is gorgeous," Paul spluttered as he treaded water.

"Yes, and in the height of summer it gets warm all over the bay; you can stay in for hours," Michelle said.

Her hair floated in waves behind her, and a salty drop of seawater slowly trickled down her finely-honed nose. Her small tongue licked the top of her lips and she bobbed up and down, also kicking water.

Oh, no, Paul thought and inwardly groaned. He felt a familiar hardness grow as he watched her lick her delicate lips in what he thought was a most provocative way.

"Come on, let's dive off those rocks there. There's a beauty of a spot to do it and some lovely starfish all over the bottom to watch." Michelle kicked backward, quickly followed by Tanya and Steve.

Paul slowly followed, trying to think of other things.

Michelle pulled herself up the granite rocks, climbed to the top of one, and stood poised. Paul trod water a safe distance away. His predicament literally grew as his eyes took in her long, finely muscled legs, lingered on her delicious mound, caressed her lean, flat stomach, and climbed her pert, round breasts to her beautiful face.

"Here I come, look out…wee," she cried and cleanly parted the water in a lovely dive. She rose next to Paul and smiled mischievously.

"Your turn, Paul."

"Can't dive, never could; I always do belly flops," he lied. He slowly backed off, avoiding her knowing eyes. Michelle didn't respond, and just treaded water.

Paul caught the glint in Steve's eyes and turned quickly away before he said anything. He swam hard to the beach, driving himself to his limit. He loved the feel of the water sweeping past his long arms and legs. The burst of hard exertion tempered his ardor, and he felt more comfortable when he turned around and watched the others come in.

They all clamped their arms around their bodies and ran tiptoe to the pile of towels by the logs. They rubbed themselves briskly until their red goose bumps faded.

"Ah, that feels good." Steve sighed, rubbing his face briskly with the towel.

The sun soon took the chill off, and everyone leaned back to get its full effect.

Out of the corner of his eye, Paul noticed Michelle's gaze hover over his chest and stomach, pausing only momentarily on the long, pliable swell across his navy trunks. He was pleased at her attention, if a touch embarrassed.

He felt the old familiar feeling starting again and decided to get changed while the going was good. He grabbed his towel, and both he and Steve went deeper into the pile of logs to put their jeans on.

"Look at that, Paul."

Paul turned just in time to get a glimpse of two tight, pale orbs before they were bound beneath a dark bra. Still a nice sight.

After a respectful wait, they both returned to the whispering girls.

"Ever been fishing, ladies?" Paul asked as they approached.

Tanya rolled her eyes. "Yes, it's boring; you never catch anything."

"Ah, but you happen to be in the company of two who can rival the old man of the sea," Steve countered. "Come, we've had a few this week already."

They packed their gear and were soon back on the boat. As hard as the two boys tried, they could not get a bite. Soon, they had to admit defeat under a barrage of good-humored barbs about the one that never even had a chance to get away.

"What time do you have to be back?" Steve asked.

"Oh, any time before dark, especially since we're on a boat." Michelle responded.

"Good, then we can cook you a salmon we caught on the way down. How about that?"

"Okay, but I'd like to nip up to the house first and get into something warmer; it's starting to get chilly. And I want to tell my mom not to worry about supper."

Tania nodded her agreement.

They tied up at the dock and let the girls off, then started to prepare the meal. After about half an hour, the girls came back, Tania in a lovely dress and Michelle wearing a sweater with a wide enough collar that showed off her shoulders, unmarred by bra straps.

"Just in time for an aperitif. Are you allowed a drop of wine?" Paul flourished the chilled bottle of California Chablis, which had drops of moisture dripping down the label.

"Oh, we'd love some—but don't wave it around too much," Michelle said as they climbed down into the cozy stern cockpit.

"Wow, so you did get one," Tanya said when she saw the gleaming salmon steaks all ready to go in the frying pan.

"Hey, who likes Pink Floyd?" She pointed to one of their cassettes lying on the counter.

"We both do," Steve answered over his shoulder. "There's more tapes over there in the cassette box, pick whatever you like."

"That one's fine: it's one of my favorites," Michelle said, and Paul was glad they shared a taste in music.

Paul stirred the chopped mushrooms, garlic, lemon juice, and cream in the bubbling pan. The scent pervaded the small cabin.

Time passed swiftly as each asked questions about music, school, sports, and the upcoming summer.

"Sit down, ladies: dinner is served," Paul said with a wave. He topped up their wineglasses till they nearly overflowed. Red salmon steaks steamed in the middle of an oval fish platter, and the cream cooled around it. In a side dish, potatoes and carrots ran with butter. A small plate of smoked oysters with lemon juice topped off the scrumptious feast.

Michelle took an oyster first, crinkled her nose at it, closed her eyes, and swallowed it whole. She opened her eyes with a smile and took another one, and the others quickly followed.

"Right, tuck in and enjoy. Oh, sorry, grace. Fish for head, potatoes for stomach, get the implements and let battle commence."

They all laughed at the grace Paul had learned from his dad and dug in.

"Mm, delicious. Where did you learn to cook like this? Most guys I've known wouldn't go near a kitchen," Michelle asked Paul.

"Well, my mom hates cooking and I love good food, so I've dabbled at it now and again. I even took some lessons in school. Which, I may add—" Paul gestured with his fork at his friend "—Steve here never let me forget."

"Well, Paul, I take everything back," Steve said between mouthfuls.

"I only cook on holidays and special occasions though."

All ate hungrily, and the sounds of pleasant voices and laughter wafted out of the cozy cabin, traveling across the otherwise silent inlet.

***

After dinner, Michelle wandered back to the open cockpit and gazed up at the darkening sky. The evening held a slight chill, but the air was still and the sky was filled with a billion bright stars. She wrapped her arms around herself.

"Oh, hi," she said dreamily as Paul came out to join her, leaving Steve and Tanya in deep discussion over their favorite bands. They seemed to be hitting it off well, and she was glad for her friend.

"Isn't this stellar?" Paul aimed a smile her way. "I just love the summer air; the sky is so clear and big."

"Yes, I know what you mean." They gazed up at the sky quietly for a moment, but Michelle's attention kept straying to his sharp features. He had a strong face, but friendly, even when frowning. She remembered the look of his flat, muscled stomach when he was in nothing but his swim trunks. *Umm, not bad*, she thought.

He glanced over at her, and before he caught her staring she asked, "Is it okay to go up top and sit?"

"Of course," Paul agreed and briskly followed her up the small ladder to the flying bridge.

They sat down, close enough to make Michelle feel a little self-conscious. After a couple hesitant attempts, Paul slowly put his arm around her. She relaxed and let herself lean against his shoulder. The wine gave her a warm feeling inside, and all was good with the world.

"Can I see you again tomorrow?" Paul asked.

"Yes, I'd like that." She lifted her chin up to look into his eyes. Paul took her subtle cue and ever-so-slowly moved his mouth down to hers. His breath was fresh and his lips soft. He tentatively explored her teeth with his tongue in a most enticing manner, and soon her own darted around his.

He changed position and drew her tighter to him. His left hand traced her hair, and she loved how delicately he brushed her jawline.

Her hand slipped inside his jacket and slowly rubbed the hard muscles of his chest.

Very carefully he let his hand wander down her neck, dance along her arm, and edge closer to her body.

She didn't object, and instead pressed her young body closer to him.

His fingers brushed her sweater, slowly tracing circles ever-closer to her hardened nipple. His palm spread out to encompass her. She let out a muted groan as he gently rubbed and kneaded.

Michelle thought to herself, *Watch out: this is too nice, and he's even nicer.* She was still a virgin, even after a few close calls. She had always held back, much to the consternation of her few carefully-selected dates. But this time she couldn't pull herself away.

Her fingers dug into his hard back and traced a line around his side to his flat, knotted stomach. She squirmed a little as she felt her dampness spreading like it never had before. *No, no,* she kept telling herself, but still the delicious tingling continued and she failed to resist.

Her nipples felt like they were about to explode under Paul's touch. The ease of his company, good surroundings, and the slight bravado of the wine soothed her usually-measured responses. She felt she had known him for ages. So, she just closed her eyes and went with her feelings.

Paul edged his fingers under her sweater. His breath was fast and shallow, and it became faster under her wandering hand, now tracing his stomach. His leg muscles involuntarily flexed when she brushed his now-tight jeans by mistake, and her excitement rose.

His hand, slightly chilled due to the crisp air, made her nipple tighter and swell even harder. She gently nibbled his ear to stifle the moans in her throat. Paul pressed into her and raised his buttocks slightly so that she felt the full length of him. Even through his jeans she could tell he was big; she felt it pulsate like a live thing. More surprising was when she realized she was pushing herself onto it.

The music wafted up, but no sounds of voices from below joined it.

Paul slipped his hand from under her sweater and traced a line to her knee and back, each time slipping down a little, till she felt him reach the seam of her crotch.

Michelle couldn't believe she had let him go so far, but still she could not pull away; her hips involuntarily arched forward to press even harder against his probing fingers. *Just a little more and I'll stop,* Michelle promised herself. The sensations Paul had aroused were just too strong to stop now.

She let her hand slip down and felt the top of his hardness. As his hand rubbed her, she let her own trace along his tight jeans, feeling him stiffen and grow even harder. So intense was she on her own exploration that she never felt the top button of her jeans release. But she did feel his fingers ever-so-slowly probe down to the band of elastic on her panties.

Okay, she thought, *enough is enough; this has to stop right now,* but somehow, she still couldn't move.

She felt his fingertips tickle the top of her hair, and still he crept further down. He passed her pubic bone to the first parting of her softness.

Suddenly she pulled back, somewhat startled at him, but mostly herself. *Why did I let that keep going?*

Thankfully, Paul got the message straight away, withdrawing his hand. He looked down, a flush rising on his tanned cheeks. Their eyes didn't meet as they slowly withdrew from each other and rearranged their clothing.

"It's late, we must be getting along," she whispered.

"Yes, of course, and—look, I'm really sorry that I came on a bit strong. I don't want you to get the wrong idea; I mean, I really like you a lot and…" he stumbled for the right words.

Michelle put her hand on his to quiet him. "Yes, I know what you mean. As the saying goes, it takes two to tango. Come on, we had better get going, or my dad will be having kittens. I don't want him wandering down here, so let's be off."

Their noise coming down from the flying bridge had allowed Steve and Tanya the time to disengage. When Paul and Michelle entered the cabin, the other two both looked rather flustered. Nobody's eyes met the others.

Paul grabbed the flashlight and lit their way as they rather sheepishly crept along the dock, Michelle in the lead. The lights of her parents' cottage were shining brightly as they climbed the creaking steps onto the porch.

Her mom was at the door as they entered. Michelle was relieved that she didn't seem at all alarmed. After all, she reminded herself, they were only fifteen or so minutes late.

On the steps, they all said their good-byes. As Paul turned to go, she took her chance to give him a little peck on the cheek.

"See you on the flipside. But not before ten, okay?"

And with that, she and Tanya slipped inside. She wondered if her friend had had as good a time as she had.

***

"Boy, Steve, I think we both lucked out," Paul said as they sat down at the galley table.

"Yeah, they're some choice ladies, that's for sure. You two seemed awfully quiet up top."

"Hey, we weren't the only ones. So come on, Mr. Casanova, spill."

"Oh, it was nothing much. I didn't try really too hard. She didn't seem the type for the first night, but she sure can kiss something delicious, and we had a good chat," Steve offered as reply.

"Yeah, know what you mean." Paul's heart was still pounding with the worry of pushing too far, too fast.

"In fact, it was Michelle who started everything. If my hand had gone one more inch, I'm sure we would have gone all the way, but she backed off suddenly. I'm sort of glad, really; but boy, do I have ball ache."

"Me too. Come on, I'm pooped. But hey, no rocking the boat tonight." Steve gave him a cheeky grin.

"No bets tonight, dude. I think I'd lose."

"You want some Four Seasons on to lull us to sleep?" Steve asked.

"Okay." And with that, Paul got undressed and hit his bunk with gusto.

The next day the girls kept them waiting for over an hour; by the end, they were both pacing the decks.

"You sure we shouldn't go up?" Steve asked.

"No, I'm sure they said they would come down here."

A little later, the girls came trotting down the path, both looking fresh and radiant.

"Have a good sleep, guys?" Michelle asked with a mischievous grin.

Paul coughed and spluttered a bit before replying. "Yes thanks. It's all the sun and fresh air. We were pretty beat."

Soon they were all chatting away like nothing had happened the night before. Paul was dying to take Michelle in his arms, but his own shyness and the previous night's episode undermined his courage to be so open. *Why am I so afraid?* he thought. *After all, she was pretty responsive yesterday.* But he still had a feeling that he'd better let her make the first move.

They all agreed to nip over to Fulford Harbor and wander around the arts and crafts stores—maybe even pick up some new cassettes.

Being a holiday Monday, the little village was packed with islanders and the first early tourists. All the artwork busily prepared by the craftsmen during the winter overflowed into the outdoor market. It was fascinating to see such a mix of people: poor artists, rich yachtsmen, ordinary family tourists, and lots of retired folks who had fallen in love with the quiet islands of the gulf. It didn't hurt that the islands boasted a cool climate with warm summers and very mild winters.

They all sat on the grassy park overlooking the small dock where yachts and powerboats of all sizes lay snugly tied up. Their Cokes were ice cold, and Paul lay on his back to soak up the sun.

He felt an ever-so-gentle touch on his lip and instinctively knew it was Michelle. He opened his eyes and smiled lazily. He traced the cool outline of her bare arm. Neither spoke, each absorbed in the other's silent touch. Paul was relieved that the tension had broken, and somehow knew the pace would slow.

However, Steve and Tanya were completely different: both were engaged in a deep and lingering kiss.

Michelle suddenly sat up and said, "I'm starving; let's go and get some fish and chips."

Without another word she pulled Paul up—despite his protests—and marched him to the little shop they had seen earlier. Tanya and Steve followed shortly after. Paul smiled when he saw Steve's hand thrust deep in his pocket, no doubt hiding his embarrassment, as Tanya laughed by his side.

"Hey, take your hand out of your pocket, Steve," he challenged in a low voice.

Steve silently mouthed his unspeakable reply, and Paul laughed as he tried to catch up to the marching Michelle, who was still pulling at his arm.

He couldn't believe how much food Michelle could consume. Most girls he knew kept to a funny type of diet, but obviously Michelle's cravings sometimes overtook her. He didn't know where she hid it all; he couldn't detect an ounce of fat. She slouched back after swallowing her last chip and made a face at Paul when he asked her if she would like another helping.

Afterward, Michelle and Tanya dragged them into a material shop, of all things. Paul idly poked at the brightly-colored racks of hand-printed cloth while Michelle asked Tanya her opinion over which color suited her best. Both were avid seamstresses, and Paul was impressed when he found out that most of their dresses were handmade.

Paul's heart missed a beat when Michelle twirled around while draped in a bright yellow cotton material. Her raven hair flowed around it. *How lucky can I get?*, he thought as he absorbed her beauty.

His thoughts were slightly tempered when he found out that she was short ten dollars. He dug into his pocket to rescue her when she couldn't make up her mind over which material she would have to put back.

Soon they were returning to her place. Her parents had insisted they come for supper, but Paul severely wished he could be alone with her. Tomorrow would be their last day: Michelle and her parents would be catching the midday ferry back to Vancouver.

Mrs. Simpson was most impressed when the boys offered to wash the pots; however, they were both relieved when she graciously refused.

"We'll walk you to the boat and maybe see you in the morning before you leave." Michelle opened the door for Steve, who virtually bounded out of his chair, quickly followed by Tanya.

"I'm sorry we have to go early; Dad has an important client he has to meet tomorrow," Michelle said as they walked along the docks. "I have a great idea. Interested?"

"Give it to me."

"Well, next weekend the Rolling Stones are playing in Victoria, and…well, I was wondering if you and Steve could come. I can get the car off Mom, and we can get back the same night."

"Wow, that would be great; that's the last weekend before we have to go back up island," Paul replied.

Both stared at each other until Paul slowly reached for her. Their lips touched, and they kissed in a long, lingering embrace before parting.

"Bye Michelle. See you next weekend," he whispered in her ear.

Steve and Tanya were harder to part, and Paul knew how they felt—he didn't want the magic to end. Both boys stood on the flying bridge and watched the faint light from the flashlights disappear into the woods and up to the cottage.

***

The next weekend went great, and after that Paul and Michelle saw each other as much as possible. Steve had broken it off with Tanya not long after they had made love in the back of his dad's Chevrolet. To Steve it was the chase more than anything, and their relationship faltered after the passion faded.

Paul had tried resolutely, but so far had failed to make love to Michelle. She would only let him go so far, which slightly puzzled him after their first rather passionate encounter. But he was patient when Michelle admitted that she was still a virgin. He didn't mind too much; in fact, he enjoyed the surreptitious plans he made to try to seduce her, and his anticipation mounted as the last of her walls faltered.

They didn't see each other too often, since Vancouver and Kelsey Bay, where Paul lived on Vancouver Island, were about six hours away. However, at least once a month they managed to see each other at her parents or his, and luckily everyone got on well.

Paul worked in his dad's mill during the summer break, which helped to pay for gas and ferry tickets on his forays south. He learned a lot about the forestry business, and his dad was secretly pleased that his only son took such an interest.

Paul described his meeting with Chuck Stoneman and the ideas the man had, and his dad listened with interest. In return, Paul's dad told him of the deal he had with Rand Barrett, the father of Paul's hockey rival, where they swapped pulp wood for the equivalent volume of chips. Both parties gained in their own way.

Paul was encouraged by his parents to go to the University of Victoria to take an engineering degree, which would hopefully progress him in the forestry industry. His dad had explained how rapidly the industry was changing and how important technical skills would be in the future.

Paul was disappointed to learn that Michelle was going to attend the University of British Columbia in Vancouver for a degree in biology, keeping them apart for longer.

Michelle's defenses had lasted just under a year until, on one unplanned night, they had made mad, passionate love in Paul's old Ford fastback. He loved his old Mustang, but sorely wished that it had more room. The gear knob had bruised him on that first night, and only when their lovemaking became more creative did it cease to be a problem. Because of the distance between them, their lovemaking sessions were wild, passionate, affairs. Once both had rooms on campus, they often spent the weekends together.

Paul soon got into the campus routine. He enjoyed the social activities and the university hockey team. The only blemish was that he missed Steve. Steve had joined the Canadian Forces Maritime Command, and his time was split between the base in Esquimalt and the Navy Training College in North Vancouver.

Paul was idly browsing through the Vancouver Sun one morning between classes when a heading caught his eye.

Rand Barrett, Local Forest Giant, Dies at Forty-Eight due to Cancer.

"Mr. Barrett's presence will be sorely missed in the industry he helped to create and expand. His company, West Skeena Timber Ltd., controls two pulp mills and six sawmills spread throughout British Columbia. Company spokesmen were quoted as saying that Mr. Barrett knew of his illness and had left detailed plans for its continued management. His only son, Nick Barrett, is believed to be the sole beneficiary. A special board of directors has been given interim control. Stocks at the close of the Vancouver Stock Exchange dropped slightly, but are expected to rise again after the initial shock is past."

Paul pondered the memory of his and Nick's last meeting on the ice rink a year prior and felt apprehensive at the future power Nick would hold. He was sure Nick was the type to harbor a grudge if their paths were to ever cross again.

Only a year later, during his semester break, and much to Paul's surprise, a West Skeena Timber corporate helicopter landed unannounced at his dad's Kelsey Bay mill. Paul recognized Nick immediately and went to get his father. He felt sure this visit would concern them both.

***

Nick stepped out of the helicopter, flanked by two nervous older executives, George and Stanley, carrying briefcases. He wasn't sure what he resented more: the unexpected loss of his father, or that his father had foreseen it and, without telling him, had appointed a team of special directors to undermine him. It had taken time, but eventually Nick had managed to convince these two that it was in their definite long-term interests to do this special favor for him.

"Hi Paul; long time no see," Nick said with a flashing grin. He wondered if the self-righteous bastard ever thought of him and what he'd done to ruin Nick's life. He turned to Paul's father. "And glad to meet you, Mr. Whorton."

Neither invited him inside.

"Can we have a private chat?" Nick pressed. "We have some urgent business we wish to discuss. Of course, Paul is free to join us." After George and Stanley introduced themselves, they all went up to a small, dingy office above the sawmill.

"George, why don't you begin," Nick said once he was seated across from Paul and his father.

"Well, Mr. Whorton, as you know, we have recently finished the pulp mill's expansion in Chemainus. Due to its increased capacity, we find the need to terminate the agreement you had with the late Mr. Barrett."

The senior Whorton went from zero to a hundred in no time. Nick couldn't say he was surprised, considering his son.

"Bullshit you can. Mr. Barrett and I had an agreement, and there are still two years left on it. Check! It goes right to the end of '74," the man thundered.

"Well, we quite understand your concern, but you see we only have your word for it; we can find no written instructions from Mr. Barrett about the matter. As we stated before, we now need the wood for our own mills."

Nick couldn't help a faint smile. That's what they got for not covering their asses with a contract.

"You got anything to do with this, boy?" Paul's father directed his accusation to Nick.

Nick's smile vanished at the obvious insult, but he kept his cool and looked the older man straight in the eye.

"You've had a very lucrative agreement in the past, Mr. Whorton; for both us and for you."

Mostly for them. Did they expect him to just continue handing over free wood, with only chips as payment, when he had his own mills to run?

"But to answer your question, yes: I want the wood back for my own mills. I have my own company's interests to consider. You can keep all the wood of ours you have in storage, but we expect the chips in payment by, shall we say, next Wednesday?"

It was a fair turn-around, if a little on the short side. Deep down, Nick hoped they would ask for an extension. It would be worth it to see Paul beg for something. Considering how they had treated him thus far today, though, he already knew he would turn them down. Serve them right.

Instead, Mr. Whorton scoffed, glaring down at him.

"I can see that you're not made of the same stuff as your late father. He was a real man, and his word was good. Now, take your sniveling sidekicks off my land and get back to your glass towers."

He rose from his chair and advanced threateningly around the desk.

George and Stanley, timid at heart, quickly backed off, but Nick stood in front of Mr. Whorton to stare him in the eye. How dare he compare him to his father? He hadn't even truly known the man. Nick maintained eye contact, asserting himself as the better man, before he turned around and headed for the door.

"I should have hit you harder that time, eh Nick?" Paul said.

That stopped Nick in his tracks. He felt his face flush slightly and met Paul's eyes. Of course, he was going to make this about *that* day. How could he have thought that *Paul Whorton* would ever let him forget?

"No doubt you'll have your chance," he bit out. "But in the meanwhile, enjoy your two-bit operation here while it lasts."

"Now's your chance, let's go." Paul moved forward.

"Hold it, Paul," his father said as he blocked his path. "You don't need to drop to his level. You proved it a long time ago."

"A wise decision, Mr. Whorton," Nick said, although inside he seethed. Drop to *his* level? He wasn't the one bringing up a years-old fistfight from a bloody game, for God's sake. But at least one of them had some sense of propriety left.

"Just get off my land before I change my mind."

Nick was glad to. He flicked a gesture at George and Stanley to follow him and strode out the door.

George avoided Nick's black eyes as he sat opposite him in the tight quarters of the Bell Jet helicopter. Nick was staring out of the window as the pilot prepared for takeoff. His eyes narrowed as he spotted the two small figures walk across the logging yard below.

Nick's fury with them only grew. 'Boy': the uppity bastard had called him 'boy'. *I'll show him just who the 'boy' is in this business. They'll see; this is just the beginning*, Nick silently promised as the dark forests passed beneath them.

But first, it would be wise to have some more information.

"George," Nick snapped, "Find out who handles their lumber sales."

"Yes, Mr. Barrett; I'll send the information to your apartment as soon as possible."

Nick smiled. How easy it was to wield power, especially among those who knew what you were capable of. He had made a mistake approaching his vice chairman first; as he'd found out, his attempts at taking control only made the man angry. The vice chairman didn't worry about getting on Nick's bad side: he was quite well off, so Nick supposed losing his job sometime down the road didn't really bother him.

But Nick learned his lesson: knowledge was power. With the help of a private detective, he'd found out which directors were hard-pressed for money and which had big mortgages on their houses. Yes, George and Stanley had met his requirements perfectly and, now hooked, would not be allowed to shake loose.

Thank God, he thought, *that my father left me a rather generous allowance while I complete my degree.* His father had mapped out his son's future in the company with progressive steps throughout the corporate ladder. According to that plan, it would take him another four years before the board of directors had the power to elect him as chairman, even though he legally held 52 percent of the shares in the company. But Nick wanted to speed things up a bit; he was ready. He looked speculatively at his two directors and made his plans.

Eventually, his thoughts wandered to the evening's entertainment. After all, all work and no play seemed like a waste of his university experience. Luckily his good looks, superb physique, and obvious money attracted an endless stream of chicks. Tonight's date promised to be exciting: an attractive girl who didn't mind it a little rough. However, she wasn't the one he had hoped for.

He'd seen Michelle in a restaurant in English Bay a few nights ago. She looked ravishing—just as he remembered her. Her polite but firm refusal of their date after the hockey match still stung, but he'd been willing to overlook that and try again. And so, he was doubly hurt when she shot him down a second time. She even went so far to say that she wasn't interested in a relationship with him, and that yes, she had made other plans after the hockey game that night. When he pressed her, she admitted that she was already in another relationship: with Paul Whorton.

The thought of it still made him fume. *Yes, Mr. Paul Whorton, one day I'll have you begging for mercy, and Michelle will realize what a mistake she made in choosing a lesser man like you over me.*

Chapter Four
The Seed

The seventies in British Columbia were boom years for the forestry industry. Engineering consultants worked constant overtime designing one mill after the other. Lumber, pulp, and paper prices skyrocketed and huge profits were there for the taking. The provincial government kept increasing the allowable cut across the province and rubbed their hands at the increased revenue from stumpage fees.

Only a tiny fraction of the forest in British Columbia was privately owned: the rest was nearly all crown land, which had been split up into tree forest licenses. A loose mandate was given that each company had sole responsibility for its harvesting and tree planting. This left very little area reforested, and most cut areas were left to regenerate naturally.

The proliferation of new sawmills and pulp mills meant that the level of sustained cutting was grossly surpassed. No warning of the long-term danger penetrated the haze of profits, and the glory years continued with precious little replanting being done.

Two years into his degree, Paul received a serious double blow. The first came when his father suffered a stroke. It took all the wind out of Gordon's sails and left him a shell of the man he had once been.

Paul's father and mother adamantly forbade him quitting university to come and help at the mill. They told him they were well-organized, and the present assistant manager was very good; he could easily run the mills operation for a good few years until Paul could complete his degree.

Paul's father still had most of his faculties intact and still oversaw the mill, albeit in a less active way. Major acquisition or expenditure decisions still had to pass his scrutiny. It helped that prices were so good it was hard not to make money; even with the pulp lumber they had lost from West Skeena, the balance books were very healthy. Tempting as it was, his father had not increased his allowable cut; somehow, it made him uneasy, and he wasn't a greedy man by nature.

The second blow, just like the first, took Paul completely by surprise. His relationship with Michelle had, to him, settled down into a warm, steady affair. They didn't see each other as often as they would have liked, since, for both of them, their courses were demanding, but they still met at least twice a month. In fact, Michelle's lovemaking had grown increasingly passionate the last few months, which made the bomb she dropped even more puzzling to Paul.

"Paul, I think it best that we have a break for a while, especially since midterm exams are coming up," Michelle said in a rush. They were driving back to her place after seeing a concert in Vancouver.

Paul didn't really hear her at first, or at least didn't truly grasp what she had said. She repeated it.

"What? No, I can handle the exams. Come on, let's go for a pizza."

"No, I'm serious, Paul, I do think it's for the best at the moment. I need a break and time to think."

Paul gripped the wheel harder; he didn't like the ominous tone in her voice. "Look, Michelle, everything's fine; you're only nervous about the exams. It'll pass, so lighten up. You're making me nervous."

"I mean it, Paul, I want a break for a while." She stared resolutely out the window, not looking at him.

"Shit, Michelle, what's the score? Everything's fine." Paul ran a hand through his hair. "Come on, honey, let's talk about this later. Okay?"

"No," she pressed, "I've thought a lot about this, and I know it's for the best. Besides, classes finish up in only another three months."

"That's a hell of a long time," Paul snapped. Was it another guy? He was afraid to learn the answer.

"Paul. Paul, slow down right now," she warned.

Paul started, realizing he had gunned the Mustang right past a bus and beyond. "Hey look, I'm perfectly safe. Besides, you usually like the speed as much as I do." He reached out and rubbed her leg.

Michelle lifted his hand off; he saw that her eyes were blurred with tears.

Damn, he thought, *this is getting serious.* He was at a loss for what to do. Where had he gone wrong?

Michelle kept her face averted as they drove through the towering skyscrapers of downtown Vancouver.

"Please take me home, Paul."

Paul was getting angry now. He sent the Mustang viciously round a corner, startling a few pedestrians into looking around in alarm at the sound of squealing tires.

He plucked up his courage and said, "Is it another guy? You can tell me."

She quickly shook her head, her black hair fluttering across her face. "No, it isn't; I can't explain it, but I just have to think. I love you, Paul, but…" She buried her face in her hands and wept.

"Hey, come on, honey, what's the matter?" he soothed. He slowed down as he pulled into her apartment's parkade.

After a while, her sobs stopped, and Paul took some solace as she wrapped her arms around him. Still confused, Paul led her upstairs and opened the door to her apartment. "Do you want me to go now or in the morning?"

"No, stay; you've missed the ferry. You can go tomorrow."

They got undressed and slipped into bed. Michelle snuggled close, and Paul stared at the black ceiling, his mind a confused mix of emotions. He kissed her forehead. Michelle responded and soon they wanted each other.

God, Paul thought, *I didn't realize how much I loved her till tonight. I've been a fool, just taking her for granted.* His thoughts and ardor were interrupted by muffled sobs from Michelle.

"Hey, it's okay, everything's fine," he soothed as racking sobs shook her.

"I love you Paul, believe me. It's just that…oh, I don't know; I'm all mixed up. Just be patient, please."

"Okay, okay, but can I still call you now and again?"

"Of course; in fact, I'll call you first."

Eventually he felt her breathing ease and sleep overtook her. But he couldn't sleep and tossed and turned all night, trying to figure it all out.

He left the next morning and caught the midday ferry back to Victoria. Michelle did call him later that week, but she was still adamant they remain apart.

Paul sorely missed her, and his want for her increased a hundred-fold. He was sullen and couldn't concentrate on his studies. He called Steve and told him the score. Steve couldn't believe it, eventually just putting it down to, "Women—just can't figure them out."

The months slowly dragged by, and he let reviewing for the exams slip. Tears came to his eyes whenever he saw any little reminders of her in his small dorm room. A hair beret here, an old patched pair of jeans there, a few of her favorite records, and other miscellaneous bits and bobs. Her calls became less frequent, while his became more so. Eventually, she told him not to call until after the exams had finished. He had slammed the phone down in frustration.

He only just passed his exams. His tutor, although disappointed, had tried to help, but Paul had kept his problem a secret and shut him out.

The final blow came when, even after her exams, Michelle still refused to see him. Finally, he asked again.

"It's another guy, right?"

There was a long period of silence at the other end and Paul's stomach knotted.

"Yes," she whispered, "but it's not what you think."

"Bullshit, what does that mean?" he snapped back.

"I haven't, well, you know—"

"Oh, come on, I'm a big boy; you can tell me if he's been screwing the ass off you." He immediately regretted his outburst.

"Hey now listen, Paul, that's not true. Even if I had, so what? You don't own me, you know," she said.

"I'm sorry, it's just I miss you terribly; I don't know how to fight it."

"Look, I'll call you soon, okay? Bye." The phone went dead.

He stared at the phone, bewildered. Steve was at sea on his first trials and he desperately wanted to confide in someone.

Things just got worse. Michelle soon lost her temper with his continued questions and told him not to call again.

He was so mad that he gathered up all her things, took the next ferry to Vancouver and arrived at her apartment. He didn't know how to fight an unknown enemy and it enraged him.

"Here, take your damn things; I don't want them."

Michelle just stared at the box at her feet.

"And take this while I'm at it." Paul flung the gold signet ring she'd bought him onto the floor.

"Please, Paul, don't be like this. Can't we be friends still?"

"No, I don't like sharing. It's me or him; you have to choose."

"I can't, please just give me time."

"That's bullshit and you know it; I've waited goddamn months already. So, what's the answer?"

"I'm sorry if that's the way you feel, Paul."

Paul had no response for that. He stomped off, leaving only two streaks of burned rubber on the road to show his anger.

***

Michelle was as confused as Paul, unable to understand her own conflicting emotions. She still loved Paul, but she also loved Andrew, her classmate. It had started out harmlessly enough eight months ago when they had swapped ideas for an essay. Well, things developed and soon she sought out his company more and more. It hadn't started off romantically, but Michelle soon realized she was harboring feelings for him. Paul had been her first love, but she had matured faster than Paul and looked to Andrew for his deeper views of things.

Four months after her and Paul's breakup, during which she allowed Andrew to take her to bed, she broke it off. Four months after her breakup with Paul, after which she had allowed Andrew to take her to bed, she broke off with Andrew. Deep down, she realized she had only needed to experience a change before she truly committed to a long-term relationship. She had tried to call Paul, but he had changed apartments. She thought it was fate and tried to put it behind her.

***

Over the next two years, Paul had to work hard at his studies, for the math and science in his program had become increasingly complex. There were long laboratory reports to write and endless exams, or so it seemed. He had made quite a few friends, and hours were spent in the students' bar talking about politics, world events, girls, and fishing.

Once a month, there was a student dance where he and a few of his classmates drank too much and felt awful the next day. He had enjoyed two relationships with girls from campus, but each time had broken them off after a couple months. Deep down, he still yearned for Michelle, and he was soon bored with their company; he always ended up comparing them to her.

He was envious of Steve, who by this point was in his third year at sea. When Steve returned on leave, Paul loved to hear his stories of Africa and the Caribbean. They painted the city red and ended up in a few fights when their boisterous antics were not appreciated by others. Sadly, Steve soon found himself hard-pressed in his final year, and they only got together for a drink every couple of months.

The final exams were hard, and Paul struggled to earn grades for the first time in his life. There were so many formulas and facts to be committed to memory that he reverted to his and Steve's old practice of only learning a certain percentage. But it paid off well: he passed with a comfortable margin and came out with a Bachelors' Degree in Engineering in the spring of 1975.

The forestry industry was still booming, and Paul had a wide selection of opportunities. Under the advice of his father, after a few months of searching he took a job as a junior site engineer with a new sawmill company in Terrace. He was lucky, both because he was starting at the beginning of a project and because it involved the construction of a brand-new sawmill, built to replace a thirty-year-old complex. His dad's work and his studies had only shown him old equipment, and he was fascinated with the new technology of thin kerf saws, high-strain band mills, and scanning optimizers.

He thought he knew everything about engineering after his degree, but to his dismay all the theory was practically useless to him. They had only touched on hydraulics, compressed air, drive design, gearboxes, and computers, but here he was surrounded by the very essence of engineering, most of which was strange to him.

He learned fast, though, and spent late nights studying the engineer's drawings intimately. He loved it when the other workers started to ask him all types of questions and, better yet, he had the answers. The questions grew in complexity and number as they quickly found out he always came back with an answer. The workers liked his enthusiasm, and like most good tradesmen, they loved to share their knowledge with a receptive ear.

The saw and planer mill complex was comprised of a hundred thousand pieces, which, when all put together, worked like a huge, synchronized machine. The hours were long—sometimes sixteen, even twenty hours per day—but his youth and energy drove him on. The project engineer let him have more and more responsibility, until at the final stages Paul was directing nearly a hundred men.

***

All over the province, chip and lumber prices held at record-high levels. Nick's company, West Skeena Timber Ltd., built a brand-new pulp mill at Prince Rupert at the phenomenal cost of six hundred million dollars. The company had borrowed heavily, but profits at the market's current prices were equally staggering, and the board eagerly jumped into the large capital expansion.

Nick had just barely passed his business degree and was soon fully absorbed in the vast West Skeena conglomerate. He loved the power of it. However green he was, the existing executives had no choice but to let him in on the upper corporate decision-making, knowing full well it would all be under Nick's control in a few short years.

Nick quickly made it apparent to the other directors what would happen to their future if they opposed him, and soon the decisions he made were invariably passed at board meetings. The acting chairman didn't like Nick and tried to slow his early involvement, but he was usually outvoted by the others.

And it was a good thing, too, Nick thought. His involvement had been good for the company. Not only did they now have the new mill, but Nick had also pushed for and acquired Forest Resources, a major buying and selling company of timber throughout the province. Between them and Nick's own company, they now controlled 75 percent of the Province's wood markets.

As an added bonus, Forest Resources was the very company that dealt with the Whorton family's mill. Nick felt a personal sense of satisfaction at this accomplishment, proving once and for all that even as a 'boy' he was above Paul and his father's little business.

***

Matt, the Whorton family's sawmill manager, had a frown on his face as he read the figures on the fax.

"Hey, Mr. Whorton, you should come see this. Got a minute?"

"Of course, Matt; what you got?"

"Well, we've just received the latest offer for next month's production, and it's 20 percent less than last month."

"What? Bullshit—I haven't seen prices drop in the Forest Digest. Here, let me see." An uneasy feeling settled in the pit of his stomach as he scanned the figures.

Gordon picked up the phone and dialed long distance to Vancouver. "Hi, Herb, this is Gordon Whorton here. Can you check something out for me? One of your clerks must have made a mistake on your buying prices for next month. Can you take a look, please?" He waited for the answer as he rechecked the fax they had received.

"Yes, I'm here. What? Come on, Herb, what the hell's the deal here? You and I both know those prices are low."

Herb's voice on the other end of the line sounded uncomfortable.

"Look, Gordon, I never told you, but I had an unexpected visit from my boss's executive. I was told in no uncertain terms to toe the line or my second-in-command would be sitting where I am. I'm sorry; my hands are tied."

The realization of what had happened made Paul's father slump a little in his chair.

"Hey, Herb, it's not your fault. I'll just move accounts, okay?" He placed the receiver down without waiting for a reply.

"Matt, please give Pickering Forest Sales a call and get a quote," he asked.

Half an hour later, Matt returned, and not unexpectedly the prices weren't any better. "You know who owns both the selling houses now?"

"Yes, West-stinking-Skeena, and I know whose hand this smells of. The bastard is trying to squeeze us. Well, there's a way around that. We just go to the little guys. They only buy at a few dollars less per board foot, and in the meantime, I'll find my own damn buyers. Matt, please get prices from the others."

"Okay, I'll have it together for tomorrow morning," and with that, he left him alone in the office.

Gordon Whorton felt drained and despised his body for its weakness. With a groan, he rose slowly and walked to the house.

Paul called that night, and Gordon started to explain what had happened, but another wave of tiredness swept over him and he slumped in his chair.

His wife took over. "Paul, don't you worry; your dad will be fine. He just tires easily now."

Gordon could hear his son's anxious voice echo over the phone. "Mom, I'll be home tomorrow."

"No, Matt has it under control. I'm sure he can handle it. Besides, you can't walk out now; the mill must be nearly finished."

A pause as he considered. "Okay. But look, Mom, if anything happens, call straight away."

***

Paul felt a little guilty, like he should have just gone home. His dad shouldn't even be working a full day, but he wouldn't hear of slowing down. Paul had read of the takeover by West Skeena and had expected something, but not an outright attack.

The bastard, he thought, *he's having a go at us*.

He hoped the mill they were building would be completed as planned so he could get back as soon as possible. But his mom was right: after over a year of hard work, he hated to leave now. Start-up was only two weeks away, and he dearly wanted to see the result of all his preparations.

It was an exciting time for a project. Start-up was scheduled for early October, and there were a thousand little things to do yet. Thankfully, the list was shortening fast. All the mechanical equipment was in, and the hydraulics, proper control cables, and drives were all in place. He could taste it: all that brand-new machinery just waiting for a few more bits and bobs to run. The big band mills, six-foot circular saws, kickers, and conveyor belts would soon be powered up and carrying wood.

The next day, Paul called his dad and was relieved to hear that a 3-month contract had been secured with one of the smaller buyers, who had given them a good price. Armed with this, he lost himself in his project.

Paul had made firm friends with the mechanical foreman from Terrace. His name was Manny Raposa, and Paul had nothing but respect for him. He had a minimal education, but he had fifty millwrights on the project and knew everything about anything to do with a mill. No matter how pressed Manny was, he always took the time to explain things to Paul.

Manny, in turn, was impressed by Paul's quickness and enthusiasm. He only had to ask for specific drawing data or where something was, and within a few hours he had the information that he needed to direct his crew.

Manny had so many men to direct that he couldn't keep up with the hundreds of drawings to be studied. Paul, however, had an eye for drawings and data. He sorted through the mass and passed on the specific information Manny required.

In this way, an interdependency developed. Each was aware of the other's strengths, and combined, they were an incredible team. The project engineer let them at it when he saw how much extra work was accomplished.

Over the six months, Paul and Manny had come to know every nut and bolt. In reality, they were the heart of the project. Men worked for them easily, as both were cheerful and produced results.

To Paul it was a magic time. During the last week leading up to start-up, Paul had arranged for all the main personnel to tackle their own machines. They loaded programs into the computers, adjusted lasers, tweaked hydraulics, fine-tuned fast-acting air cylinders, and put test pieces of wood through their machines.

By Friday night, the reports were in: they were at least 98 percent ready for Monday morning. The mill would be empty except for Manny and a ten man 'fix it' crew of operators and vendors.

Paul assured the Project Engineer and Mill Manager that they may as well go for it: a project of this size would never be 100 percent ready. They took his word for it, and Paul spent a restless night. A thousand details spun around in his head, and soon he gave up, turned on his light, and finished his latest Wilbur Smith novel. He waited for the sun to rise before driving down to the mill.

Soon the hour was at hand. Paul climbed into an operator's cab that overlooked the log in-feed area. Manny joined him and slapped him on the back. Neither spoke. Instead, they watched as the first large log loader slowly trundled up the slope to the empty log decks.

A front-end loading machine to carry the wood, not unlike a huge insect on wheels with massive steel pinchers, loaded twenty tons of tree-length wood from the loader onto the steel-plated log decks, which were the size of two tennis courts. The deck plating jarred as the logs spilled onto them.

Two thirty-horsepower motors started up and, slowly, ten parallel lengths of thick chain jangled into motion, pulling the logs along. The logs spread out as they were dragged toward the first machine. Paul and Manny smiled at each other.

The operator pressed a button, and the compressed air cylinders picked the first log up, rolled it over, and dumped it into a conveyor chain. The first process was to take all the bark off the log. The conveyor pulled the log through a four-foot diameter ring with whirling, steel-tipped arms to peel away the bark in tightly-curled spirals. The log came out the other side stripped bare.

The log's stripped flesh fell into a trough below. The whole mill was in effect two layers: the bottom layer was crisscrossed with conveyors that took all the waste, such as the bark, for further sorting; the top was where the logs themselves were processed.

The waste material would enter a machine, called a hog, which would pound the waste wood into smaller pieces that could be easily processed in a pulp mill. In this way, the 10 percent of a log's volume of bark and waste wood could be sold at a profit to the pulp mills.

Paul breathed a sigh of relief as the tail of the stripped log cleared the debarker. The log dropped into another conveyor and passed through a hoop that scanned the log's diameter. The computer whirred as a hundred solutions of how best to cut it were computed.

An eight-foot circular saw pivoted down from overhead and cut into the wide fir. The log trembled as its first twenty-four feet was severed.

The first piece was automatically swept off onto a large, inclined deck that led up to the mill. The rest of the log continued to be slashed to length. In this automated way, six logs per minute could be processed.

An overhead scanner had determined the required depth of the cuts and the chipping head moved into position in the path of the approaching log. The huge band mill buzzed, and chips flew off as the log entered the sharp knives. The chipping head produced a predetermined flat face, and the band mill behind it cut to a thickness accurate within two thousandths of an inch. A lumber board, twelve inches wide by two inches thick, peeled off onto the bed of circular steel rolls.

The band mill had teeth on both faces; this time all it had to do was reverse to slice off an eighteen-inch-thick slab. The log was rolled, repositioned, and the carriage ran back again until the whole log was reduced to varying thicknesses of boards and cants—a cant just being a very thick board that needed further processing.

The boards kicked off automatically to a machine called an edger, while the large cants went to a different machine. Some of the cants were slightly rounded on two faces, which needed to be removed before being made into boards that could return to the edger.

The edger consisted of various foot-long circular saws that could be moved across the incoming boards to any position desired by the computer. A scanner determined the exact profile of the board and decided which tapered edge needed removing by the saw. The waste pieces fell below, while the finished board was ejected onto a transfer table. There, it was eyed by an operator for flaws, who in turn either returned it to the edger or sent it on to be sorted.

Once past the scrutiny of the prime sort operators, the boards passed under the final scanner. Here, each board's final length was calculated, and an overhead trimmer cut the board to exact length.

The steady flow of lumber, of up to one hundred pieces per minute, entered the sorter. The sorter was a series of seventy bins that only accepted a certain combination of thickness, width, and length. Kick arms automatically dropped the boards into one of the huge bins. Once full, the whole bin was lowered and taken to a stacker. The stacker neatly stacked the boards in layers until a large, four-by-eight-foot package had been produced. After a predetermined drying cycle in the kilns, the package went to the planer for final processing.

The planer was a separate building with its own seventy-bin sorter. Here, very fine shaving heads skimmed all four sides of the board to smooth precision. Each board passed through a mist of chemicals to prevent bacterial growth. Then, the final stack of wood was end-pressed and wrapped with heavy protective paper bearing the company logo.

On that first day, there were only minor interruptions to the flow. Paul and Manny's meticulous attention to detail had paid off. Everything ran a bit slow, but all the operators were nervous and warily watched the flashing consoles, groping for the right buttons. The resulting small volume was due to the operators' inexperience with this new hi-tech machine, rather than any failure of the equipment.

There was only one surprise. Paul, Manny, and the mill manager were leaning on the overhead catwalks watching the logs being pushed through. They all saw the moment that a log jammed. Another log pushed behind, and the high-tension band reached its twisted limit.

Everyone ducked as it snapped with a rifle crack. The blade, now free of its constraints, ripped through its protective hood. Sparks flew as it writhed against the metal framework like a deadly snake. Chunks bounced off in all directions, and the electric motors screeched now that they suddenly had no load to bear.

The operator, over one hundred feet away in an insulated cab, didn't realize what had happened, and more logs kept coming.

Paul and Manny ran down the catwalk and reached the cab at the same time. At any moment, the other three bands could explode as logs started to pile up.

The startled operator had just spotted the problem on his overhead TV monitor and was wildly looking for the kill button. Paul slammed his hand down on the big red button just before Manny, and the hum and throb of machinery died.

"Holy shit, did you see that band?" Paul exclaimed breathlessly.

"Yeah," Manny said.

"Hey Tom, what the fuck were you doing? Sleeping, or what?"

"Hey, I was busy loading the next log. I haven't got time to look at all four cameras at once."

"You mean you never heard the saws whining?"

The operator gave Paul a confused look.

"Whining? No. At least, not until you came in. Guess the insulation is just too good in here."

"Right. Manny, let's put a microphone in every cab so the guys can hear the machines."

"Good idea, I'll get on it."

Everyone sheepishly laughed at their previous frantic antics, diving out of the way as the saw below them buried itself into steel. Luckily no one had been hurt, but everyone knew that if a piece had hit him, only severed limbs would have been left.

From that moment on, the overhead walkways were rarely visited, and even then, only for short periods.

Overall, the shift had gone well, and at the end Paul wrote down everyone's comments on minor revisions or changes. That night, a busy shift of electricians, welders, and millwrights hit the prioritized list before the next morning's operation.

After three weeks, the only minor thing that remained was for the operators to gain confidence and reach full production rates.

Paul started to relax as the mill's personnel took over, and reluctantly he realized that his job had ended. Manny had promised him a fishing trip when they were finished, and now was the time. He had heard of the legendary fishing in the area Manny was taking him to, but up until now he hadn't been able to tear himself away from his baby.

Manny called early the morning of their trip—early enough that it was still dark. Paul excitedly grabbed his Barbour jacket to keep off the morning's drizzle.

"Wow, what a beauty, Manny. I bet she can really fly," Paul said when he saw the aluminum jet boat in the gloomy car park lighting.

"Thanks. I've got all the tackle already, so we're set. Let's go fishing," Manny called from the driver's-side window.

Soon they were off in Manny's truck, the boat trailing behind them. "What river are we hitting?" asked Paul.

"Oh well, let's see, there's about four which are good at this time of the year. The Coho are running, so it should be good."

Paul nodded. He pointed to the hints of water they passed from the road.

"Are these tributaries of the Skeena River?"

"Yes, between here and Prince Rupert there's a half dozen. As we cross them, I'll see what height they're at and pick one with good flow and color."

"What size are the Coho? I've heard these northerners are big."

Manny nodded with a vigorous grin.

"Last year, I had one on which I reckon would have gone over thirty pounds."

"Holy mackerel, that's nearly a record. Biggest one I heard of was thirty-six down by Victoria."

"Yes, there's record fish around here: salmon over a hundred pounds, steelhead over forty, cutthroat, dolly's…you name it, we got it. Next time, if you have a spare week, we'll nip down south to the next inlet. There's only a small First Nations village there, and the fishing is untouched. We couldn't keep them off the hook last year."

"That must be Stikeen River then. I heard that's part of the last Tree Forest License in British Columbia."

"Yes, but there's a hell of a gorge at the mouth: huge, solid cliffs that don't make it easy for logging. But someone will go for it when we run out of old growth here. Now that that new West Skeena pulp mill at Prince Rupert is up and running, I bet it won't be long."

"You ever met a guy called Nick Barrett? About my age, but the bastard virtually owns Skeena Timber."

Manny gave him a look.

"No, but I heard of him. Some of the guys saw him when they were working on the new pulp mill. Apparently, he gives everyone shit, even the guys who have been there for years. I reckon he likes to throw his weight around or something."

"Me and my dad have had our run-ins with him. The bastard shut us out of the two big buying houses, so we had to go to the smaller guys."

"Really? What's he got against you?"

Paul gave him the run-down on their history.

"What, so now he hates you? Well, I can see he don't take to losing too well. Best to keep clear, especially since he's in the same business."

"Ah, the big shit doesn't scare me, but yes, I'll watch him. As you say, it's unlikely I've seen the last of him."

"You know, that reminds me. When we were up the Stikeen last year, we saw one of the West Skeena choppers buzzing around the valley. Bet you they're eyeing it up for acquisition." Manny shook his head. "Shame, because that valley is sure beautiful, and I'm not kidding. There's this one tributary we went up and saw a bunch of trees the likes of which I've never seen before. They were monsters, like those we must have had hundreds of years ago."

Manny gestured beyond the windshield. "There was this one which must have been, oh shit, at least three hundred feet tall, with a butt the length of my boat. There's an old log jam there with a small pool, which had loads of Coho in it. Reckon I'll take you there one day."

"Hey, just say the word. I'd love to see an untouched valley. Can't be many left now, eh?"

"No, there's a few pockets left, but I think that's the last that's a complete watershed. How about next spring? I've been dying to try it for steelhead. One of the older guys at the First Nations village says they catch them in the main river around the middle of April."

"Super, I'll come up next spring for sure," Paul said.

Manny pulled the truck off onto a small dirt road next to a fair-sized river.

"We'll try this one; it looks the right height. It's called the Exchamsiks," Manny said.

The jet boat was soon launched, already full of rods and fishing tackle. The early morning mist gave off a diffused light, and drops of moisture hung from every branch and twig. The river's glassy surface snaked down between two high bluffs to disappear around a bend.

The engine burbled to life, and Manny eased the boat's red nose upstream. As the mists started to clear, they could see distant, snow-clad peaks in the swirling gaps.

Paul was thrilled to be on such an adventure. He imagined scores of gleaming silver Coho. The jet boat only drew three inches of water, and Manny skillfully maneuvered it around bends, past submerged logs, and over riffling shallows.

The roar of water crashing over submerged rocks announced the presence of the first set of rapids. Manny slowed the boat, keeping her stationary against the current, and planned his path.

"Shit, we're not going through there, are we?" Paul asked nervously. He viewed the white water and seemingly impassable boulders up ahead.

"Ah, no problem. Hold on, here we go."

Paul held on as the bow reared up, and they shot forward into the main chute of fast water. Manny drove her at over twenty knots. Paul instinctively shouted a warning about a huge boulder that lay in their path.

Manny laughed and deftly steered her just slightly to the right. The boulder swept past their side, just grazing the gunnel. Spray washed over them as they hit boils created by submerged rocks.

Paul's heart was in his mouth, imagining jagged edges beneath the blue green waters. But after a few more twisting turns, they were suddenly gliding through a wide, smooth pool.

"Damn, that was tight, but hell, you sure got close to some of those rocks," Paul said.

"Yeah, you have to sometimes, where there's only narrow gaps to pass through. But I know every rock and boulder." Manny gave a self-deprecating laugh.

"I sure have hit every one while learning the river."

The mist now covered only the tops of the steep mountains. Waterfalls cascaded over the sheer sides of the peaks to disappear in the steaming old growth below.

The cold air felt good on Paul's skin, and he licked his lips of moisture from the water that came over the bow. Old logs poked out of the river everywhere, and the odd piece of bank crumbled and splashed into the river as the boat's wake hit them.

Manny killed the throttles quickly.

"Look," he whispered.

"Yes, I see him," Paul said.

A big black bear, its coat glistening, was feeding on an old salmon carcass. When their boat glided closer, it looked up, sniffed the air, and then bounded off, its bulk rippling with all the fat it had put on to get ready for winter.

"Wow, that was a huge bear. Did you see him run when he spotted us?" Paul could barely contain his excitement.

"Yes, and we'll probably see more since the salmon are running. Keep your eyes peeled," Manny said as he hit the throttles again.

The bends, ripples, and pools blurred into one as they probed further up the valley. After a few bends, they surprised a female moose and her calf grazing by the riverbank.

Paul felt himself relax, and soon the once-important details of everyday life seemed insignificant now as nature's splendor passed him. He had an urge to just climb that peak or explore that valley.

Manny eased back on the throttles, and the hull scraped on fine sand as it rounded the inside of a bend. Manny had spotted a shoal of fish under the far bank.

"Right," Manny said as he secured the boat, "Use this rod and cast as near to the far bank as you can. Be sure to let it sink slowly."

Paul cast the blue-and-silver spoon in a smooth arc. The spoon splashed and sank. He got nothing that cast, but Paul felt his mouth dry with anticipation and tried again.

"Got one," Paul yelled as his rod lurched. A bright, silver bullet cartwheeled out of the water by the far bank.

"Holy mackerel, look at that go," he said as the reel screeched in protest. The fish jumped again, then swam back fast—too fast for him to keep up. The line passed him. Then, the fish turned and raced back to the other side. The rod bent double as the tension increased.

The fish made several more powerful runs back and forth before it started to tire. Paul eased the fish onto his feet.

Manny grabbed its tail. "Bet that's a good fifteen pounds, Paul. Not bad for your first northerner."

"Down in Kelsey Bay we'd kill for a fish like this."

They gently released it, and with a quick flick of its tail, it sped across the gravel bottom to disappear into the blue-green depths.

Manny landed the next three, and Paul had another beauty of nearly twenty pounds before the shoal was spooked.

Paul absorbed the wilderness, and his love for it deepened. He kept thinking what it must have been like before man began to rape it. *Then again,* he realized, *there must be a balance somewhere.*

A few pools further up and another half-dozen bright fish later, they sat on a gnarled old log for a sandwich and beer.

"You know, Manny, this sure is God's country. We really don't realize how lucky we are."

"Yeah. But if you think this is nice, wait till you see the Stikeen: you'll have an instant orgasm."

They pulled the boat out after an exhilarating two-hour run downstream, weaving and running rapids.

The next week back at work dragged for Paul. The mill's personnel were taking over. He made his decision, and that Friday Paul packed his bags, said his good-byes, and caught the afternoon flight to Vancouver, where he could connect to another flight to the island.

The Boeing 737 took off and climbed steeply over the wide Skeena River Valley. Paul gazed out of his window, resting his forehead on the cold, thick glass.

God, he thought, *there's hardly any areas not cut.* Nearly every valley had been logged, from the high slopes to the far headwaters. Brown slashes ran vertically down inclines: the fragile topsoil, now denuded of gripping roots, couldn't absorb the heavy rainfall and slid away.

What troubled Paul even more was the lack of replanting. *Surely, they can't go on like this,* he thought. He felt a bit guilty, because the mill he had just helped to create could gobble up an area the size of a football field every day.

We've got to slow down or something. His mind wandered back to old Chuck Stoneman on Saltspring. *There now, surely his method could be adopted here, but on a larger scale.*

He spent the next month at home helping his dad. Unfortunately, his father had deteriorated, and every day he became more frustrated as he had less energy and lost more and more of his speech.

Paul comforted his mom when he caught her silently weeping in the kitchen one day. She admitted that seeing her husband slip away bit by bit was killing her.

Paul had a solution. "Maybe I should stay here full-time. I've learned a hell of a lot, and Dad can't do it all anymore."

The next day his dad agreed and Paul was immediately put on as the assistant plant manager. Paul soon became absorbed in the daily running and maintenance of the mill. Prices kept high all year, but it still galled him that they didn't get top dollar for their lumber; they were hog-tied by Nick's strangle hold on the lumber market.

After six months, Paul rang Manny up where he lived in Terrace to confirm their promised trip. He felt okay leaving for a week in the spring, since his dad had stabilized over the last half year and even seemed to improve a little.

So, in mid-April of 1977, Paul started off to Terrace for their trip to the Stikeen Valley, the last untouched temperate watershed in the world.

Chapter Five
The Valley

It took them a full day at cruising speed in Manny's twenty-six-foot Chris Craft to enter Eagle Channel, into which the Stikeen River spilled. Here, eighty miles south of Kitimat, there were no signs of the devastation of clear-cut logging. Instead, tall stands of Douglas fir and hemlock covered the slopes like a green blanket. Bald eagles soared overhead, and herring dappled the sea's flat calm.

The jet boat, tied with a long lead and rubber shock absorbers, trailed behind them. Twelve jerry cans of gas lay lashed to the gunnels, just in case they didn't bump into a fishing boat that would let them replenish their tanks.

Paul had an eerie feeling of déjà vu as he viewed the towering peaks and large valley that opened up to the east. They dropped anchor as they approached an unspoiled beach and let the silence of the wilderness envelope them.

"This is just, well, I can't describe it. Just fantastic, just fucking fantastic," Paul said.

"I know what you mean, Paul. It's one of my favorite spots. There's only one small First Nations village in the whole area of about fifteen hundred square miles. Most of the young people there leave for Terrace, Prince Rupert, and Kitimat. It's a pity, because the unskilled ones that can't get jobs often become drunks and just end up in jail when they get into trouble. They would have been better off staying, but the lure of big money seems to draw them in every year."

Manny tugged on the anchor, making sure it was secure. "Sometimes I think our system isn't as good, what with all our stress and greed. Have a good look around, because I bet within a couple of years this place will have logging roads, a camp, and eventually no more trees, just so the rest of the world can benefit from timber and paper."

"It doesn't have to be that way," Paul replied. He told Manny about the alternative logging he had seen years ago on Vancouver Island. They debated back and forth, Manny playing the devil's advocate, but Paul had reasonable solutions and even figures to back him up.

Paul became more and more enthusiastic about his method, and soon Manny started to catch his eagerness. It was something that would have a minor impact on the wilderness, yes, but it would be sustainable and employ locals, bringing money into a community.

"Well, it sounds nice," Manny said. "But unless one of the big guys picks up on the idea, we'd still better get in our enjoyment of the area while we can."

The next morning, they anchored the Chris Craft in a sheltered cove and loaded the jet boat full of gas and supplies. They planned to go up the main river and stay the first night at the First Nations village.

The deeply-laden boat entered the wide estuary, and soon they could see where the river channel entered the inlet. Ahead, the mountains closed together until it seemed they joined. The river, meanwhile, disappeared among the thick-wooded valley bottom. It was a large river, up to quarter of a mile wide where it entered the sea.

After they had cruised along its placid flow for a while, they found that the river narrowed to only a hundred yards across, where it spilled in boiling white sheets out a steep, rocky gorge.

"Wait, *that's* the Stikeen?" Paul asked when he saw the turbulent waters ahead.

"Yeah, no problem. Don't worry: it looks a lot worse than it is. There's plenty of room, even when it narrows further up," Manny replied.

"Well, you're the boss, so let's go for it." Paul gripped the windshield tight.

Manny opened the throttles wide, and the jet boat leaped forward. Soon the sun was hidden behind steel-sided cliffs. The noise grew to deafening proportions as the water crashed over hidden boulders. Within minutes, they were soaked from the pervading mist.

Thick moss hung off the cliffs in this world of perpetual moisture. The standing waves reared four feet high in places, but the jet boat easily climbed them and slid down the troughs before repeating the process again.

Up ahead, a boulder the size of a large house split the river in two. To the right side the water was angry and unpredictable as it sped over hidden rocks.

The left-hand side was no wider, but it was smooth, fast rapids; that was the side Manny steered for.

"Hold on: this is the worst, and then it's clear sailing," Manny shouted over the roar of the waves.

Paul ducked as the boat took a large wave over the bow and drenched them both in icy water. Manny had the boat giving its full three hundred horsepower, and yet the going was still slow against the current.

The waters pulled them toward the left-hand side of the gorge until Paul could have reached out and touched it. Manny expertly weaved from one side to the other, picking the least current and avoiding the larger waves and whirlpools.

Paul was about to ask Manny to turn back when suddenly they leaped out of the torrent and entered fast but glassy water. The roar of the rapids diminished as they entered a long, undulating pool.

After about a mile, Manny pulled back the throttle and let the boat drift.

"Listen," he whispered.

Paul couldn't hear a thing, except for the occasional drip of water near the river banks.

"To what? There's nothing here," Paul said.

"Yes. It's amazing, isn't it?" Manny said.

Paul listened more intently and let the quiet fill his soul.

"You know, not many people have been up here by boat; it's hard to find a good path around those rapids," Manny informed Paul.

Paul was suddenly struck by the enormity of it all. To him, it was like they had entered a vast cathedral. He looked up the steep-sided mountains surrounding them. High above there was a cliff of bare rock. He could see where the river had once been from the smooth curve worn into it. Paul wondered about the vast time it had taken the river to gouge out this lower portion of the river. He felt awed and didn't want to break the magic of the moment.

The noise of the engine snapped him out of his thoughts. Soon they were heading upstream again. They passed a few more rapids and swirling whirlpools, and Manny had to dodge a large tree that had come down with the last rainfall. Soon the river slowed, and it widened into a smooth, glassy surface.

"No wonder no one has tried to log this valley before," Paul said. "Putting in a road to bypass the gorge would take years and cost a bomb."

"Yes, but with the other valleys running out of pristine timber, it won't be long until it becomes viable. Then it will just become another wasted valley the public never gets to know about," Manny predicted.

The boat climbed another rapid, where a large eddy hugged the left shore. Paul knew the salmon would lie in this eddy, collecting their strength before running upstream again.

Once through the rapids, the valley opened up. It was huge, and the river now meandered from side-to-side in large, sweeping bends. Hazy snowcaps on the far distant mountains could be seen, and Paul imagined the large glaciers and snow packs they must contain: a remnant of the last ice age. Those ice packs supplied the water for the river as they melted and carved their path to the sea.

Paul's thoughts were shattered by the whirl of helicopter blades, which swooped down low over them. They instinctively ducked as the downdraft hit them. From its green livery, it looked like a West Skeena chopper and Paul wondered what it was doing up here.

"Shit," Manny said. "Hopefully they're only up here for a scenic trip or something."

They felt a little cheated after their hair-raising trip up the wild river, only to be interrupted by the helicopter. They continued in silence.

In the distance, Paul spotted smoke rising across a large meadow from some small houses, which he assumed to be the First Nations village. As they closed in, he could see that some of the houses sorely needed a paint job, while others were left abandoned with broken windows or holes in the roof.

Manny deftly maneuvered the boat against a small, wooden jetty. They were greeted by a couple of curious children wearing tattered jeans and baseball caps.

"Hi, you up here fishing?" the older one asked when he saw the fishing rods sticking out of their holders.

"Yes," Manny answered. "How's it been?"

"Have to ask my dad. He's been catching a bunch in his nets," he replied.

"Come on then—you can lead me to your dad, if that's okay," Manny said. Then, when the boy hesitated, he added, "Or one of the other men who have been fishing here."

The youngsters bounded across the meadow to one of the larger houses. Paul and Manny followed at a more sedate pace. The boys stopped outside the house in front of a man cleaning fish to get ready for smoking. He dropped his knife and approached Paul and Manny.

"Hi there. I'm Manny, and this is Paul. Pleased to meet you."

"I'm Tom." The man clasped their hands warmly. "You men come up the river in the jet boat?"

"Yes, we just arrived. We were wondering what the fishing's been like?"

"Well, if it's steelhead you're after, your timing is good. See?" He led them to the rows of fresh fish on a large, cedar-planked table which stood in front of the house.

"Wow, those are beauties all right." Paul said as he admired the large, silver fish.

"I was here a couple of years ago, and one of the locals told me about the great steelhead fishing here, so we're here to give it a bash." Manny added.

"Yes, I think I remember someone telling me we had some visitors. I was at a conference in Vancouver at the time. We don't get many visitors up here. Please, let me show you my village."

"Thank you, we'd be honored."

They both followed Tom as he walked them around the village, where they were soon joined by other curious villagers.

It was sparsely inhabited, mostly elders and grandchildren left. Even the children's parents had left to the cities to try and make some money.

"What do you do for schooling and supplies?" Paul asked.

"Well, that's part of the problem," Tom said. "We only have one native teacher here, and it's difficult to teach such a large spread of ages. The government has been trying to pressure us to leave the village and move to Terrace, since there are no roads to this valley. So, a chartered float plane brings in the supplies once a week and a doctor once per month."

He gestured to the wooden jetty, where they had industrial-grade coiled rope and tie-offs. "It makes everything very expensive, and our government assistance only just covers our expenses. Luckily the fishing and hunting is still good, and the village here has some great soil; we grow most of our vegetables in the spring and summer, a lot of which can be stored for the winter."

He passed a ball back to one of the children, who had resumed their play now that the strangers had been introduced.

"I'm afraid the lure of the cities continues to take our people. No doubt one day we will have to bow down to the government and move, but while I'm chief, I will try and get us to stay."

"Oh, you're chief then?" Paul said.

"Yes, Chief Tom Wolf Salmon of the Stikeen people."

"Surely with all the wood in the valley, your people could log and then stay in the valley?" Paul asked.

"Yes, we tried that a number of years ago, but the government said it wasn't our wood to sell. We continued to log, but the government threatened to cut off our financial assistance. So, the men became bored again and left the valley. Our claim to the land of the valley has been gathering dust for decades."

The chief sighed heavily. "And it will until the Federal Government recognizes us as first peoples, returning our right to all resources in the valley. I'm afraid once the government lets out a Tree Forest License for here, then it will be too late; the valley will be stripped of trees."

He gazed out at the horizon. "We only cut for subsistence, but the large forest companies would use up all the wood with no intent for sustainability; they are only controlled by greed and growth."

"Has one of the forestry companies been over here to access the valley?" Manny asked.

"Yes, a party of officials from West Skeena Timber were here only a few months ago. They spoke of good jobs, a road past the gorge, and money in the community, but we rejected it; this is our land. They wanted us to relinquish our claim in exchange for employment."

Tom crossed his arms. "They also spoke of a large sawmill, and by the size of it, we didn't think the valley's wood would last more than 20 years. That would then leave us in an even worse position when the jobs dried up: we'd have no forests to hunt, and the river would be polluted by sawmill waste. The young man who led the party didn't like that much: he became very angry and accused us of stopping progress."

"Was the young man's name Nick Barrett, by any chance?" Paul asked.

"Yes, a man I did not like or trust," the chief answered.

"I know him," Paul admitted. "He will have control of West Skeena soon; he is very ambitious. I can see why they want the Tree Forest License: the new pulp mill they built in Prince Rupert will need more wood to sustain it. I heard their forest license up north is running out of wood faster than they predicted. Lumber and pulp prices are very high at the moment, so the government would support a large operator here, since it means more taxes to them. Any other companies been around?"

"No, I don't think so. Why do you ask?" the chief inquired.

"Oh, I'm just curious, that's all." Paul answered. He reminded himself that that was as far as he could get: curiosity. Despite that, he was still anxious to see more of the valley and see if the quality could sustain a selective, less destructive method than the traditional clear-cutting.

Tom invited them for supper. They were fed wonderful arrays of fresh vegetables to go with the fresh steelhead. They talked most about the fishing and wildlife in the valley. The chief's daughter was called Wind Walker, and Manny instantly fell in love with her dark eyes, easy smile, and quick mind as they talked about life here in the valley.

After supper, they said their thanks and retired down to the boat, where they crept into their sleeping bags. Paul's mind kept spinning at the possibility of selective logging and wondered if that was something Chief Wolf Salmon and his people could get behind. He also admitted to himself it would be nice to beat Nick Barrett to the punch. The obstacles would be enormous, but boy, what a challenge: to show the industry what could be done without destroying the environment.

After a while, the sound of running water and the gentle sway of the boat lulled him to sleep.

***

At the crack of dawn, after eating a hearty sandwich and a sweet cup of steaming hot coffee done on the Primus stove, they untied the boat and headed upstream to Emerald Creek. A very fine mist covered the valley. As they passed a log jam, they interrupted a heron's early morning prowl for small, unsuspecting fish.

Paul expertly assessed the dense forest that spread up the valley sides as far as the eye could see. The stands of straight Douglas fir, cedar, and balsam were pristine examples of their species. They passed beautiful stands of such trees, some of which were over eight feet in diameter. Paul had to crane his neck to see their lofty tops.

He could just imagine the beautiful timber that could be harvested from them. With carefully-planned selective logging, this valley could sustain the industry forever with no clear cuts or landslides.

However, two large problems faced such a venture. One was for a relatively low-volume cut, how could a mill be built up here and still support the staff to run it? In addition, a road would cost millions—easily over a hundred million, Paul estimated. A vast volume of wood would have to be cut to pay for it.

He had neither the influence nor money for such a venture, which didn't even fit his idea of sustainability. *No,* he thought, *what am I even considering this for? It's a dead duck of an idea.*

Manny hugged the south bank, and Paul soon noticed that the water had taken on a more opaque, greenish-blue color. A bend in the river was approaching, behind which towered even taller trees than those that surrounded them now.

"Nearly there, Paul. Just around the bend we'll enter Emerald Creek. Not far up you'll see trees like nowhere else in the world; not even Cathedral Grove."

Paul gave Manny a dubious look. He had visited the grand Cathedral Grove near his home on Vancouver Island when he was young. The small park had been left unlogged, and contained some of the largest trees in the world. He remembered marveling at their height; the display plaques set out for visitors boasted that some were over eight hundred years old.

As they rounded the bend, a small valley opened up to the south of them. Soon, the mouth of Emerald Creek came into view, and Manny slowed the boat down to a crawl. He maneuvered the boat around gnarled old roots and logs that had been swept down in previous high waters and floods. The water color of the river now completely separated as Emerald Creek joined it. The Stikeen was still a greenish-blue filled with glacial silt, but Emerald Creek was completely clear; Paul could see right down to the gravely bottom as they neared the creek's mouth.

The current picked up speed as they entered the main creek. Up ahead, Paul could hear the unmistakable sound of rapids. They turned the corner to see a frothing, ugly-looking set of rapids.

Manny slowed the boat down and studied them as he calculated the path he would take.

"Hold on tight," he said. He pulled down on the throttle and the boat jumped up in eagerness. They went hurtling into the rapids at full speed. Only a small amount of spray came aboard as Manny expertly weaved his way past submerged rocks.

Soon they entered calm waters in a large pool. Another bend swung to the left, and beyond that Paul could see the tops of impossibly high trees.

"Wow," Paul said when he saw them up-close for the first time. They crowded a large bank piled high with age-old tangled logs. The water swirled around them. Even small trees had started to grow on the huge log jam.

Beyond the jam Paul got his first look at the Big Fir. Its trunk must have been at least 12 feet wide at its base, and its top was beyond easy measure: maybe even over 300 feet tall.

"Man, that's magnificent." And just to its left was a huge balsam, and there a hemlock and a cedar.

"These things dwarf those in the Cathedral Grove. Come on, let's anchor and take a closer look." Paul said.

After tying up the boat to a sturdy log, they carefully climbed over the log jam. Soon it turned to a carpet of green. Paul noticed that the grasses had been blown flat in a wide circle, and there in the center were the telltale signs of a helicopter's runners. Paul felt a prickle of irritation that someone had been there so shortly before them.

As they approached the base of the Big Fir, the overhead branches produced a cool, deep shade. The bark was a rich red brown, wrinkled like a crocodile's skin. Paul spotted a lighter patch and approached.

Someone had tried to carve their initials in the thick bark.

Paul could just decipher them: "NB." Paul swore as he made the connection. How could that jackass have desecrated such a tree?

"That's Nick Barrett, isn't it, Paul?"

Paul just clenched his fists into knotty balls. His feet crushed a pile of bark beneath the freshly-carved initials.

Paul went to a swampy black piece of earth nearby and returned with a handful. He carefully wiped it over the marks until they were covered up. "Think of it. This tree has been here probably over a thousand years, and that fucking moron puts his initials on it." Paul said.

Paul's good mood had evaporated. Even so, as they walked deeper into the shade, he couldn't help but be amazed at the trees' size and diversity. By some freak of nature, this grove had survived the intermittent forest fires and floods over the centuries. Both men realized what a treasure this grove was—probably the last of its kind in the whole of British Columbia.

"Come on, Paul. Let's get some fishing done before lunch," Manny said.

As Paul followed Manny past the Big Fir, he estimated it had enough wood to build four three-story houses. He heard a soft thud at his feet. It was a fir cone. He picked it up and examined the tiny seeds trapped in its surface cracks. It was those minuscule seeds that could produce such an enormous tree as the fir in front of them. Paul carefully put the fir cone down on the ground and continued after Manny.

A mile further upstream they pulled up to an enticing-looking pool. On the far bank, there was a deep channel which just spelled fish to them.

Paul cast his float upstream. Typical of steelhead fishing it went straight down, not going downstream more than a couple of feet.

A fish exploded out of the water, arcing up over three feet high, then sped downstream nearly to the end of the pool. Paul tightened his drag on the reel and felt the fish turn.

His line went slack; the fish had decided to rocket upstream. Paul frantically wound his reel as fast as he could so that the fish wouldn't be able to spit the hook.

"Faster, faster, Paul, I can see the line, and its right across from you. Don't let it run again, or you're going to lose it." Manny advised.

The rod arched and the powerful trout took off downstream again. The line sang with tension, and Paul arched his rod backward, trying to turn its head. Slowly, the fish turned and sulked in the deep water opposite him.

After another 10 minutes or so, the fish began to tire. Paul eased it closer to him.

"Wow, that's a beauty, Paul," Manny said as he deftly took the barbless hook out from the fish. It lay on its side at his feet. Manny gave the fish to Paul while he took a photo with his silver SLR Pentax camera they had brought for just such an occasion. The fish's scaly sides were marked with a faint rainbow tinge, which earned its freshwater compatriot its namesake: rainbow trout. The only difference was this trout had been to the ocean to feed before coming back to spawn, usually after about four years: thus, its larger size and new name.

Paul gently lowered the fish into the icy water to release it and watched it glide slowly back into the depths.

They caught six more fish in the pool until the school scattered, so they decided to move upstream to the next run.

Their timing was perfect: the fresh rain from a few days before had enticed the waiting fish to enter the Eagle Channel in the thousands. Unlike the five species of Pacific salmon, which all died after spawning, the steelhead could survive the vigor of spawning and return to the ocean to come back year after year.

Paul took over the wheel when they entered the slower water. He loved the sensation of weaving in and out of the deep and shallow pools, watching the gravel glide beneath the boat's draft. He was awestruck at the sight of the smaller valleys that joined theirs; their sides were sheer and the tops of the mountains were covered in mist and cloud.

Manny read off the map they had brought.

"Jade Creek, Two Lakes Valley, and Misty Mountain Gorge."

Emerald Creek was a fair-sized river when compared to some in Europe, but the landscape here was so big that it had been thought of as only a creek by the early explorers who had named all the valleys and waterways.

After a quick lunch of sandwiches, Manny said the day was fine enough they could try to reach the lake. In these northern climes, rain clouds could swoop off the Pacific at any time and sock the land in for days.

Manny pointed to a majestic spire of rock up ahead.

"Look, that's Diamond Peak," Manny said. "That mountain has a glacier coming down its northern face. It feeds the lake, which in turn supplies the creek."

Paul thought how aptly named it was: its sides were nearly sheer, and it had a Matterhorn-type peak which rose high into clear blue sky. Near the top, a few ice packs clung precariously to its steep sides, where they would remain throughout the summer.

Early in the afternoon they came to a place where the creek split into smaller channels. Manny took over the wheel, picking one of the two. They slowly crept up it against the swirling currents.

Before them lay Emerald Lake, which shone a vivid green-blue. The unique color came from the glacial till: a super-fine powder that hung suspended in the water and reflected the light into green and blue.

"Hold on, Paul, we're going to have to jump a few small logs," Manny said. Once they were pointed out, Paul saw the partly-submerged logs blocking their path. They had come down the lake and gotten trapped at the creek's narrow exit.

The engine roared. The nose of the jet boat lifted, and Paul felt a small jar. Then the engine screeched as the impeller came out of the water. They landed with a splash at the other side and entered the pristine lake.

"Bet they don't do that down south, eh?" Manny boasted as he pointed the boat's nose to the far shore.

The lake's surface was like a mirror—only a few ripples marred its surface from their boat and some swimming ducks near the shore's edge. White streaks lined the steep slopes where small avalanches had cascaded down the mountain during the winter. The accumulation of snow had not melted into the icy waters, but had instead formed small, floating glaciers, which clung to the sides of the bare rock. They headed toward one of the bigger ones on the south side of the lake.

Manny saw a hole in the huge pack of ice and headed into it very slowly. White light filtered down on them as the cave opened up before their boat. They marveled at the bluish-colored ice that lay over fifty feet thick above their heads.

The metallic clank of the boat's aluminum sides hitting the cave's icy walls echoed eerily as they continued toward the spot of sunlight up ahead. Manny had turned off the engine, and they pushed themselves along, fearful that any undue noise may cause the roof to cave in. The ice creaked all around them as the spring's sunlight heated its outer surface. By mid-summer, it would totally disappear.

Once outside, Paul spoke for the first time since entering the cave.

"This must be one of the most beautiful places on earth. To think hardly anyone comes out here. It's downright spectacular; in fact, it's absolutely…"

Paul made a small pumping action, which caused Manny to burst into laughter.

"Hey, keep away from me, you mad horny bugger," said Manny.

"Listen." Paul cupped his ear and turned to the north.

"Pass me those binoculars a minute, Manny."

Paul scanned the far shore and looked up the mountain. Soon he detected a small dot on the far slopes and passed the binoculars to Manny to take a look.

"Must be that chopper we saw yesterday, eh?"

A muffled crack broke the silence of the valley.

"What was that?" Paul asked.

Manny continued to track the helicopter. "The bastards must be shooting at something. Funny, but they're too high for deer or elk. You can get goats up on those slopes, but it's too early in the season to get a hunting permit for them. Come on, let's take a closer look."

***

In the helicopter, Nick swore. "Keep the damn thing steady; I could have had that one." He'd been so close: rock from the slope had splintered just inches from one of the goats, which had a magnificent head of horns on it.

"Sorry, Mr. Barrett, but there's a big updraft here; it's not easy to keep steady."

Nick glared at the pilot's excuses.

"But I will try again if you want," the man amended.

Nick switched to rapid fire on the multi-action Remington rifle he'd had made special order for him and pressed the trigger as fast as he could.

The dark-haired First Nations man in the back shouted, "Hey you got one, yee-ha!"

One of the copper-topped bullets hit a slow, fat ewe in the stomach. She wasn't the one he'd been aiming for, but her lack of speed put her in the line of fire. A large, red stain appeared on her creamy flanks, and she lost her footing on the slippery rocks. One hoof struck thin air, and she lost her balance completely.

Nick smiled as he saw her inevitable fall. She cartwheeled five hundred feet before she hit a ledge; the impact broke bones, and her brains left a pinkish-white smear on the dark rock. She kept bouncing down until she hit a large scree deposit another thousand feet down. Her body jack-knifed over and over until she eventually came to a mangled, bloody heap among some boulders.

A fully-developed baby goat, now dead, poked out grotesquely of the ewe's split abdomen. Nick shrugged as he quickly reloaded the rifle with another 10-round magazine. So that's why she had been so slow. He drew a bead and fired another burst at the fleeing male he had his eyes on.

A bullet shattered its back leg, and it crumpled down with the shock of the impact. The ram scrambled to its feet and tried to bound to a ledge ten feet away. With only one back leg working, it missed badly and crazily tumbled down like its mate.

"Got the bastard, I got it—what a shot," Nick screamed over the engine's noise. High on the feeling of success, he swung his rifle over to the last of the fleeing goats. But just as he squeezed the trigger, the helicopter swung to the left and he fired high.

"What the fuck," Nick screamed at the young pilot beside him.

"Sorry sir, but I couldn't hold it any longer." The pilot kept his face averted, but he looked a little queasy. Although small gusts did rock the craft, he had flown it expertly up till now. He must not be much of a hunter.

Nick decided to grant him a reprieve.

"Right, let's go down. I want the horns," Nick said.

***

Manny and Paul were now close enough to see a goat fall almost a thousand feet to the rocks below.

"That's definitely not right," Manny said, shaking his head. "No way they're hunting for the meat. Even trophy killers are more careful—they're not likely to get any intact horns after a fall like that."

"Come on, let's go over there. I want to catch the bastard in the act," Paul said. "Get the camera out. I don't think they've seen us. And besides, the helicopter needs level ground to land on—they'll have to scramble up to the goats from there."

Manny passed Paul the Pentax camera, which he clutched close to his body as they approached the scree where the tree line stopped.

"Shush," Manny whispered as he saw the helicopter. They both flattened to the ground. "There: look up at the top right." Manny pointed.

Paul adjusted the two-hundred-millimeter zoom lens and the distant figures came clearly into view. As he clicked the shutter, he could imagine a knife trying to release the shattered horns from the scalp of dead sheep. He took photos of Nick and the First Nations man that was with him, both now busy at their work.

"Take some shots of them going into the helicopter," Manny advised. "That way, there will be no mistaking their identity, not with that big logo on its side."

Nick came down carrying a broken pair of horns. He looked to be swearing at their condition. Paul sighted him square in the lens and smiled to himself.

"Hey, what the hell…"

Paul and Manny jumped to their feet in alarm at the sound of the voice. A man, the pilot by his headset, had approached the lake with a small canteen, clearly intent on grabbing some water. His face was just as surprised as Paul and Manny felt.

Paul saw Nick and his companion look their way. He and Manny bounded down the slope back to the boat.

"Quick damn you," he heard Nick shout. "I need that camera. No, no buts! If they got pictures, your license won't be worth a damn, got it?"

Paul pushed the nose of the jet boat out into the water. They both heard the helicopter's engines rise to a crescendo. Paul saw it lift among the trees behind them. After a couple hundred yards, the sound grew deafening and both men ducked as it swooped low over them. The downdraft buffeted the boat, and Manny nearly lost control. He recovered, quickly adjusting the side slip.

"He can't do anything from here," Manny said. "He's just trying to frighten us. So why are we panicking?"

"I know," Paul said, "But I'm sure he recognized me, and there's no lost love between us. If we stop out here, they might, too."

"Maybe you're right. I certainly didn't like the look of that sidekick of his. If we don't stop, we'll be back in the First Nations village before dark. They wouldn't dare try anything there, and maybe we'll learn who he is."

***

The helicopter continued to buzz them to no avail. Nick swore to himself. He had to think of a way to stop them and get that camera. He looked down through the Plexiglas floor and saw the jet boat slow.

The more he watched them, the more he suspected that the face he'd seen through the trees belonged to Paul Whorton. Nick swore again. What, was the bastard following him? What other reason did he have for being in such a remote place?

Nick scanned the area and ordered the pilot to a ridge he had seen about two miles downstream. He smiled as he thought of a solution to his latest problem. His stomach lurched as the helicopter dipped its nose and accelerated, soon reaching over a hundred and twenty miles per hour.

Nick reasoned it would take the interlopers quite a while to reach their location, since they would have to negotiate a number of bends and minor rapids on the river.

The helicopter blew up a flurry of sand as it landed just downstream of the bend he had picked.

"Pass me the chain saw, Raven Eater," he ordered his companion.

Raven Eater nodded approvingly when he realized what Nick was about to do. The bend he had picked was perfect. It was a sharp ninety degrees with a hard rock face dropping into deep water on the far side. Tall trees on the inner edge hid the last part of the turn from any boat coming downstream.

Nick strode to a nearby tree and pulled the starter cord. The chainsaw buzzed to life. The teeth of the saw buried themselves deeply into the young, but tall, Douglas fir, and yellow sawdust blew out behind him. He quickly cut a large 'V'-shaped groove on the side he wanted the tree to fall.

Satisfied, he went to the other side and made another cut just above it. He stepped back as he heard the inner fibers crack.

The tree's distant top lagged behind as the heavy trunk gathered momentum. The trunk cleaved through the water and sent up a large wave downstream.

Perfect, he thought as he viewed his handiwork. The higher bank on the other side supported a good fifty feet of the tree's top, while the remainder drooped completely across the river, blocking off the inside bend. Only a small gap of six-by-three feet was left open below the far bank, and he thought that far too small for the boat to pass through.

"Good job, Mr. Barrett," Raven Eater said. "That should stop the bastards, alright."

"Look, Mr. Barrett, I think this has gone far enough. Why don't we just offer them money for the film and their silence and be done with it?" the nervous pilot asked.

Nick scoffed.

"What, and just trust them to keep their word?"

Not likely if that really was Paul Whorton. But it was good to keep his options open if it wasn't.

"We'll get our chance when they stop in front of the blockade," he said.

***

Paul scanned the horizon for the helicopter. He was worried when he couldn't see it. After about a mile due north, they heard it behind them.

"Might want to pick up the speed again," Paul advised.

Manny complied—he was adept at maneuvering the little jet boat among the rapids, even at break-neck speeds. Remembering the far rocky shore, he chose the inside bend along the sandy beach.

Paul looked behind them and ducked instinctively as the nose of the chopper bore down on them again. Manny kept his attention straight ahead to make the high-speed corner, which would have been tricky at the best of times, never mind nearly at full throttle.

With a great downdraft, the whole helicopter suddenly blocked their vision right in Manny's chosen path, not three feet above the creek. Manny swerved hard to the left toward the far bank. They were still doing about twenty miles per hour. He corrected to take the more dangerous outside bend.

"Holy shit," he screamed when he saw the top of the tree caught on the rocky bank. It completely blocked their path.

Paul quickly looked right and thanked the pilot for his mistake. The log on the inside bend rested on the sandy beach, and Manny wouldn't have seen it until it was too late. There was a narrow opening under the log that Manny aimed for as he cut the engine—even so, they wouldn't stop in time.

"Duck," Manny shouted.

Paul quickly crouched low, bracing himself for the inevitable.

The high-pointed bow hit the lower part of the log and crumpled, leaving a deep scar in the soft wood. The impact lowered the boat's nose, but not enough. The windshield exploded when it collided with the log, and the top half of the console bent over Manny's head.

The boat bucked, kicking the stern up as the bow was forced down from the jarring impact. Paul felt the log brush his back. The rocky bank slashed at the boat's sides, and water spilled through a six-foot gash in the left-hand side.

They might have made it if it hadn't been for the steering cable, which had become caught on the smashed console. It jammed and swung the jet boat hard to the left into the rocky bank.

The boat's bottom ripped like paper on the jagged rocks. Manny screamed when one of them hit his bent knee, smashing his kneecap before it continued to cleave his skin down to the bone.

Paul was luckier; he had fallen sideways, and the rocks just grazed his left foot and ripped his runner off.

The boat came to a jarring halt as it wedged itself on the block of the V8 engine. Manny and Paul were thrown into the icy water, and the boat was driven under by the power of the swift current.

Paul grabbed Manny by the shirt collar and kicked hard toward the easier current of the inside bend. Manny was unconscious, and Paul became alarmed when he saw the widening red cloud blooming out from his left leg. He hoped it was better than it looked.

He kicked even harder as the current bore them downstream, and soon he felt bottom. He hauled the limp Manny ashore on the soft sand, coughing and retching up the water he had swallowed in his struggle to get them ashore.

***

Nick winced when the boat collided with the log. *Damn*, he thought, *those crazy bastards really booked it round those turns*. They must really have wanted to beat him down the river. He was glad the pilot had warned them of the inside bend—he wasn't sure they'd have survived if they had hit the log head-on at those speeds.

He distracted himself from his guilt with the pleasant knowledge that the boat had sunk in the fast water, and the camera with its damning evidence was now lost forever in the swirling currents.

He saw the two figures on the sandy beach downstream. He hoped one of them actually was Paul Whorton. Would serve him right, that fucking moron.

"Let's clear off," he ordered the pilot. Their work was done.

"We can't just leave them there; what if one of them is injured?" the pilot said.

Nick rolled his eyes.

"They're all right; and besides, the point is to get out of here, not stick around. If we don't go back, past the village, no one will know we were here. Just write up in your log that we headed north and keep your mouth shut; there'll be a big bonus in it for you. They can't prove a thing, and you get to keep your license, so wrap up and get the fuck out of here."

Nick could feel the pilot's silent disapproval, but the helicopter still rose, turned, and headed due north, well out of sight of the downstream village.

***

Paul nearly panicked when he saw the extent of Manny's injured leg. The white bone of his kneecap was speckled with blood, and the red fluid seeped out to stain the sand.

Paul ripped his shirt off and tore away a sleeve at the arm. He pressed it hard over the gaping wound, and soon the bleeding slowed. With the other sleeve, he covered it and wrapped it tight.

Manny stirred and feebly moaned a bit.

Night wouldn't come for at least two hours, but Paul knew he'd have to be busy before then. He shivered in the cool air. Across the river, he saw the shadow of the boat in the icy depths. In the front compartment, they had all their extra clothes and food wrapped up in tight plastic bags.

Glancing back to see how Manny was doing, Paul returned to the creek and dove in. The water was so cold it gripped his chest, but soon he was above the boat. The engine had sucked the boat's stern downward and the bow poked out of the water.

Paul reached up into the front compartment and with frozen fingertips tried to undo the latch. It didn't move. He tried again, warming his fingers first. He stepped up on one of the broken bench seats and heaved. It opened. A plastic bag fell out and floated down river before he could grasp it.

He half-closed the door to stop more from spilling and felt inside. His fingers soon had the grip of his airline bag and he pulled it out. He hung it over a piece of jagged aluminum that had once been the boat's sides and searched for more.

Next, he found some food and cursed his laziness for not wrapping it better—it was soggy to the touch. He lowered himself back into the water: it was an effort not to shrink back from its icy grip. With his booty held above his head, he struck out for the far sandy shore.

The current swept him fifty feet downstream, and he had to trudge back to Manny's side. He was shivering uncontrollably and fumbled open his airline bag to put on some dry clothes. The socks would wait.

He carefully stripped Manny and re-clothed him with the remainder of the clothes. Relief filled him when Manny opened his eyes.

Manny met Paul's eyes and looked down at the bloody bandages on his knee.

"How bad is it, Paul? It feels like hell."

"Oh, you have a nasty cut, but it'll be okay," Paul lied.

Paul was pleased when Manny stopped shivering and tried a joke about his oversized clothes. Manny barely managed a grimace and told him in no uncertain terms who he thought Paul's ancestors were.

"Damn," Paul said when he realized he would have to return to the boat to get some type of rope to make Manny a splint. "You stay here and rest. I have to go for another swim. I'll be back in a moment."

Paul braced himself and undressed. Not far downstream of the boat, he found a rod and reel and took the two hundred yards of fishing line it contained. It would do what he had in mind.

"What're you shivering for?" was his welcome from Manny.

Paul put his dry clothes back on. "Right, we're going to build some type of shelter for the night, so pass me that knife of yours."

"Hey, Paul?"

"Hm?" Paul was busy gathering branches.

"Do you think that trunk fell naturally, or did that son of a bitch just try to kill us?"

Paul sighed. "I don't know—Nick is a crazy bastard. Whatever his intent, he left us stranded; he's going to pay for this, you watch."

Paul surveyed the makeshift camp he'd made from driftwood and overlaid fir branches. He prayed it wouldn't rain overnight. He helped Manny hobble over to the shelter and tried to ignore the other man's sweating brow and deep furrows of pain.

Manny caught his dragging leg on a stump and screamed.

"Shit, sorry, Manny. Come on, just a little further and you can sit down."

Manny closed his eyes, gasping in lungful's of air as Paul gently lowered him to the ground. Paul realized Manny wasn't going to be able to walk out, even with his help.

As dusk came, Paul dragged over some fair-sized limbs of driftwood and tightly lashed each one together with fishing line. Once he had a wide enough base, he added another layer to it. "Wish this was as easy as it is in the movies."

"It will never float," Manny jibed.

"You just watch, buddy, it'll be like the fucking Titanic."

"I know; that's what I'm worried about."

Paul stopped when it became too dark to see and joined Manny in the shelter.

"Thirsty, Manny?"

"Yeah. Pass a can of Coke out of the bag."

Silence hung heavily over them. It was a moonless night, and soon a myriad of stars above were the only faint light. Paul shuffled closer to Manny when he heard his teeth chatter and forced him to take his sweater. Soon he heard Manny's deep breathing and was glad for him.

Paul, however, couldn't sleep in the cold. His feet especially were freezing. The night seemed unending. As dawn crept over the far horizon, his head throbbed. He decided to do something to distract himself from his discomfort and went over to the raft. He rolled up his jeans and tried to push it into the shallows. His feet sank into the sand. It didn't move an inch.

"Idiot," he said to himself. "You should have built it closer."

He dug the clinging sand away from both sides and slipped some small branches underneath. After an hour of grunting and sweating, he reached the shallows and the raft lifted off the sand. Paul sat back and breathed hard. Sweat cooled on his brow.

"Aaagh," Manny screamed as he woke up.

Paul raced back to the shelter and held down the struggling Manny. He became alarmed when he felt his friend's forehead: it was burning hot. Manny's struggle had reopened the wound. Luckily, he had fainted, so Paul re-bandaged it.

Paul wolfed down some soggy sandwiches and swallowed a can of Coke in one draft. Manny woke and stayed still this time.

"Shit, Paul. I can't believe the pain."

Paul gripped Manny's hand and nearly cried as he looked down at his stricken friend.

"Hey, it's not all bad: look what I found yesterday." He pulled out a bottle of Crown Royal. Paul thought what the hell: Manny may as well dull the pain while he could. It would take a fair bit for them to reach the village and get help. Paul took a neat swig after Manny and felt its warmth slide down his throat.

"Let's mix it with the Coke; it'll last longer." He passed it back to Manny. "Well, are you ready for a cruise, my friend?"

Manny's eyes pleaded with Paul to not move him, but there was no other choice. Manny made the first move and struggled up to his elbows.

"Come on, then. Show me Titanic, and may all who sail her be blessed."

Paul struggled in the soft sand to lower Manny gently onto the small, wooden raft. Manny looked dreadful, and his knee was grotesquely swollen.

Paul pushed off with a long, stout pole and hoped they would float. He questioned the soundness of taking Manny with him, but he couldn't bear the thought of leaving him all alone in his dreadful pain.

"Hold on," he said. "I'm the one driving now." He pushed harder, and the ungainly craft moved slowly into the current.

Manny lay on his back and closed his eyes.

Paul fought to keep a straight line but failed: the raft turned broadside in the current and caught on an underwater boulder. Water splashed Paul's legs, and he pushed with all his strength to push the raft's nose around.

Another half-submerged rock approached. It caught the nose and slewed the raft sideways. After a few more close calls, they entered a long, slow stretch. Very slowly Paul began to read the current and avoided trouble well in advance. They made good time, and the morning sun's weak heat began to dry off their damp clothes.

"How far out, Manny? Do you reckon?"

"Oh, at this rate we should be there next year," he said.

"No, I reckon we're near the Big Fir, and from there we have it beat." He saw Manny's grimace and the perspiration on his face. "Do you want me to stop for a while, or are you alright for some more?"

"No, I'm dying for a shit so keep going; I don't want your help." Manny replied.

Paul laughed hard; he couldn't help but admire Manny's spirit.

They ran a few more rapids, and sometimes Paul got into the water and manhandled the raft in the shallows.

A few hours later, Paul gave Manny the last of the Crown and Coke. He spotted the large trees around the next bend and sighed in relief. Not long afterward the raft entered the main river, and he began to angle it across to the other side.

All was going well until he tried to push off with the pole again and nearly fell over; he couldn't reach the bottom.

Damn, he thought. *The gorge is only about three miles away. If I can't get to one shore or the other, we'll go straight down it; this raft won't survive that—and nor will we.*

They continued straight down the center of the river. As soon as Paul saw the village, he cupped his hands and shouted. He didn't see anyone around the dock; there were only a couple of children playing by the houses. He watched helplessly as they passed, yelling harder. He gave up as the village passed from sight.

He tried to use the pole as a paddle, but to no avail. Fear settled in when he noticed the current pick up speed. They were still in the middle of the river. Up ahead he saw the dark, deadly cleft of the wild water gorge. He broke out into a cold sweat and was glad Manny was unconscious again. He resisted the urge to wake him.

Just then he heard the murmur of an engine and looked back up the river. He recognized Chief Wolf Salmon in a small jet boat and waved frantically. He jumped for joy when the bow rose, speeding up toward them.

Paul looked back at the gorge and saw the big boulder that split the river in two. It loomed larger, and he began to doubt they would be reached in time before they entered the first boiling rapid.

***

Wolf Salmon pushed the throttle harder. He hadn't believed the young boy when he'd said he had seen someone riding a raft. He decided to check it out only because he knew they had visitors in the valley. He now urged the engine faster and hoped the raft wouldn't be forced down the gorge before he could reach them.

Paul was trying to ward off the large boulder with what looked like a fir branch. Instead, he slid backward and the raft hit with a jarring crunch. He let go of the makeshift pole and grabbed at Manny, who was lying on the raft. The man didn't move on his own, even though he was about to be rolled off as the current pushed the edge of the raft down. Worry filled Wolf Salmon.

He was only fifty feet away when the raft popped up under the strong, relentless current and grated along the side of the boulder. They were going to be swept downstream.

Wolf Salmon closed the gap swiftly and threw Paul a line.

"Tie it on, quickly," he yelled. He saw the first of the white water and swung the bow back upstream. He eased open the throttle and felt the jar as the slack was taken up in the tow rope.

The stern of his jet boat sunk lower as the engine revs rose. Even at full throttle, the raft didn't move—if anything, the bow began to sink.

Wolf Salmon made a quick decision and swung the boat around yet again. The jet boat bumped the raft's side and water slopped over it. They had entered the first of the standing waves of the white-capped rapids.

Manny groaned in pain as Paul virtually threw him into the jet boat. Paul slashed the tow rope holding the raft with a knife he held. He could hardly keep his feet as the raft rocked wildly in the rapids. Paul jumped and landed in a heap in the bottom of the jet boat next to Manny.

Imperceptibly, the jet boat crawled upstream, now eased of its load.

Wolf Salmon glanced back and saw the raft disappear in the first of the six-foot standing waves. Before it was totally lost to sight, he saw the bow break up. "What the hell happened," he shouted over the engine's noise.

"Long story. Tell you when we get ashore; we need to get medical help for Manny. He needs hospital attention as soon as possible."

Wolf Salmon switched on the VHF radio and told his wife to contact Terrace hospital and get a helicopter over to the village.

***

Eight hours later, Paul listened as the doctor explained that Manny's leg could be saved, but they'd had to fuse his knee since it was so badly smashed.

It would limit his mobility in the future, but it was the best they could do. Manny was resting for now, but Paul had one last thing to do before he could sleep.

He repeated his story to the bewildered RCMP officer, describing the helicopter and Nick Barrett as one of the occupants. He didn't know the identities of the other two. The officer promised that the investigation would include sending someone to check the tree they had crashed into, to see if it had fallen naturally or not.

Paul was set up in a motel in Terrace so that he could check in on Manny. As soon as his head hit the pillow, he fell instantly asleep.

It rained hard during the night and was still pouring come the next morning. The clouds were dense and menacing, and the forecast was for the same for the next two days. On the third day, after the skies had cleared, Paul was asked to return to the station. An officer had been sent to the valley via helicopter.

Paul read aloud parts of the report the officer had compiled. "The alleged tree could not be found; signs of a damaged watercraft discovered among rocks. Further wreckage could have been swept downstream by flooding. The river was still in flood condition, and the helicopter could not land. Further investigation required once terrain returns to normal conditions. At this point, there is no evidence of a criminal act found on site."

Paul processed that for a moment.

"Okay, what about the helicopter we saw there? It belongs to Nick Barrett's company," he said.

"Sir, we talked to the pilot, and his log showed he was north about 100 miles. He has denied everything you alleged."

"The lying bastard," Paul said. "What about Mr. Barrett?"

The officer quirked an eyebrow.

"He admitted being in the helicopter with a Mr. Daniel Raven Eater but, as I said, they were north of you—nowhere near the valley. They were looking for a new logging site. There was also no sign of anyone hunting on the chopper: no meat, no trophies; not even any blood. Mr. Barrett did have a rifle with them, but it is licensed to his company, to be used in rural locations for defense against wildlife."

Paul opened his mouth to protest, but the officer held up a hand.

"I'm sorry, sir, there is nothing else I can do; at this point, your accusation cannot be substantiated. Mr. Barrett has mentioned that you two have a history, and he is sorry that you are still harboring a long-time grudge against him. He did say he is not going to sue you for defamation if you let the issue go."

The officer paused.

"If this continues, however, he would be well within his rights to do so."

Paul was not to be placated.

"So, what you're saying is that lying bastard is to be believed, but not us, eh? Thank you, officer, and good bye."

***

Paul said his goodbyes to Manny after a few more days, with a promise to visit again soon. Only those close to them believed their story. Paul had tried to confront Nick, but that hadn't gone any better: he had been thrown out of West Skeena Timber corporate headquarters by three burly security guards without even seeing Nick Barrett.

Nick's obvious disregard for nature, and the idea that Nick was in the area to look into logging, motivated Paul to visit the Ministry of Forests while he was still in Vancouver. The idea of sustainable logging appealed to his sense of adventure, and he wanted to find out more about the government's plans for the valley.

He avidly read the official description of the Tree Forest License and its recommendation it be opened to potential companies for logging rights. The valley's extent was huge, and had some of the last major stands of Douglas fir, hemlock, cedar, and balsam. However, Paul was only twenty-five; he couldn't finance a multi-billion-dollar operation with a full-blown sawmill and logging roads. He had a bit saved in the bank, but that only amounted to maybe ten thousand dollars. He felt dismayed and frustrated.

Lumber prices dropped as the housing market slumped, and new units and renovations decreased. His father was forced to accept lower and lower prices from their buyers, but the major companies still flooded the market with what was now over-production. Six months passed, and the healthy bottom line soon turned to red. Paul and his father started talking about cutting down to only one shift.

The whole of British Columbia was affected by the loss of jobs and corporate income: most of the lumber market was sent to the States. Soon, all mills were forced down to a single shift, and yet inventories still increased due to the lumber depression. The economy was still a system of boom and bust, and after five years of boom the bust had arrived.

Forest companies braced themselves for the lean times ahead. Many had spent large amounts of capital to increase production when profits were high, and the interest payments now began to hurt. Some of the smaller independents closed their doors altogether and went on a maintenance-only program, waiting for better prices in the future.

General public opinion didn't have much sympathy: many had heard of the huge profits once reaped, and those who lived in the Greater Vancouver area did not see the hardships for small-town inhabitants further north who dealt with lowered wages or none at all.

After half a year of struggling, Paul's father had to shut down to a maintenance-only operation as well. Paul left for Vancouver, where he found a job at a consultant downtown. He only landed the position because he had been involved in the building of the last major sawmill and his father knew one of the partners. He was disappointed in the small projects he was assigned, but even so felt fortunate he had a job.

Paul soon gained the respect of the whole office: he knew not only design but operational considerations of construction. Many of the assignments were just proposals for future projects that could eventually go ahead when the economy rebounded.

Luckily the recession didn't last long, and within a year Paul was doing overtime as some jobs turned into actual projects. Running mills increased production and the closed ones started up again. After each job, Paul always spent time on-site as the company's site engineer. His father's mill was soon on two shifts again as the housing market in the US boomed. His father's health had improved, so Paul stayed in Vancouver for a while longer.

Paul's salary nearly doubled as he took on more and more responsibility. He loved this aspect of engineering, and took a great thrill in starting a project from a blank piece of paper and turning it into concrete, steel, and equipment that produced a valuable product. However, companies were still only getting back on their feet; no new mills were being built just yet.

More and more articles appeared in the province's newspapers about the state of the forestry industry. A few TV documentaries were released that highlighted the unsustainability of the present industry. Some were scathing in their remarks, and green parties began to blockade logging roads to save the last watersheds in their area.

***

During the last four years, Michelle had been employed as a research assistant in the Western Wilderness Committee. It was a grassroots organization that wanted the overcutting of forests to be halted. She loved her job, even though the wages were very low.

Unlike most of her classmates, Michelle hadn't gone to work for the forestry companies. She chose this career path after one of her holidays on Vancouver Island, where she saw some of the vast clear-cuts of forest stretching for miles.

In her mind, the trouble was that a lot of old-timers still ran the industry; they would go against their advisors about not overcutting because a fat bottom line was too much to ignore. Short-term profits ruled their operational plans. They had been cutting for a hundred years, and they still believed it could continue. However, they ignored that the rate of cutting throughout the province had also accelerated vastly.

As more and more people traveled the province on holiday, they saw the clear-cut areas from the logging roads they were allowed to use on the weekends and voiced their concerns to the newspapers. Now, damaging articles appeared nearly weekly. The government had to take heed. Greenpeace, a large environmental movement, even managed to get an injunction to stop logging altogether in a small valley in northern Vancouver Island and the news spread internationally.

Some of the activists went too far, even for Michelle, in their ever-increasing demands to stop logging in vast areas of the province. Public pressure grew so strong that legislation was introduced to force a percentage of each Tree Forest License to become permanent public parks, with no logging allowed. Michelle realized that much of BC's economy depended on the forestry industry, including tens of thousands of jobs. However, she believed that some areas should be left untouched for the generations to come.

She was writing an article on just that topic, and had gone out to do some of the research personally. She and the executive committee had just come back from the Stikeen Valley where the local First Nation chief, Wolf Salmon, had invited them to see an untouched watershed that had never seen any logging.

Chief Wolf Salmon was smart enough to realize that unless he did something soon, his people's ancestral home would be let out to one of the huge conglomerates. Already he had become alarmed at the increase in interest in the valley; he had said they had recently seen a number of helicopters exploring the area. Prices had again reached record heights, and the gleam of huge profits loomed large in the eyes of forest companies.

Chief Wolf Salmon hoped that support from organizations like hers would help their cause, and so had given Michelle the grand tour. For her part, Michelle had fallen in love with the valley. She had especially loved Emerald Creek and the magnificent trees in the grove.

She viewed the glossy photos in front of her and picked the best for the article. This valley was a treasure beyond compare. After all, it was only one of hundreds, and if it could not be protected then something was grossly wrong with the whole industry.

She reviewed the final layout on her computer, with maps and photos inserted to go along with the text. Michelle had spent hours in the library poring over old documents and maps, and was proud of the final result. She had tried to stick to the facts, but some emotions came through in her descriptions of thick moss carpets, shimmering ice peaks, and mountainsides clad in blankets of trees. It was a true, comprehensive listing of the valley's natural treasures.

She hoped the article would be enough to prevent it from being lost forever to the buzz of chainsaws.

Michelle had her article complete in less than two weeks and already the printers had copies ready to go as flyers in all the major newspapers. The committee had over six thousand ordinary members, and she hoped the impact of the four-page glossy flyer would bring more pressure to bear on the government to protect the valley.

The papers had been distributed on Sunday to over a quarter-million readers. On Monday, the phone went crazy. They received generous donations and many questions on how they could help. She and the office staff told them to write letters to their members of parliament.

That Friday, Michelle watched a short interview with the Premier of BC: reporters had been waiting for him as he left the parliament buildings.

"Mr. Premier, is it true that the last TFL in BC is about to be given out for tender? Will the government be expected to subsidize some of the huge costs of logging roads to the remote valley?" asked the newsman.

"Answering your first question. Yes, the closing date for the TFL tender is June of 1980. We shall carefully consider all proposals which meet our strict criteria. Second, there are no plans for subsidization; all costs shall be borne by the successful candidate," the Premier answered smoothly and continued to his waiting car.

Michelle nodded in satisfaction. Public pressure would force the government to detail the benefits internally and reconsider why the TFL was out for tender in the first place.

***

Meanwhile over town, Nick was deep in a meeting about fiber inventory for their currently-held licenses.

"You mean to tell me that in twenty years the trees where we logged eighty years ago will only be fifteen inches in diameter? Our average right now is thirty. That, gentlemen, is unacceptable; it constitutes a loss of about one-third the fiber, and our mills will begin to starve for wood."

"Yes, Mr. Barrett," his chief forester said. "You see, old prediction analysis models were overly-optimistic. These statistics are from recent surveys we have just conducted. I am afraid the old model did not consider that the growth rate drops dramatically at higher elevations. Slopes constitute about two-thirds of the volume in an average valley that we hold titles to. At our present rate of cutting, the only way to keep the mills in fiber is to cut down our production of lumber," the chief forester explained.

"Hell, you're talking about eight mills, mister—all of which turn good profits. What do you think is paying off the expansion loans we still have on the books? The new environmental laws are going to cost an extra three hundred million per year just to meet regulations. We need those lumber mills producing full-bore, not shutting down."

"Not all of our TFLs are in that bad a shape, but the trend is alarming, I must say. We have to do something. The Rupert mill will have to cease production within five years unless another source of lumber is secured."

His forester quickly moved on under Nick's withering glare. "I would suggest we obtain TFL 41, the Stikeen Valley. Build a new mill at the valley estuary and shut down the one in Rupert."

Nick bent his head down, deep in thought.

"No," he said eventually. "It would cost too much money, and where the hell would we get the labor that far south from Rupert? There's only a few drunken natives in that run-down village, and the mill would need about two hundred employees."

Nick leaned back and shook his head, sure of himself now.

"No, I think the only viable answer is to get the license and haul the wood north by barge to the existing mill. We can even divert some of the wood down to our pulp mills on Vancouver Island. How long would that TFL last at, say, two million cubic meters of cut?"

"According to new predictions? Forty years tops," the forester replied.

"Fuck, we're damned if we do and damned if we don't." Nick slammed his hand on the table.

"What the hell—we have to do it to survive. Who cares if the valley is cut by then? It'll give us time to recuperate. Let's go get that license. I want a full log-hauling cost analysis done and a budget for the old mill at Rupert to be upgraded. Have it on my desk by next week."

He left without waiting for a response. He had to talk with the chief financial officer. Interest rates were high, and the debt load they had incurred over the years worried him greatly. As long as pulp and lumber prices remained high, they would be okay, but lows always happened, and they needed to save for the bad times.

He heard what the chief financial officer had to say and swore.

"Fuck it, I can't pay over fifty million dollars a year in interest year after year."

If the prices increased just five more percent, then he could order maximum production from all mills and pay off the huge loan as fast as he could. It looked like TFL 41 was the only way to make that happen. At least, they were in an ideal position for the bid, since their company was in the area already.

He knew his lawyers could draft a very compelling response to the upcoming request for proposals for the license. The bid had to be in by the end of June, which gave him a further four months to prepare and enhance their chances. The promise of more jobs in Prince Rupert and taxes to the government put them in a good position; no other company had a mill anywhere close to the TFL.

***

Paul read the article on the Stikeen Valley that he had borrowed from a friend at work. He recognized a lot of the photographs and was amazed at all the other information about the area, including wildlife, native culture, and the impact large-scale logging would have on the valley.

Boy, someone sure did their homework, he thought, and he scanned the credits for its author. The name immediately pounced out at him: Michelle Forney, BSc in Forestry from the University of British Columbia. He whistled softly. In his mind's eye, he pictured Michelle the last time he had seen her. An aching loneliness engulfed him as he remembered the precious time they had spent together. How time had flown.

Eventually, though, his thoughts went back to the valley and the work he had been conducting. For two months, he worked on a detailed estimate for a floating sawmill designed for custom cut lumber: a product that brought in only the highest prices. He thought it was perfect for the valley.

Steve had given him the idea of using an old supertanker for the platform, thus saving millions of dollars in site preparation, concrete, and structural building.

He had overcome the huge cost of logging roads with the unique idea of using a small airship called the Cyclotron to transport logs to the floating mill. The Cyclotron was a type of zeppelin, like a smaller Goodyear blimp, and was powerful enough to lift a payload measured in tons—more than enough for the relatively low production he had planned.

He had seen one in a hangar in Oregon during a class trip one semester. Now, it just lay as a tourist oddity. The company who had financed it had gone bankrupt, and no companies had taken it up. He was sure it could be purchased cheaply from creditors.

Paul scanned the plans of the floating sawmill and knew it had everything required to process lumber at the lowest possible cost. Most of the equipment he had estimated for was second-hand, since after the last decade of expansion most mills in the province had a surplus.

He figured a crew of twenty could run the operation. They could come from Terrace on a two week turn-around, just like the oil patches in Alberta—they had no problem attracting employees, albeit at higher wages than he could afford.

Steve had even said he would be Chief Engineer. His Navy training meant he could run all the main engines and generator. Paul was also sure that Manny would love to be involved, although as of yet he hadn't told him of his dream. He realized it was still only a dream, but it filled his leisure hours; he liked the challenge of coming up with something unique.

What kept it a dream was still financing: twenty-two million. A huge amount in his eyes. However, he knew some investors might be interested if the return was good enough.

That weekend he went home and took a plan of his layout with him. He showed it to his father for the first time that Saturday evening to get his professional opinion.

His dad showed a keen interest, and soon they were into talks of optimum recovery, flow, piece count, size of machines, and other details.

"Who's this for anyway, Paul?"

"Oh, it's not one of our clients. It's just an idea of my own that I had: how I would log the valley sustainably for ad infinitum."

Paul's father clapped him on the shoulder.

"Well, it's a hell of a concept, and I really like it; well done. I'm surprised it's never been attempted before for the coast logging operations."

He scratched his chin, looking down at the plans.

"The logging roads alone in that area would cost a fortune, and half a mill's operating costs are normally just getting the logs to the mill. Of course, the concept of specialty cutting for finishing lumber isn't new, but this has the right size to it. Japanese buyers, in particular, would be all over you for the cedar. How much were your capital costs again, including converting a supertanker at a Vancouver shipyard?"

"With the changes you recommended? I reckon about twenty-four million and change."

His father leaned forward. "You know, our mill has been doing pretty good now and I've had three offers to buy it. Do you really think you could do this? And more importantly, would you go for it full-bore?"

Paul wondered at the direction of his dad's probing. He answered carefully. "The figures I estimate are within five percent; and yes, I would love to show the big boys how to really do sustainable logging. Our mill here is great, but you built it, and now Matt seems to have it down-pat—he's doing a fabulous job running it for us."

"Yes, Paul, but you know there is always a big place for you here; family is family. And anyway, one day it will all be yours."

Paul covered his father's hand with his.

"I know that, Dad, and I appreciate it. But you know I have to do something on my own first. I'm sorry, but it's the way I feel at the moment."

"I know—I felt the same at your age. Think you can leave these drawings and notes with me? I may have a few more ideas, and I want to show them to your mom as well. I think you're on to something. I know she'll also be proud of you for coming up with the unique idea."

"Yes, no problem."

Paul didn't think about it much the following week until, out of the blue, his dad called him at work.

"Paul, are you coming over again soon?" his dad asked.

"Well, no, I hadn't planned to. Anything the matter?"

"Err, no, not especially. But why not nip on over anyway? Your mom says she'll cook a sirloin roast."

"Okay—you have me sold on the steak alone. See you late Friday, then?" Paul hung up, wondering what had gotten into his dad.

"Old age, I suppose."

That Friday, Paul caught the late afternoon ferry from Vancouver. It had been a long drive, and it was past midnight by the time he arrived in Kelsey Bay and climbed the stairs up to his room. His parents had left a note that they'd see him at breakfast.

"Hi Mom," Paul said as he hugged her from behind the next morning. He breathed in the aroma of frying bacon and tomato-and-mushroom omelet: his favorite breakfast.

"Away with you, and sit down. It's nearly ready; Dad will be down in a minute. Can you pour the coffee, please?"

They chattered idly over breakfast. It was not until the end of the second cup of aromatic coffee that his dad broached the subject of why he had asked Paul over.

"Paul, me and your mom really like this idea of yours. We have a proposition to make to you."

Paul put his coffee down.

"You know that since my stroke I just don't have the heart for business like I used to; I want to spend some quality time with your mom since…well, you never know."

Paul touched his dad's shoulder and saw his eyes glisten.

"I know, Dad, and soon, I promise, I'll come over for good and take over. I just need a little more time doing my own thing."

"No," his dad interrupted. "Let me finish. You know those offers I was talking to you about last week? Well, we really started taking them seriously: the prices may never be as high again, and they were way above what I thought our little operation was worth."

Paul cut the air. "You can't sell, Dad; you and Mom built this place up from scratch—it's been your life."

"We're both in agreement," his mom interceded with a hand on his shoulder.

"We feel like we've earned a bit of peace and quiet; and anyway, we won't be completely out of the picture."

"What do you mean, 'not out of the picture'? You mean only sell a portion, or what?"

His dad leaned over.

"No, we'll sell the whole lot, but toward a partnership in the new mill you've thought of."

Paul was silent for a while. "What? The mill I thought of?"

His mother smiled. "Your dad and I want to back you on the floating mill and be partners with you, silent, sort of, while you run it."

Paul gaped at them. "Wow, are you serious, or what?"

"Yes, deadly serious. Here's how we see it."

His dad cleared the table of plates and brought out the plans Paul had left him. From the notes in the margins, it looked like he had worked on it a bit more. His voice took on an eager note that Paul hadn't heard since his stroke. He explained some of the fine-tuning he'd done.

"Well, say something, son. What do you think? Let's show how the woods can be cut forever and still make a healthy profit."

Paul was choked.

His mom came up behind him and squeezed his shoulders.

Finally, he managed a hoarse whisper.

"It'll be the best darn mill in the world, apart from this one, of course. What was the highest offer, if you don't mind me asking?"

His father beamed.

"Twenty-six million, and we get to keep the farm and one hundred acres. One of my stipulations, which they agreed to, was that if they close the mill down, they would do remedial work to the land and plant trees."

"Shit, Dad, that's awful close to the budget."

"Ah, I reckon you could talk business with the chief of the Stikeen Tribe, what was his name? Yes, Wolf Salmon. He goes to the aboriginal minister and they get to put in, say, four million, if they can get it. That leaves us more than enough of a nest egg. I may even be able to get one of my buddies to invest more."

"Wow, I can't believe you. You're really serious about this—no joke, now?"

"You bet your bottom dollar, son. The biggest problem we have to the whole scheme is time: time to get the proposal in, to get the financing in order, and to fight the big boys. I can tell you, it's going to be a dogfight."

The rest of the night was spent going through what the proposal format and content should be. They reckoned they couldn't compete with the big boys in dollars but the ace up their sleeve was the environmental benefit. That and, if Paul could get them on board, the support of the tribe.

Paul's dad suggested that Paul get hold of the Western Wilderness Committee and form an alliance. They could set aside a good portion of the valley as an untouchable park or recreation facility that the Committee could swing as a business of their own. Paul swallowed hard at the prospect of meeting Michelle again.

"I suggest you call up Chief Wolf Salmon and set up a meeting with him, too. Without him, I don't think the government would entertain our proposal seriously. But with all the adverse publicity the tender has generated, I think we have a good fighting chance. I'll pay for all the flight costs, but can you get off work as soon as possible?"

The rest of the day was like a daydream for Paul. His mind whirled at all the work to do, but he was giddy as a puppy. He got tipsy with wine over the juicy sirloin his mom cooked that night. All their spirits were high with the anticipation of a new and exciting adventure.

Paul said his goodbyes the next morning with copies of their revised plans in hand. He also had a list a mile long of the next steps to be taken before the tender deadline.

Paul knew time was tight, but he savored the late nights it would take. He just hoped asking for a couple of weeks holiday from work on such short notice wouldn't be a problem. They only had six weeks to do everything.

Paul was refused the time off. Reluctantly, he gave his notice in April of 1980 and jumped into the project with both feet, praying he hadn't burned any bridges if they lost the bid. He had ten thousand in his savings account.

He worked hard putting the formal proposal together. The main theme would be sustainability, minimal impact to the environment, and the tribe's involvement in the project. He had already arranged to fly up to Terrace to meet Chief Wolf Salmon, who had sounded eager to hear more about what Paul had briefly told him.

His dad, in the meantime, had the contract for sale of his mill all agreed to, although he had put off the final decision date to after the tender proposal. The purchasing company didn't know of their plans, and although they could back out anytime they wanted, Paul didn't see it as much of a gamble.

More pressingly, Paul wanted to meet with Michelle in private to tell her about his idea. He wanted to hear what she thought before he approached the Committee formally. Michelle's and the Committee's views seemed so far apart from his that he was nervous at them even taking his proposal seriously, let alone accepting it.

But his argument was sound. He called Michelle directly to break the ice before they were required to meet in office surroundings.

***

Michelle was just polishing up another article when her incoming line flashed.

"Hello, this is Michelle, how may I help you?"

"Hi Michelle, it's, uh, it's me. It's Paul." The voice was familiar—oh-so-familiar—but the hesitant speech wasn't. That and the shock of hearing from Paul out of the blue left her unable to respond.

"Hello? You still there?"

She pulled herself together. "Yes, yes; I'm here. Just a bit of a shock after all this time. How are you?"

"Oh, not bad. In fact, I'm doing great. How about you?"

"Super, super; keeping busy, you know."

"Congratulations on that article you wrote about the Stikeen Valley. It was damned good, and you got a lot of public support."

Oh, was that what this was about?

"Thank you. It took a lot of research, but I did my homework. What are you doing these days, anyway?"

"Well, funny you should ask. I just quit my job from the consulting firm I was working for, and am now doing something far more important."

Michelle smiled. Classic Paul. He loved to add a bit of drama to the moment.

"Oh, and what's that?"

"I have an idea concerning the Stikeen Valley, and I want to talk to you about it. Can we get together for lunch or something?"

"Well, I'm rather pushed at the moment; we have a tight deadline to meet on our defense proposal. Can it wait for a couple of weeks?"

"No. You see, it concerns the Tree Forest License bid coming up, and I think your committee would be very interested in what I have to propose. I've been to the valley and fallen in love with it; I don't want the status quo of clear-cut logging anymore."

Michelle was surprised to hear that he had seen the valley first-hand. As a consultant, what did he have that could change the valley's outlook?

"Well, okay then. When and where?" she asked.

"How about The Bistro at Lonsdale Quay? Say, twelve o' clock the day after tomorrow?"

"Okay, I'll see you there."

"Great. Bye."

And with that, Paul hung up.

Michelle raised her eyebrows as she slowly lowered the receiver. She wondered what was so important for Paul to call her. She pictured his face—blue eyes, ruffled hair—and shivered at old memories. She was a little mad Paul had upset her world after such a long time, but was forced to admit she was looking forward to seeing him again.

She tried to finish her work but to no avail; she couldn't concentrate anymore. After a fruitless hour, she powered down her computer and got ready to go home.

Chapter Six
Preparations

The morning of his meeting with Michelle came. Paul fussed around for most of it, achieving little work as the hour approached. He cleaned up, straightened a painting on the wall, watched ships come and go in the harbor, and generally drank too much coffee. The early spring weather was warm, and the view from his twelfth-story apartment room was glorious.

He checked his watch for the tenth time and took one last look in the mirror before grabbing his briefcase.

On the road, Paul smiled and dropped a gear. He loved the throaty sound of the exhaust on his old Mustang. He took the lower road, which wound around the curving coastline. A few kids waved to him as he sped past them in the red roadster.

It was mid-week, so he easily found a spot in the parking lot at the Quay. He looked at his watch: he was a good ten minutes early. Seagulls squabbled over the clear water for a few scraps of apple thrown in by a young girl and her mother.

Paul passed the outside fountain and glimpsed a sea bus heading across the water to downtown Vancouver. He walked up two levels to the entrance to the Bistro and sighed in relief because he couldn't see Michelle. He managed to get an outside table on the balcony and promptly ordered a Bacardi and Coke to steady his nerves.

He glanced at his watch: five minutes past twelve. Knowing Michelle, she would be another ten minutes. His tongue explored his even white teeth. *Good, nice and clean*, he thought. *Shit, what am I doing? I'm not on a date. This is strictly business.*

He was busy admiring the lines of a Cunard cruise ship entering the harbor when he heard her voice behind him.

"Hello, Paul. Sorry I'm a bit late."

Paul jerked his head around and awkwardly got to his feet.

"Hi Michelle. Nice to see you again. Here, have a seat." He pulled out a chair for her.

"Thank you," she said and sat down.

The sun shone in her midnight waves of hair, which tumbled down to spread over her white cardigan. Paul tore his eyes away from the delicious mounds beneath and met her eyes. Michelle smiled nervously and he smiled back.

"Would you like a drink?" he asked.

"Yes, please. Just an orange juice."

Paul caught the attention of the waitress.

A pregnant silence followed as each tried to avoid each other's eyes. Paul shuffled around in his seat. His breath was quick and shallow as his mind raced.

Damn it. She's even more gorgeous than I remember. The years had filled out Michelle a bit, turning her once girlish figure into one of a beautiful young lady in her late twenties. He felt a flush heat his cheeks as he watched Michelle's gaze follow his arms and shoulders.

"You know, I really meant it when I said I enjoyed your article on the Stikeen Valley," he said. "Did I tell you I have been there as well?"

"You mentioned; when did you go?" she asked politely.

"A couple of years ago, me and a buddy of mine from Terrace went fishing up there. It's a beautiful place; so wild, yet serene at the same time. We went up Emerald Creek and saw the most magnificent trees I've ever seen in my life."

"Oh, I know the ones. You mean those monsters just by that huge log jam. The big one by the edge is just beautiful."

"Yes, that's right. I reckon that Big Fir is over a thousand years old," Paul said.

Michelle smiled, chin in hand, and gazed out over the harbor.

"Paul, can you imagine what it must have been like all along the coast here, hundreds of years ago? You know, before all the logging started? There must have been many trees like that." She shook her head sadly. "And now there's just a few spots left. They're disappearing faster and faster as the furthest reaches are being logged."

Anger flushed Michelle's cheeks. Paul recognized the fiery glint in her eye.

"You see, Paul, it just has to slow down, or there'll be nothing left. I'm going to fight those big forest companies the whole way. Not one tree will be cut in the Stikeen, not if I can help it." She slapped the palm of her hand on the table and the glasses jumped.

Boy, Paul thought. *This is going to be tougher than I thought.* He decided to let the matter in hand wait a while longer.

Paul sidetracked the conversation away to news of past friends, since it seemed safer ground for the moment. The food and warm sun made good companions and soon both were relaxed. Paul felt himself slide easily into Michelle's company; it was as if the years hadn't been long. He ordered coffee for himself and strawberries and cream for Michelle, who squealed in delight when she saw them beautifully arranged on a frosted plate.

"I see you haven't lost your appetite any," Paul chided.

"Umm, just can't resist these." Her pert white teeth sank into one of the juicy strawberries. She caught the dripping cream with a cupped hand.

Paul squirmed in his seat and eased the tightness in his jeans, which threatened to embarrass him. *Time to broach the subject.* He took a deep breath.

"Michelle, do you remember what I told you about that old logger on Saltspring Island?"

"Mm, I do." She popped another strawberry into her mouth.

"Well, I believe his method of selective logging could be sustainable on a larger scale. I've been doing a lot of work on it and I reckon you'd be interested in the idea. Here, take a look at this." He slipped her his plans of the site and a brief description of the floating sawmill.

Michelle took the small binder and looked through it.

"Yes, very nice, but what's it got to do with me? You know my views of logging, and they aren't the same as yours; they never will be."

"I know. But since we last saw each other, I've seen a lot of the forest go to waste, and like you, I want to do something about it. Look again at the inlet the ship is on and tell me if you recognize it." Paul had purposely not put a name on the map.

Michelle lifted the map closer and her eyes widened.

"Paul, is this where I think it is?" she demanded.

"You tell me where you think it is."

"It's Eagle Channel, by the Stikeen River Valley, isn't it?"

"Yes, just a mile west of the mouth."

Michelle tossed the binder back across the table. It landed squarely on Paul's plate.

"Now hold it, Michelle; you haven't heard what I have to say. Calm down and give me a chance." he said.

Her eyes flashed a deeper green and her cheeks flushed.

"Just you dare, Paul Whorton; just you dare," she challenged.

Paul held up his hands.

"Please, Michelle, just listen to me for a few moments. Then, if you still disagree, then that's fine. Okay?"

She huffed.

"I'm listening, go on."

"You know all the big boys are bidding for the license, and I reckon even with the publicity your article made, the government is still going to award it to one of them. There's just too much money in it for them to make the whole thing into a park."

"They have to, though: it's the last one…"

"No, they don't. Now please, just hold on for a few more minutes. I know the industry intimately and what you're up against. Take West Skeena Timber, for instance. Since Nick Barrett took over the reins, they've increased their cut in every area to pay for the new pulp mill they built in Prince Rupert."

Michelle looked down; her arms crossed.

"He's aggressive, Michelle, even more so now, and he has the best chance of getting that license. My aim is to stop him and the others by getting the license myself. I don't want the valley screwed up any more than you, and that's precisely why we should join forces for the bid."

Michelle jerked her gaze up. "You're kidding me, aren't you? We're on opposite sides of the fence, and you know it."

"Look, I still believe there's a very important place for forestry in BC: it employs one out of six people in the province, so it's naive to think it's just going to go away anytime soon." Paul immediately regretted taking an aggressive stance but ploughed on when he saw Michelle about to respond.

"You see, with my plan of selective cutting, I can employ local labor in the valley. In addition, I can save the valley, not destroy it; with what I have in mind, you'd hardly notice any logging at all. In fact, I don't even plan to have any logging roads scarring the landscape."

"And how do you expect to log in there without miles of logging roads all over the place? It's impossible terrain."

"Oh, but I do have a way. Just hear me out a bit longer."

He told her of the Cyclotron airship and the details of his cut volumes, flipping to the relevant pages in the binder as necessary. Michelle probed here and there with probing questions, but Paul had reasonable answers to them all and the time swiftly passed.

"Well, what do you think now?" he asked.

Michelle sat silently for a while and gazed across the harbor.

Please, please, Paul wished silently.

"What about the tribe? Have you approached them yet?"

"No, but I know the chief from my trip with Manny. I'm sure he'll be receptive: my aim is to have the tribe fully involved by training them as operators. After all, no matter what way you look at it, it's their homeland. I really believe that with their backing and your group working with us we can build a healthy logging industry and still keep most of the beauty of the valley untouched for generations to enjoy."

Michelle ran a hand through her hair.

"Look, Paul, this is too deep a question to answer here. But I'll put your proposal forward to the committee members and then let you know. Okay?"

"Great." Paul beamed and impulsively squeezed her arm. His hand lingered on her softness. Only reluctantly did he release her. "Can you get back to me as soon as possible? The bid closes in June, which is coming up fast. If you agree, then we'll go see Chief Wolf Salmon straight away and try to get him on board as well."

"Okay. But as I said, I'm not sure we can go for this. It is logging, after all, and most of our members are dead against it. But I'll give it some serious thought."

She looked at her watch. "Now, I really must go. Here, take this for my share." She pressed twenty dollars into Paul's protesting hand. With a flashing smile, she was gone.

Paul couldn't take his eyes off her tight jeans and marveled at their contents as they swayed deliciously to the door.

"Bye," he called and finished his coffee before paying the bill. All considered, it had gone rather well.

***

Michelle left her meeting with Paul quickly, her mind racing in reverse. Paul's persuasive arguments had sounded convincing, but they went against her convictions. She just needed to get away and think. Plus, she admitted to herself, she still felt a strong attraction to Paul. She must not let that cloud her judgment.

Back at her apartment she threw her bag onto the sofa, stripped down, and stepped into the shower. As the water beat down on her, she went over Paul's arguments again. She sort of agreed with him that by joining forces they might stop the large forest companies from getting the license and stripping the valley.

Her thoughts wandered to Paul's handsome features and felt a familiar heat rising. She'd had a couple of casual affairs since Paul, but they'd always fallen short for her. She quickly turned the shower to cold then stepped out, dried herself roughly, and thought how close she had come to compromising her convictions.

"No, you damn well can't have the last valley: none of you," she said to the empty room.

***

Two days later, Paul's illusion was shattered. Michelle called and told him that after discussing the proposal with some of the other committee members, their consensus was that they couldn't support any commercial logging venture in the valley.

Paul moped around for days and couldn't concentrate on his work. His dad called him to check how things were going.

"I'll be over at the end of next week to look over the final format, okay?" His voice echoed over the line, breaking Paul out of his fogged mind.

"Err, yes; just give me a call the day before." *Shit. Better get to work.*

Paul dug straight into the pile of paperwork, trying to condense it into a concise document. He was revising the budget for the tenth time, and kept coming back to the ship. He realized that he couldn't just estimate this: the potential room for error was simply too large.

140

He called Steve, who was luckily home on leave, and so they could meet up.

Paul laid his plans on the table.

"Well. Any thoughts on the type of ship we need? And more importantly, how much?"

Steve asked a few questions regarding the minimum size of vessel and condition needed before answering.

"At the time of the oil glut in the early seventies, hundreds of oil tankers were literally mothballed and left to anchor in inlets all over the world. Since then, about seventy percent have either been re-commissioned or scrapped; but that still leaves a lot of tankers. I did some digging, and made up a list of about twenty or so when you told me roughly what you were looking for last week. Some of these should do."

He handed over a faxed sheet from Lloyds of London. It showed each vessel's name, type, tonnage, and other details, including the owner's particulars.

"Boy, you really are something, man. How the hell did you get this?"

"You'll never believe me if I told you."

"Go on: try me."

Steve shrugged. "I went out with a sweet little Wren—that is, one of the women recruited for the Maritime Command—and kept in touch with her in England. She actually became one of the first female officers, and boy, Paul, was she ever a brick house: legs up to her armpits and tits to match."

"Forget that. Just tell me how."

"Oh," Steve said, and shook his head. "Well, she left the Command and joined Lloyds of London as an appraiser. She did a bit of digging for me when I called her as a favor. Pretty good, eh?"

Paul chuckled. Leave it to Steve to get help from an old flame.

"Yes, great. Now, how much?"

"I faxed a couple of the companies who own some of these ships and received a few replies. Here they are." He passed them over to Paul.

They ranged from vessels able to handle 100,000 tons of weight to supertankers over 1,000 feet long, one hundred feet wide, and able to carry up to 400,000 tons.

"Well, it looks like if we can get one of about 250,000 tons for around $1,300,000; that would fit my criteria and budget," Paul said.

"As it happens"—Steve whipped out another fax from Esso Petroleum with a flourish—"the tanker *Hibernia* is of 255,000 deadweight tons and has an asking price of $1,500,000 US."

"Mm," Paul mused. "Why is it proportionately more than the others per ton?"

"I asked the same question and they faxed back some more details." He passed Paul a second page.

As Paul read his eyes widened. "Boy, sounds like just the ticket, eh?"

"Yes, apparently she was in great working order when she was decommissioned. They've kept her in the same condition in hopes of the oil boom coming back."

"Are these prices representative of what's out there?" Paul asked.

"I pored through dozens of world-wide magazines, but the others are really just for scrap—you would have to spend a lot to get them back in working order. For instance, the ones in India and Taiwan are just rust buckets; I doubt you would get them here in one piece, never mind the cost of repairing all the generators and main engine," Steve replied.

"Well, okay, we'll bank on her: I'll put $1,500,000 in the budget."

To celebrate a little, they went to Sailor Hager's pub, which had a spectacular view of downtown and served a decent pint of homebrewed beer. The first pint of draft slid down smoothly, and with a smack of his lips Paul promptly ordered two more.

The lovely server gave them a saucy smile along with their drinks. Both pairs of eyes followed the provocative sway of her behind as she went back to the bar.

As Steve continued to make eyes at their server, Paul lost himself looking out across the harbor.

"Hey, Steve, wake up, you horny idiot," Paul prodded him. "Just look across town, will you?"

"Yeah, what about it?" Steve answered.

"Shut up and get educated, you three-legged goober. Do you realize that before the white man came here, that city across the harbor was once massive firs and cedars that grew taller than most of these skyscrapers? Can you imagine the sight?"

Steve chuckled and took a pull of his beer.

"So, you've said. You've already got me on your side, remember?"

Paul continued without really hearing.

"Think about it. A forest of trees like the Big Fir up in the Stikeen—and maybe some even more impressive." Paul stared across the darkened waters of the harbor.

He felt himself transported to the longboat of Captain George Vancouver as they rounded the first narrows and set eyes on the magnificent protected harbor. Sea otters watched them pass, floating on their backs among waving fronds of kelp. A small tendril of smoke to the north showed signs of a native village.

As the oars dug in, each man looked around in awe. In all their travels, they had never seen such massive trees, which stretched as far as the eye could see. One straight trunk would mast a hundred gunner of His Majesty's Navy of the line.

"Hey, wake up, Paul." Steve tapped him on his shoulder.

"Err, yeah?" Paul groggily replied.

"You okay? It looked as though you were miles away."

"Actually, I was over two hundred years away. I'm fine, really." Paul replied.

"Ah, you're a dreamer, Paul."

"Let's go before I really get a taste for this beer." Paul said.

Each put ten dollars on the table to cover their drinks. On the way out, their server, whose name-tag said Gwen, crossed their paths.

"Night, boys. Having an early one?"

"No, just starting. Any suggestions what two lads like us might do for the rest of the evening?" Steve replied.

She gave him a sly smile. "Well, as it happens, I do. Ever been to Hippos on Third Street?"

"No, never heard of it," Steve lied.

"Well, it's pretty good on a Thursday night. My shift ends in half an hour, and a friend of mine and I will be heading over there, so…" She left the invitation unsaid.

Steve gave Paul a secretive smile. Paul tried to feign indifference, but his interest had been piqued.

"Well, tell you what; I think we will have another couple of pints. By the way, is your friend as smashing as you?"

Gwen blushed before replying.

"Have to wait and see. Same again?" She went behind the bar to get their drinks.

"Look, if she's a dog, then you get her, all right?" Steve continued to push Paul back to their vacant table.

About a half-hour later, Paul noticed Steve frown mid-sentence. He expected the worst as he turned to follow his stare.

Gwen stood there with her friend. "This is Steve and—"

"I know. Hi Steve. Long time no see." Michelle looked Paul straight in the eye and smiled.

Paul's shock at hearing her voice quickly cleared up.

"Hi Michelle. Boy, this is a surprise. One minute we don't see each other for years, and the next, it's twice within a week." He pulled up a chair for her.

Paul saw her hesitate and his heart slowed down. But she accepted his offer and sat down.

"Well guys, since you seem to know each other, I'll go get changed. Be back in a minute."

Steve broke the awkward silence with a cough.

"Well. Can you believe meeting each other like this? Do you still see Tanya?"

Michelle's attention briefly returned to Steve.

"Yes, I see her now and again. She and her husband live on Vancouver Island now. They have two kids."

"Well, next time you see her, tell her I said hey, and I'm glad she's doing well. She was a bit special. Remember that glorious summer? It seems like a million years ago now."

"Actually, she mentioned you quite a few times," Michelle said.

Gwen came back and sat down.

"Wow, you really meant it when you said you were getting changed. Stellar outfit, Gwen." Steve said.

Michelle rolled her eyes and pointed at Steve.

"Watch him, Gwen. I've known him for a long time, and he's a charmer."

Steve gave them his most innocent smile.

"Ah, come on, Michelle. I'm not. Give a guy a chance, won't you?"

Michelle told Gwen how they had all met years ago.

"Must be fate. So, what do you say? I think you should hardly waste the chance. And I'm dying to dance—I haven't been out for ages." Gwen stood up, ready to go either way.

Paul looked over to Michelle and gulped, afraid of her answer.

"Come on, Michelle. For old time's sake," Steve said.

Paul's breathing slowed as Michelle nodded and stood up. Gwen gave her a squeeze on the arm and smiled.

Outside, Steve opened the door for Gwen to his 1968 E-type Jaguar.

"Ooh, Michelle, you're right: he is a charmer," she said.

"Have to squeeze in the back, you two," Steve said with a wink for Paul.

"You haven't changed much, Steve." Michelle smiled.

She hopped into the cramped back seats. Paul let her get comfortable first and then got in beside her. There was no way their hips wouldn't touch and Paul was very conscious of it.

Gwen praised the look of the dash and asked what all the knobs and dials did—the modern, American vehicles she was familiar with didn't have them. Steve turned the ignition on and the twin overhead cam engine burbled, then growled to life. Gwen squirmed in her seat. Steve turned on the lights and the dashboard was filled with pin pricks of yellowish light.

"Hang on, girls. This is Alpha Centura, taking off for the wonderful planet of Hippo," Steve warned.

He looked over his shoulder as the 240-horsepower engine rose. The car shook with suppressed energy. With a squeal of rubber, the top-down roadster shot like a bullet onto the wide road. The acceleration was terrific and all four heads snapped back as Steve changed gear.

They screamed past another car on the inside lane. Paul and Michelle involuntarily held each other as the acceleration forced them backward. Michelle's long hair streamed behind her as they gathered speed, her eyes wide.

"Slow down, you mad bastard," Paul said with a laugh. "You're just showing off to make me jealous."

"Yeah, and I love it," Steve said as they passed another car. The speedometer was registering over sixty miles an hour and climbing.

The road wound gently and came to an intersection. The engine roared even loader as Steve deftly double-clutched down. He saw a gap in the traffic and the Jaguar leaped into it.

"Sorry about that folks, but I just become an animal when I get into this beast. Look at that beautiful long hood."

"Next time, remind me to take my car," Michelle said.

"Yeah, at least we would get there in one piece, you maniac," Paul added. Everyone laughed, relaxed now that they were doing the steady speed limit; the wind just caressed their cheeks.

The city lights beckoned as the foursome crossed over the spectacular Lions Gate Bridge. A cargo ship passed silently a hundred feet beneath them, destined for far distant lands. The early autumn night had a slight chill to it, which even the powerful heater couldn't overcome. But unless it was raining, Steve always had the top down.

Gwen stroked the long hood of the Jaguar as they walked toward the neon-lit Hippo Club. The blaring noise hit them as they entered the dim interior.

"Lead the way, girls," Paul said over a song by U2.

They squirmed and weaved their way across the dance floor and sat at a curved corner nook where it was a bit quieter. They ordered drinks and chatted for a while. Gwen and Steve hit it off easily.

Paul plucked up his courage.

"May I have the pleasure of this dance, Michelle?" Paul smiled when she rose off her seat.

The tune by Billy Joel happened to be one of their favorites. Other couples noticed the handsome pair as they danced to the lively song, and soon the dance floor was full.

After the song, Paul and Michelle squeezed their way back the bar and chatted breathlessly. Steve and Gwen came back to join them.

"Hey, guys, I suggested to Gwen we go and see the city lights from the top of Cypress. Do you want to go?"

Steve mouthed a hidden 'No' to Paul.

"Err, no, you two go. Michelle and I can catch the sea bus later." He winked at the smiling Steve.

"Now remember this, Gwen," Michelle sternly told her friend. "This guy is a real Casanova, and make no mistake."

"Think I can handle him," Gwen replied.

"Bye," Steve said and, in a flash, both were gone, Gwen in the lead.

"Last drink, Michelle, or do you want to go home?" Paul said.

"Yes, let's go; my ears are ringing."

Neither of them spoke much as they crossed the harbor to the North Shore. Paul walked Michelle over to her car.

"Well, Michelle, I had a wonderful time. Friends again?"

"Of course, Paul; we never really fell out."

"Note I didn't mention the bid all evening?"

"Yes, I know, and you must have been disappointed but…"

"Ah, I know it was a long shot, but I figured what the hell."

Michelle was about to step inside her car, but stopped.

"Look, do you want a coffee?"

Paul's heart thudded. "Thanks, I would like that. I'll follow you, okay?"

"I don't know. You still driving that old Mustang? Better keep up. My little bug goes like stink." She laughed as she pulled the door shut.

All the way over to downtown Paul couldn't help but think about Michelle—her smile, her laugh, her driving passion—and how much he was really still in love with her, even after all this time.

Michelle had a lovely apartment in the West End overlooking English Bay. Paul admired the smartly-furnished foyer as they waited for the elevator. His nostrils flared as he entered her apartment and took in the lovely scents which pervaded the room. Cedar, rose petals, and a lingering perfume hung everywhere, but not too strongly. Posters adorned most of the walls, all of luscious forests and towering mountains.

Paul followed Michelle into the small but comfy kitchen.

"Can I help with anything?" he asked.

"Yes, please: can you pass me a couple cups from that cupboard?"

In the confined space of the kitchen, they couldn't help but touch. After one such brush, neither moved, frozen in time, waiting.

Paul gulped and turned Michelle slowly by the shoulders. He stared into her lovely eyes and slowly bent forward to kiss her gently: just a fleeting kiss. Michelle leaned into his arms and put her head onto his shoulder. There they remained for a time, simply enjoying the close intimacy.

Paul felt the heat rising as fingers stroked hair and lips touched necks. Neither spoke, but they became more ardent, their kisses now more intense. Slowly, without parting, they made their way into the living room.

Later, Michelle lay snuggled up to Paul, twiddling the hairs on his chest. Words weren't necessary. Their lovemaking had been intense, each rediscovering their secret places.

"Come on, let's go to bed," Michelle said.

Paul watched her shapely silhouette disappear into the bedroom. He rose and felt himself start to rise even harder than before.

Eventually in the early morning, both fell asleep, exhausted and content.

***

"Shoot," Paul exclaimed when he woke and saw the time. He scrambled around the living room looking for his underwear.

"Michelle, where're my undies?"

"Try the hall, I think." She tittered. "Do you have a plane to catch, or do you want breakfast?"

"Oh, I'm sorry, Michelle, but I promised to pick up my dad from the ferry this morning and I'm going to be late. Oh, what the hell. I'll put on the coffee we never drank last night." He went into the kitchen in his now-found underwear.

Michelle joined him in his shirt, which only just covered her dark crotch hairs. Her nipples poked out hard.

Paul gulped his coffee down and tried to hide his growing hardness.

Michelle blushed as Paul caught her lingering stare and met her halfway. Michelle traced the growing outline of his penis through his underwear until it poked out the top. She slowly stroked it. Paul ran a hand through her hair and with his other, massaged her already-taut breast.

Half an hour later, Paul retrieved his clothes and dashed out the door.

His father was waiting in the arrival's foyer.

"You're late, son." He frowned. "And look as though you never slept a wink last night."

"Right on two counts, Dad, and I'm sorry. I'll explain in the car." Paul had always been frank with his parents, so he told him about meeting Michelle again, although he left out some of the finer details.

"Well, it's a pity she couldn't get the committee to join us."

"Ah well, she tried. How's Mom and the mill doing anyhow?"

"Both are doing great. She told me to give you this." He handed Paul one of his favorite candy bars.

"So, how well do you know the chief up in the valley there, Paul?"

"Not too well, but I know he has no love for the big forest companies, especially West Skeena Timber. Apparently, they have been enticing some of the younger men who are left to help survey the valley, promising good jobs to them if they get the license."

"When did you tell him we were coming up?"

"Oh, I spoke to Tom Wolf Salmon last week, and he said he would be glad for us to come up and see him anytime."

They drove in silence after picking up Paul's bag from his apartment and wound their way through the towering office blocks of downtown Vancouver.

The airport terminal was fairly empty and they quickly passed through check-in and security to their plane.

"Come on, Dad, this is our gate."

They boarded the Canadian Pacific Boeing 737 bound for Terrace. The powerful jet taxied down the runway. Paul always loved takeoff, and watched the asphalt swiftly disappear beneath the wheels until they climbed into the air.

The whole of the lower mainland slipped beneath them, and the mighty Fraser River snaked down toward the sea. The Fraser was still one of the largest producers of salmon in the world, and had once fed the armies of England in her colonial days.

The jet banked to reveal Harrison Lake below them, which shone an impossible green-blue in the late-spring sun. Snow still lay in deep gullies. At its head, a large glacier fed the lake. Spreading patches of cleared forest pockmarked the landscape, and winding logging roads twisted up the steep mountainsides.

Now and again, the tan-colored roads were cut in two by massive landslides, where the shallow soil had let go of its tenuous grip on the underlying rock. With the forest cover gone, the snow melted five times as fast in the summer and sometimes avalanches rushed down the steep slopes.

"Paul, that's one thing your Cyclotron will eliminate," his dad commented as he pointed out one particularly large slide. "On terrain like this, no matter how careful you are, there always seems to be damage. I think your way of air-lifting the logs out to the mill is economically sound; better yet, it will please the public to no end."

"Hell Dad, I know you've tried really hard to minimize damage on your lands, and I bet the roads you built cost a damn sight more than they could have. Using the Cyclotron should create some huge savings in that regard. In fact, I'm considering adding another one to the budget to allow for better turn-around and maintenance."

"Well, better to put it in now rather than later," his dad advised.

Paul went back to staring out of the window. The mountains passed underneath them in rows, like soldiers marching toward the sea. To the west long, winding fjords cut into the hinterland, sometimes extending for miles from the sea. Snowcaps of dense, sparkling ice cloaked the higher peaks and spread out like tentacles down the valleys. They ended in raging rivers, colored dark brown by the suspended rock in their waters.

The landscape was so vast that Paul couldn't imagine the tenacity of the early explorers like Mackenzie, Fraser, and Thompson who explored it with little help or provisions.

While these explorers roamed, further south a young botanist, David Douglas, made a new discovery of flora.

"I rejoice to tell you of a new species of Pinus, the most princely of genus, perhaps even the grandest of vegetation. It attains the enormous height of two to four hundred feet with a circumference of fifty feet and fir cones of twelve to eighteen inches long. The trunk grows remarkably straight and destitute of branches until near the top where they form a perfect umbral. The wood is of fine quality, yielding a large quantity of resin."

This description was soon the topic of conversation in England. The wooden hulls of England's fleet were never short of spars and timbers. They'd thought there was an endless supply of timber, but it was being finished off faster than any had imagined.

"There it is, Dad." Paul leaned back to let his dad look out of the small window.

"Where, where? There's so many valleys down there."

"Just over that peak: you can see the beginning of the valley where it's joined by one from the south."

"Ah, I see the one you mean now. That's the Stikeen River there, eh?"

"Yes, and you can see the glacier which still feeds the river—it's a little hazy in the distance."

Both watched the valley pass beneath them, undisturbed since the last ice age fifteen thousand years ago.

Ten minutes later, their plane taxied into the tiny airport. Mountains completely encircled them in a shimmering ring of white and green slopes.

Manny was there to meet them and after furious handshakes they loaded their bags into Manny's red Ford pickup. Paul noticed his stiff left leg and felt a twinge of guilt. "Good to see you again, Manny. I see the leg is better than we thought, eh?"

"Yes, I worked my ass off and managed to get some movement out of it. But I won't be running the Olympics, that's for sure. But I am fishing again: I had a twenty-pound steelhead the other day."

"So, when do you take us?" Paul's dad asked.

"Hey hold it, Dad; we've come here to work, remember."

With that, his dad sat back in the rear of the pickup. Manny's new wife, Liz, met them at their rancher just outside of town, which they had built on the edge of an escarpment that granted an excellent view of the snow-clad mountains. Introductions and congratulations were made, and soon everyone was relaxing over steaming cups of hot coffee.

After a hearty roast of moose and red wine, they sat in the living room and got down to business.

"So, Paul, how goes the battle in the big city," Manny asked.

"Well to start, the Western Wilderness Committee is not on board, but I tried."

Manny nodded sadly, but he didn't look surprised.

"Number two, West Skeena Timber has made a media blitz on the local TV channels, raging on about how great they are at replanting forests, which is total bullshit. They want the public to think they have the environment as a first priority. Three, I haven't a clue if Chief Wolf Salmon will support us over the other parties when the crunch comes."

Paul rubbed his neck. "So, apart from an uphill battle, I suppose it's alright."

"Good." Manny said.

"What?" Paul asked.

"Well, if it was easy, we all wouldn't be here trying to beat the bastards." He laughed and filled their empty glasses. "While you guys have been doing your budgets, I've been doing some digging of my own." He passed Paul a twenty-point list. Silence followed as Paul and his father read them.

"Manny, are you sure of your facts and figures here?" Paul's dad asked.

"I haven't got a degree or nothing, but I've made my life in the logging industry, and I reckon I know a thing or two."

He pointed to item number five.

"This is a big one: logging costs are expected to be in excess of twenty million dollars, based on two hundred and fifty miles of roads that require numerous bridges and the blasting of steep mountainsides. At today's market value, a full quarter of this license's lumber inventory would be needed just to pay for the roads."

"How did you get these figures?" Paul asked.

"Well, I figured them on a pro-rated basis of West Skeena's average road costs, and applied them to a large-scale map of the valley."

Manny had also laid out the costs of traditional clear-cutting, from financial notes such as the logging roads to environmental ones like the impact landslides would have on the salmon population.

"Okay, I see your point," Paul said. "This is dynamite stuff, and once included in my proposal should help our cause a lot."

Paul and his dad added to the discussion, and in the end, they refined it to ten major points that highlighted the impracticalities of traditional logging in the watershed because of the valley's remote and rugged terrain.

As usual when Paul and Manny got going the time flew. Soon it was 2 am and Paul's dad was on the verge of sleep. Paul helped him downstairs. He came back up to find a full glass of rye and Coke. Manny sheepishly grinned as Paul saw the glass.

"No, Manny, last one. We've got to get up early and do some work."

However, talk turned to fishing, and it was another hour before they went to bed.

Paul woke with a slightly throbbing head and groaned.

"Shit, we never learn." He painfully got out of bed and had a cold shower, which luckily helped a great deal.

Two hours later they were heading down Douglas Channel out of Kitimat, towing Manny's new jet boat behind. The huge aluminum smelter in Kitimat disappeared behind them as the boat sped down the channel. The sea was calm and the sky an unbroken blue. The towering mountains rose majestically out of the indigo sea on either side of them.

Paul breathed in the fresh air and smiled. He loved the sea and reveled in the sight of the boat's curling wake. The Chris Craft heeled to port as Manny aimed its bow south toward another deep fjord. Over the drone of the engines, the occasional croak of a raven or screech of an eagle could be heard from the thick forests on either side of them.

Manny eased back on the throttles and switched the engine off. The sudden silence awoke Paul from his daydreaming.

"What's up, Manny?"

"Look up at that small inlet to the left."

Paul and his dad were silent. Instead of a dense blanket of green cedars and hemlock shrouding the valley's sides, bare granite glistened with moisture. Only the occasional gray stump was visible. No wildlife inhabited the valley and silence hung heavy on the air. The small river was brown and laden with silt.

"Five years ago, that valley was green. Now for ten miles it's bare. The river running into it is fouled. It used to teem with salmon and steelhead, but last year we only hooked two instead of dozens. I love where I live, and I know every penny I earn is from the forestry industry, but shit. Stuff like this has to stop before it's too late. The bastards don't even replant. Can you guess which company owns it?"

"Manny, what about all that wood over there?" Paul pointed to a pile of timber that lay tangled all over the sides.

"Well, they class that as 'pulp wood'. They say it would cost them too much to get rid of it, so they just let it sit there and rot. They don't even allow anyone else to utilize it. It's a big monopoly, and they want to keep it that way. No matter how small the company that wants to buy, they say no."

"Shit, if I left my log license like that I would be shot—never mind being able to sleep at night," Paul's dad said. "With the small license we have, I have to get every last scrap of wood from it. Does this type of thing go on a lot up here?"

"Yes, but the general public never sees it. Only commercial fishermen and a few sports fishermen like me."

Manny waved a hand inland. "Whenever they have a lot near a public road they cut in small batches and replant in a year so they can tout how great they are at protecting the environment. Hell, even the forest commission turns a blind eye to the waste: technically, they should be fining them for not using the pulpwood. Trouble is, the fines are a joke. So, the practice still goes on. I know a lot of small operators who are starving for wood, and yet here maybe twenty percent is left to rot. It's a crime for sure."

"Let's go, Manny," Paul's dad said. "I've seen enough."

Paul's jaw set into a hard line and he frowned.

"I'm going to beat the bastards to the punch and show them how to really log and still make a profit: just you wait and see."

Four hours later they pulled up to the aging dock at the head of Eagle Channel. Here the First Nations had a fish camp and a few houses which the commercial fishermen lived in. Wolf Salmon was there to greet them.

"Pleased to meet you, Chief. It's Tom, isn't it?" Paul's father clasped Wolf Salmon's hand strongly. "My son has told me how you saved his life last year, and from one father to another I thank you with all my heart."

"No problem. Between you and me, it took me back to my younger days. I only wish we had been able to catch the men that did it. We all know it was those West Skeena devils, but there was no proof. They've been here the last few months promising this and that, but I've seen their logging practices and want no part of them."

Wolf Salmon led them to one of the fish cabins. It lay on a small escarpment and had a fantastic view of the inlet and mountains beyond.

"Please, be seated. Help yourself to smoked salmon and beer—or juice, if you prefer."

Paul tried a piece of the proffered fish. "Umm, this tastes good."

"It's chum salmon, which is the best for smoking. Our people have cured it this way for centuries. Sometimes the whole village comes to the mouth of the river here to help smoke what we catch in the fish boats."

Paul broke off another piece of the pinkish, crumbly fish. He liked the strong, salty taste of it.

There was a knock on the door, and the chief rose to answer it. A tall, dark-haired native with a muscular frame entered. He had very dark brown eyes and looked around the room before walking up to Paul.

"Paul, Mr. Whorton, Manny, this is Daniel: or, as he would prefer, Raven Eater."

Paul met the man's firm grip with his own. Raven Eater's eyes bored into Paul's, and the pressure on his hand increased. "Pleased to meet you, Paul," Raven Eater said levelly.

"Same here."

"I asked Raven Eater to join us, as one day he may become chief."

"I take it then, Tom, that you don't have any sons to pass the title on to?" Paul's dad asked.

Wolf Salmon's shoulders visibly sunk as he spoke. "No. I had a wonderful son, but he drowned while fishing on the river about five years ago."

Paul was watching Raven Eater, trying to place why he and his name seemed familiar. He saw a faint smile when Wolf Salmon mentioned his son. Raven Eater caught Paul staring at him, and the trace of the smile vanished.

"I'm sorry to hear that," Paul's father said somberly. "Do you have any other children?"

"Yes, a wonderful daughter named Wind Walker." Wolf Salmon's eyes glistened with tears. He looked over to Raven Eater with a strange look on his face.

Paul didn't like the look of this man, and was uneasy in his company. He tried to quickly change the subject. "Well, Chief, let's talk about what we're here for."

Everyone sat down in front of the roaring fire. Paul explained his plans for the valley and the local people's involvement in it. He thought he rather eloquently laid out his plans to obtain the forest license and his wish for the First Nations people to be involved in the sawmill's modest operations.

"And in conclusion, Chief, I hope you will ask your people to back me in my bid. I wish for us to become partners in this venture for the last TFL in British Columbia. Together, we can show the other companies how it should be done."

"Paul, your case deserves serious consideration," Wolf Salmon said abruptly. "I will think on it deeply. But now I'm afraid I must go, as I have other matters to attend to." With that, he rose to his feet and waited for them to do the same, gesturing to the door.

Paul was shocked. When they were speaking earlier, it looked like the meeting would go well. Now he seemed in a rush to get rid of them.

"But Chief, surely you have some questions regarding the bid?"

Raven Eater walked in front of the chief and replied for him.

"You heard him, Paul. He will consider your proposal and we will get back to you."

The door shut behind them. The three men shared a bewildered look at the turn of events. Paul thought he heard angry voices as they retreated down the path leading to the dock.

"What the hell!" Paul's father said once they were back in the boat and out of earshot. "Last time we spoke, Tom was delighted we wanted to come up and see him. Now that Raven Eater character shows up, and suddenly he sends us on our way."

"Yes, you're right, Dad. There's something weird going on, and it starts with that guy: I'm sure of it."

Paul stopped short as memory hit. "You know, Manny, I think it was Raven Eater with Nick Barrett that day. He sure has the same build and long, dark hair. And the officer said there was someone who flew out with Nick and his pilot—I think his name was Raven Eater."

Paul's stomach knotted as he relived the events. *Yes, of course it was him,* he thought. *I should have guessed.*

He turned back, but Manny grabbed his arm. "Paul, listen: leave it. We have no proof. And besides, let's not tip our hand before we know what's going on between him and the chief."

Knowing Manny was right, Paul nodded. The camp was quiet; nobody else was around. A raven croaked eerily from the dark woods.

"Well, lads," Paul's dad said. "Let's at least do some fishing while we are here and salvage something out of the day. Maybe we can come back and try to speak with the chief when Raven Eater is not around."

They pointed the bow into the inlet, still towing the jet boat behind. Manny switched on the depth sounder. At about one hundred feet from a rocky bluff, he stopped the engine and let the boat drift.

"Well, there should be halibut and lingcod down here, so let's get the rods out and give it a try."

Both Paul and his dad fixed up their rods at lightning speed. The rods were short and stiff, and each had heavy-duty reels.

Paul put on a herring, released the drag, and let the weight carry it down to the bottom. The rod tip sunk down and jiggled a bit. He slowly wound it up. "Got one, you guys; but I think it's only a small one."

Paul heaved the fish over the side and it writhed on deck.

"Great, it's a lingcod; perfect for eating," Manny said. He quickly unhooked it and bonked it on the head.

The afternoon went quickly but they didn't catch any halibut—only more delicious lingcod and a couple rock cod.

The tide started to turn, and Paul let his bait down for the last time. It hit bottom and he lifted it up and down to attract fish.

"Damn, I'm caught on the bottom," he said. He yanked the rod, trying to free it.

The line started to move sideways. Paul checked the rocks nearby and realized it wasn't them drifting.

"Hey guys, I've got something big here, look."

Both Manny and Gordon turned just as the line started peeling off the reel. Paul leaned back on the rod and tightened up the drag to no avail: the line was still going fast into the depths.

"Holy shit, I can't stop it."

"You have a big halibut, there. Quick, Mr. Whorton: pull up your rod and I'll get the engine going so we can follow it."

Gordon did as he was told, and soon the engine burbled to life. Manny eased onto the throttle and the boat followed the halibut's progress beneath them. Paul started to gain some line as the tension eased.

"Keep going, I'm gaining on him," yelled Paul in his excitement. He leaned back on the rod. Slowly, he felt what was on the other end of the line draw toward him. But then the reel screeched off the line and he lost all he had gained.

"Here, Mr. Whorton, you take over the controls: just follow that fish slowly. I'm going to get the harpoon. Paul has a very big fish there, and we don't want to lose him at the boat."

Manny went into the cabin and came out with a six-foot-long harpoon with a three-pronged barb. He tied some yellow nylon rope to the end and then propped the harpoon on the gunnel of the boat. Next, he disappeared into the cabin again and came out with a small handgun.

"Shit, what's that for?" Paul exclaimed when he saw it.

"To kill the halibut. If you bring a big one into the boat before its dead, it can thrash about and damage the boat—or us."

The battle see-sawed between Paul and the fish for over an hour, and still they had not seen it. Slowly, though, Paul had gained a lot of line, and the bottom-hugging halibut was now being pulled up toward them.

"It's coming. You should be able to see it soon. I've nearly got all the line back." Paul said. In fact, he could see a dark shape where his line cut the water's surface. He felt the rod buck now and again, but the movements were slower and weaker now.

"Right, Paul, just a few more feet and we have him. Here, Mr. Whorton, when I harpoon him and bring his head above the water, you shoot him between the eyes."

Manny climbed over the gunnel and stood there, poised, the harpoon ready to strike. The dark outline of the fish became clear. The halibut was over six feet long and came up with its large mouth open.

Paul gave one last heave, but the line went slack.

"Shit, it's gone!"

Manny thrust the harpoon as hard as he could at the now-disappearing halibut. It missed the mark by a couple of feet and all watched as the big fish slowly sank into the depths again.

Paul inwardly groaned and lowered the rod. He wound the limp line and examined the end.

"Look at this, guys." He passed the end of the line to them to examine. It had stretched to nearly nothing and was now as thin as a spider's web.

"Hard luck, Paul. That's one of the biggest I've seen for ages. About the same size as the largest I've landed, and that one weighed over two hundred pounds. Those big ones are the females though; they're not great to eat, so it's no big deal. At least you got a great fight out of it."

"Sure did. Would have been nice to see it a bit closer, though," Paul replied.

"Ah well, son, you'll remember that one for a long time, I bet."

Paul smiled up at his father. At that point, they all agreed it was getting on and they should anchor for the night.

On the way up the channel, Paul pointed out the site he had chosen for the sawmill. It was ideally situated about a mile further from the fish camp. Only a few feet away, the rocky cliff side dropped steeply into the water to create an over hundred-foot drop-off. The cliffs gave way to a lower, flatter area which carried on for a good mile inland before the mountains rose up.

They decided to anchor by the rocks for the night. They feasted on fresh lingcod, potatoes, and delicious sweet peas, enjoying the silence of the inlet around them. All were tired and they went to bed early to get ready for the long day ahead.

Early the next morning, Manny got the jet boat ready their trip upstream. They dodged in and out of tangled tree roots swept down by the last rains and entered the gorge.

After an exciting trip up the rapids, the boat eased into the main current of the river and headed up into the valley.

"You're right, Paul. It makes sense to use the Cyclotron up here. A road over that gorge would cost a mint," Paul's dad said.

Paul stood up and raised his head above the windscreen. Manny purposely bumped his shoulder and Paul looked up to where his eyes were pointing. A thin ribbon of milky-green water on the south bank broadened as they approached the mouth of Emerald Creek. The two waters joined in a confused mix of swirling eddies. The trees seemed to sprout from all around them. They blocked out the early-morning sunlight, filtering its rays through their dense branches.

"Well, Dad, this is Emerald Creek. Home of monster trees and the most beautiful valley I've ever seen."

"Well, from the looks of things so far, the valley appears to have a healthy mix of species; definitely a good size to them."

Manny warned them to sit down as he opened the throttles and turned directly into the heavy current. Paul kept looking back at his dad and was pleased to see he was enjoying the wild ride immensely.

They were all a bit wet by the time Manny guided the jet boat past the rapids downstream of the Big Fir. Paul heard his dad's sharp intake of breath when he saw the first grove of trees up ahead. The cedar boughs hung over the river on the far bank, and further up the mighty firs reached for the heavens in a tight knot of dense green. The Big Fir came into full view as they gently rounded the bend. It and its companions dwarfed all those around.

"Paul, you didn't exaggerate. Those are the biggest trees I've ever seen in my life, and we have some monsters on the island. I remember seeing huge ones in the Nimpkish Valley as a kid, but they don't compare to these guys."

Manny threw the anchor onto the beach and they all stepped ashore. Paul noticed fresh deer prints in the pockets of glistening sand. They climbed over the decaying old log jam and entered the cool shade of the Big Fir. The ground underfoot was soft as a carpet from a deep layer of pine needles freshly deposited last autumn.

Gordon stood under the Big Fir and slowly looked up. The gnarled bark writhed up its immense length. The uppermost branches couldn't be seen even while leaning back.

"Paul, this bark must be over two feet thick," his dad said. He put his hand in a deep groove in the tree's trunk. "And look over there, that's a humongous balsam, if I'm not mistaken."

Paul followed him further into the grove. The north side of the balsam's trunk was covered in thick moss and old, broken boughs stuck out along its height.

Manny joined them and pointed to an old cedar that rose out of the forest floor. Manny paced around it, counting as he did so. "Nineteen, twenty. That's nearly fifteen feet in diameter if it's an inch," Manny said. He hopped back to them over the mounded roots. The base was like an octopus, made up of ten gnarled roots that joined together to form one huge trunk reaching for the sky. The trunk split into branches over two hundred feet up. At the base, there was a hole about eight feet high.

"Hey, Paul, this must have been a nursery log. Look at the hole left by the rotting parent tree." Paul's father patted the trunk.

The deeper they explored the grove, the more magnificent trees they found. As they silently wandered through it, Paul was reminded of a cathedral: the air was heavy, sounds were muted, and stately spires reached for the heavens. They met back at the boat some half hour later.

"Paul, we must fight like hell to save this. It's unique, and by God there aren't places like this left anymore." A gleam overtook Gordon's eyes, but was quickly extinguished again.

"Yes, it's a special place alright. I knew you would like it. But there's even more upstream. We'll show you the rest of the valley; then we can make camp for the night and have a nice meal of our fresh-caught cod. Maybe even dig into the rye and Coke."

His dad nodded and soon the jet boat left the gentle giants behind.

***

Three miles upstream, a rag-tag camp of broken beer bottles and half-empty cans of beans lay scattered in the sand around the smoldering embers of a fire.

"Get back you," Wind Walker screamed as she brandished the end of a broken bottle. Her scant clothes were ripped, and the sight of her near-exposed breast only gave more ardor to her attackers. Her back was hard up against an old tree stump, and her retreat was blocked.

The man in front of her had yellow, rotting teeth and a pockmarked face. He preferred to go by the name Black Bear. He feigned a grab, but the broken bottle Wind Walker held caught the soft skin on his arm. "You bitch, you'll pay for that," he shouted as blood trickled from the wound.

Joe Coyote, a squat and muscular bulldog of a man, stood back as Wind Walker made another lunge with the bottle at his companion. Both had been drinking steadily since early morning. Raven Eater had delivered the girl to them the day before with strict instructions that they not harm her, but boredom and booze had gotten the better of them. Wind Walker's exquisite figure and long, dark hair had nearly driven them mad and now, a dozen beers braver, they were after their prey.

"Stay here—don't let her get away." Joe strode off back to the boat and returned with a large landing net.

Wind Walker shivered when she realized his intent. She looked around wildly for an avenue of escape, but Black Bear stayed close, ready to pounce. She could smell his rotten breath as his black eyes roved her body. She tried to cover her embarrassing state of undress.

She swallowed hard as her second captor approached with the landing net outstretched. Her vision clouded as the first tears welled, but she forced them back and bared her teeth in defiance.

Wind Walker dug her toes into the soft sand and kicked as hard as she could. The tiny particles showered Joe Coyote, and he tore at his eyes as the sand blinded him. As she expected, Black Bear looked behind at his blinded companion and she struck.

With a back-handed upward sweep, the jagged bottle caught him full in the cheek. The white gleam of bone was very quickly covered in blood.

She ran. Bounding over logs like a fleeing deer, she kept her attention on the river ahead of her, putting everything she had into her sprint. She heard the sounds of pursuit, but kept going without looking back.

An old log jam barred her way and she hopped from one to the other. One of the logs crumbled into tiny fragments, and she felt her ankle bend over at a sharp angle.

"No please," she cried as she gripped her throbbing ankle. She had been so close to escaping. Now, real terror settled in as she realized she was like a wounded animal just waiting to be caught.

She rose and ran on, every step jarring like a knife as her torn ankle tried to carry her slim figure. She dove to the left into the dark forest.

Wind Walker heard Black Bear swear viscously back on the beach, but even closer was the faint crack of a snapping branch behind her. She froze even lower in the bed of salmonberries where she hid. She hardly dared to breathe, yet her lungs felt near to bursting.

A shadow passed her in the undergrowth. "Come on, baby, we only want to play a little: not hurt, just love. You come over now before I get really angry."

She pressed harder to the ground and sensed him pass further into the forest. Her only hope was concealment—and maybe the creek. Yes, the creek where the current would sweep her downstream far faster than she could hobble.

Ever-so-slowly, she rose from her hiding place. She glanced around, and when she saw nothing, she crept back toward the creek.

Her injured foot cracked a twig, and she heard Joe run her way. She broke cover and prayed she could make it to the creek in time. Her feet hit sand: not fifty feet away lay the safety of the creek and its swift current.

She saw Black Bear a fraction too late, and he slammed into her at a full run. They both fell heavily; the glass bottle flew from her hand. She saw the gleam of steel: Black Bear held an eight-inch hunting knife.

Frantically, she rose again to run. But Black Bear still held onto her skirt, ripping the hem. His other hand grabbed her now-swollen ankle. She dug her nails into the soft sand, but had nowhere to go. Black Bear's hard, calloused fingers writhed up her squirming leg. She kicked hard and heard a groan, but his grip didn't ease.

Suddenly, her head was viscously snapped back by her hair. Joe Coyote had doubled-back to them.

"Now we play for sure, little one," he said, slowly pulling her up to her knees toward him. Her hair was wrapped tightly round his fist. She felt his hands tear at her blouse.

Behind her, Black Bear ripped the back of her skirt down. He ran his hand down the small of her back into the cleft of her cheeks, roughly forcing her legs apart. With one quick rip he tore her panties off; the elastic left a red smear around her small waist.

"Hold her hands behind her back," Joe barked as Black Bear continued his probing. His dark eyes flashed on his pockmarked face, but he did as ordered.

Wind Walker's shoulders were yanked back hard as she was forced down to her knees. Joe fumbled with his jeans zipper. Wind Walker closed her eyes as he pulled out his thick, swollen member.

Behind her, Black Bear groped between her legs, spreading them apart with his knees. He smiled as he saw her dark pubic hair and his fingers dug into her harshly.

Wind Walker still had her eyes closed, and she screamed as the fetid smell of Joe's breath hit her nostrils.

***

Manny killed the ignition.

"Listen," he said.

Paul and his father fell quiet.

"There: you hear it?" The sound repeated itself: an unearthly scream, rising just upstream from them.

The jet boat started up again and shot upstream. Manny cut the rapids dangerously close to the bank, a hidden rock scraping the hull.

The jet boat broke through the last of the rapids. Fifty yards upstream, three figures could be seen in odd positions. Two jumped up as the boat closed with the shore, yanking up their jeans.

Manny kept the throttles open till the last minute. Both he and Paul immediately saw what was happening and got ready at the bow to pounce as soon as the boat hit the beach.

Manny leaped over the side and missed Black Bear by inches, but not before receiving a slash on his right arm from the knife the man held.

Paul did the same, catapulting straight into Joe Coyote, who hadn't expected such a fast approach. Both stumbled back. Paul rose to his feet, and Joe crouched low with his hands up, ready to strike.

Paul was so busy looking at his hands that he wasn't watching Joe's feet. His head snapped back, and pain lanced through his nose: Joe had kicked him full in the face. He tasted blood and in a reflexive response swung a hard right, which caught Joe full in the sternum. Joe grimaced in pain as he staggered back.

Paul momentarily froze and glanced to his left. Joe followed his gaze, then realized his mistake—too late. Paul kicked hard, followed by a fist to Joe's shoulder. Paul's fist hit rock-hard muscle and suddenly he was even more wary of the squat figure in front of him.

Joe lowered his head and dove at Paul, catching him in the stomach. The air left Paul's lungs in a painful whoosh. A fist like a rock hit him hard on the temple and his vision blurred. His arm was caught, and Joe's muscles squeezed down hard.

Paul winced at the power of the grip. Unable to break free, he swung madly as Joe groped for his throat. Fingers dug deep into Paul's flesh, crushing his Adam's apple. He began to choke noiselessly.

He looked for help from his companions. Manny had gotten the better of Black Bear and was in the process of pummeling the now-prone but flailing man. His dad had stopped the boat and now had the girl in his arms as she shivered uncontrollably.

Paul was slowly being brought to his knees by the time his dad looked up.

"Paul, Paul," he screamed. He let go of the girl and ran toward them, grabbing a knotted piece of wood as he did.

Joe Coyote saw Gordon Whorton approaching fast and released his grip on Paul. Paul tried to speak, but no words came out. Darkness crowded in on his vision.

The next thing he knew, Paul's head was in his dad's lap.

"Paul. Paul, it's me: it's okay," his dad said as he easily stopped Paul's flailing arms. Paul relaxed when he heard his father's voice. "Manny, go see to the girl; I've got Paul here."

After a moment, Paul sat up unaided. He heard the rumble of a motor from upriver.

"Quick, back to the jet boat; the bastard is going to get away," his dad yelled.

They half-carried Paul and the girl back to their boat as another came screaming around the corner.

The first shot shattered the windscreen, and they all hit the sand. Paul saw Black Bear slowly rise to his feet right before a bullet hit him. Half his head flew out behind him in a bloody red mess, and his body fell heavily to the sand.

Manny leaped over the side of their boat and reached for the rifle he kept inside. Another shot rang out, and a hole appeared only inches away from his face. Without aiming properly, Manny fired at the blur of the receding jet boat. But the escaping Joe Coyote held the throttles open and bore toward the rapids. The boat disappeared behind the rocky bluff of the rapids.

"Come on, let's go," Manny shouted.

"No, get on the radio and warn the village," Paul's dad ordered.

Manny tried, but he only got static. The intervening mountains were too high for the signal to get through.

Paul lay against the boat's side, painfully feeling his throat. Wind Walker shied away from his dad's protective hold as he gently whispered to her.

"Manny, take her and wrap her up into one of the sleeping bags," he said.

Paul slowly rose and all three struggled for a few minutes to push the boat over the sucking sand back into the water.

In a barely-heard whisper, Paul said, "Right, Manny: hit her."

The boat roared to life. The strong current caught the bow and the jet's rooster tail showered the dead figure of Black Bear with spray and sand. Gordon held on protectively to the now-quiet Wind Walker as Manny hit the bends at full throttle. They swept past the Big Fir, down the last rapids, and entered the main river.

"Right, Paul: up or down?"

Paul saw some unusual waves upstream and was just about to answer, but his dad spoke up. "Back to the village; this girl is hurt." He gestured to the blood that flowed down her legs into the bottom of the boat. Paul looked longingly upriver as Manny swung the bow downstream toward the village.

They radioed ahead once they were in calling distance, and by the time they reached the village a small crowd had assembled at the dock. Wolf Salmon was there to meet them and the first to help tie up the boat.

"Chief, did you radio the hospital helicopter and the police?"

"Yes, soon as you called."

They gently passed over the injured Wind Walker and she was helped up to the chief's house by a couple of women.

"Who did this to my daughter?" Wolf Salmon asked.

"Sorry, we don't know them. But one is dead and the other has gone upstream in a jet boat," Paul hoarsely said.

"If the police helicopter arrives soon, they may be able to catch him before he runs to ground," Manny said.

"Chief, where is Raven Eater?" Paul's dad asked.

"Gone as soon as you radioed. He took one of the boats and headed downstream."

"I think you know something more about this and him, don't you?" Paul's father crossed his arms sternly.

"Yes." Wolf Salmon's shoulders sagged, and he watched the women lead his daughter to his house.

"He said no harm would come to my daughter if I met with you as arranged, but I was not to give you any hope about supporting your bid for the forest license."

"Do you know who he's working for?" Paul pressured. "I'm sure he wouldn't be doing this of his own accord, would he?" If Raven Eater *was* the one in that helicopter that day, Paul had a pretty good idea who it was.

"No. I asked him, but he said it was no concern of mine."

"Okay, Tom. In that case, may we have food for three days, gas, and one of your best guides?"

The chief blinked. "Why do you need this? It's no fight of yours, and soon the police will be here."

"Look, you know this is about the license. And when someone tries to kill me, it becomes my fight," Paul said.

"Paul, you can't do this; it's a matter for the police now," his dad interrupted.

Paul touched his father's arm. "Look, Dad, if I am to ever succeed up here, I have to. I can't just drop it and go home." Paul curled his hands into fists. "After all, if we hadn't come up here, none of this would have happened. You stay here and tell the police all that happened and send them upstream straight away, okay? Oh, and get them to send another contingent down to the river mouth and get that bastard Raven Eater."

"Okay, but you be careful: no damn heroics." His father raised a warning finger. "Just wait for the police if you spot him. That man is a murderer now, and he may try and ambush you."

"We'll be okay, Mr. Whorton," Manny said. "We'll just run him to ground and let the police do the rest."

All the provisions and extra gas were loaded into the boat, and they were introduced to their guide, Richard. Wolf Salmon passed Paul a rifle. "Just be safe, eh?"

As Manny swung the boat's bow into the current, they heard the sound of helicopter blades over the trees. The hospital helicopter landed on the village field alongside the police helicopter, and Paul's dad headed toward them.

Manny eased the throttles open, and soon their wake receded upstream. The Stikeen River ran broad and deep. Its swirling surface hid old glacial moraine and underwater tree trunks. Smaller tributaries, some just tiny streams, joined at intervals along its length. Their guide, Richard, pointed out the ones that were likely, or ones they could ignore because they were too wild and fast for even the most powerful jet boats.

In the far distance they heard the helicopter, but it hadn't spotted anything yet.

"Manny, radio them and ask them to look out for a camp for the night," Paul said.

The light was fading fast, and soon it would be too dangerous to continue upriver. Around the next bend the helicopter guided them into a small bay. They slid the boat onto its small beach. They were met by Sergeant Thomson, who was eager for more details, the RCMP pilot, and Paul's father. For the next hour, the three men explained in detail what had happened to them earlier in the day.

A pair of officers had been sent to retrieve the other man's body and investigate his death. Considering the danger, the sergeant urged Paul to turn back, but he and Manny adamantly refused. At the very least, the sergeant insisted on coming with them in the boat, to which Paul and Manny agreed.

Everyone took turns on watch in case the fugitive tried to escape back down the river. With a full moon no boat could pass them, even if it just drifted on the current.

Paul took a liking to the guide, Richard, and they talked about his people's history during his watch. Some of his people were originally of the Nass Valley, further north, but after a great forest fire about 300 years ago they moved to join this village.

A fish cannery had opened in the inlet, and the people were virtually enslaved to the slash of knives, the soldering of cans, and the packing of millions of canned salmon. Colossal tons of fish were harvested, until one year only a trickle returned to spawn, leaving the village without food and work.

Over the twenty years the cannery had been open, most village workers had laid down their bows and nets, thereby losing the skills necessary to hunt successfully in the wild land. They barely survived. Missionaries had tried to make farmers of them, and nearly succeeded. However, the markets were too far south, and even the missionaries left.

Then Indian Affairs took over, and they managed to get half of the remaining inhabitants to move. A hard core remained in the village, and to this day steadfastly refused to move. In the last twenty years, the salmon had returned in historical numbers and a few people made some extra money at commercial fishing and trapping.

Paul gazed across the creek in the moon's light. This was the home of the Kermode bear, a legendary white bear that roamed the creek's upper reaches and mountain meadows. The coat of these black bears ranged from pure white to a pale, tawny brown. Paul imagined its ghostly form silently slipping through the trees, occasionally stopping to sniff the air before disappearing again into the gloom of the thick forest.

Dawn crept up on them slowly, its faint glow silhouetting the Seven Sisters mountain range to the east. Their razor-sharp peaks pierced the early-morning glow, and Paul felt like he could see every nook and cranny: the air was that crisp and clear. Stars still shone behind him as the stark colors of the sunrise turned the river's mist an iridescent yellow. All was quiet: only the constant rippling and gurgling of the stream broke the stillness.

"Wakey, wakey, campers. It's a fabulous morning and breakfast is on," Paul said as he woke the others from their slumber.

"Fuck off," Manny replied as Paul stripped off his blanket. Paul laughed and stoked the fire. The lonely, eerie cry of a loon echoed in the distant mists of the river.

After a cup of steaming black coffee, they all talked strategy and agreed that Joe Coyote couldn't be that far away; if it hadn't been for the failing light yesterday, they may have spotted him upriver.

Paul's dad was talking to the helicopter pilot as they both studied a map of the area. They waved their goodbyes before they took off, the small Bell Jet's rotors swirling the river's mist.

Paul, Manny, Richard, and the sergeant got into the boat to head upstream. As the sun's rays grew stronger, the mist faded away, revealing the river ahead of them.

After another mile, another river joined the Stikeen to swell its banks. It was the Kalum, or mud river, which got its name from its coffee-colored waters.

"Slow down a minute, Manny," the sergeant asked as the radio crackled to life.

"Please repeat."

"We have spotted a boat about five miles upstream of you, but can't see anyone around."

"Ten-four. Just scan the area, and we'll be there soon."

Paul's heart raced as the jet boat sped upriver. The Seven Sisters loomed closer, and they spotted the helicopter hovering over a small tributary which flowed in from the north. Manny edged the boat into its turbulent current and the splash of icy water woke them up in a hurry.

Just around the next bend they spotted the boat. It slewed around in the current, half-full of water. Its bottom had been pierced by a boulder. Manny deftly picked his way in and out of boulders and hit the beach. Upstream, the creek narrowed even more until only white torrents remained: there was no clear passage for a boat of any size.

"Sergeant, any idea why he would come up here?"

"Well, my guess is that he's heading for a hunting cabin up the valley; it was built some years ago. He knows we would find the boat by helicopter, so my guess is he's trying to get out of the valley by foot."

"Well, you're probably right," Richard said. "That's Hell's Gorge, which is impassible by boat. The river narrows considerably, and the current is at least twenty knots. Only the salmon and steelhead can pass to where the river meets up with the glaciers," he explained.

Paul and the sergeant examined the abandoned boat and saw it was empty of provisions except for an empty bottle of rum and some spent cartridges, which the sergeant picked up as evidence.

"This guy plays for keeps. We had better be mighty careful up here in this thick bush; he could ambush us easy, and we would never see him."

The sergeant gazed out from the shore.

"Let's see. The nearest town is Terrace, but that's over fifty miles away, over the Homothka Glacier. He must be heading there, but shit: that's a hell of a hike."

"This guy is pretty fit, I can tell you," Paul said, rubbing his neck. "Besides, he doesn't have much choice."

The helicopter landed. Paul's dad and the pilot would remain at the boat to stand guard, just in case Joe Coyote decided to double-back. The helicopter would be useless to spot him among the heavy tree cover, and the pilot wanted to reserve fuel if they needed help down the road.

"Don't worry, Paul," his father said. "We'll make camp on the other side of the main river. So, go on, and be careful, son."

Manny, Paul, Richard, and the sergeant entered the dark forest. A well-worn path led up toward the hunting cabin. Soon they reached the cabin's clearing.

"Right. Split up: two to the left and two to the right," the sergeant ordered. "And no heroics if you spot him. When we get close, I'll use the bullhorn to call out to him."

After five minutes of inching their way closer, they had the cabin surrounded.

"Anybody there," the bullhorn echoed.

After two more attempts the sergeant rose, revolver drawn, and walked up carefully to the front door. Paul held his breath: the sergeant presented a sitting target to anyone in the cabin.

The sergeant climbed the last few steps up to the porch and nudged open the slightly-ajar door. "Okay, come on up: there is nobody here."

They all entered the cabin. Cans of food were strewn across the floor, obviously from someone in a hurry who didn't mind leaving a mess as he stocked up.

The sergeant picked up an empty ammunition box and frowned. "Well, Richard, you know this country. What are his chances of getting to Terrace before we catch up to him?"

"The way is long and hard; the days are short and food scarce. He will have to cross the creek many times. It is also the land of the Kermode. Is it not better to send in the helicopter?"

"Not until we get into some open space. Until then, I'm afraid we're on foot. But look, those reinforcements should be here this afternoon, so you guys can go back if you want and I will wait here."

"Hell no. The bastard will be clear gone by then and the trail will be cold. I say let's keep going. He may give in when he realizes we're so close behind him."

The sergeant nodded and radioed the pilot, updating him on the status at the cabin.

Paul walked up to his friend. "How's the leg, Manny?"

"Good. I'm not as nimble as I used to be, but I can keep going."

All day the four struggled along the creek bank. They had to cross it many times, and the cold was numbing. However, the sandy banks always had some clues as to their fugitive's path.

By the late afternoon, they had climbed over a thousand feet, and the creek was now just a mountain stream. The trees thinned out as they climbed toward the pass to Terrace. They all crept cautiously forward: it would be easy to be ambushed. Paul half-expected it every time they reached a new crest, but so far, they had been lucky. Once through the binoculars they spotted a small figure climbing up some rocky scree about two miles ahead of them.

Night came and they made camp. One kept watch while the others slept. They checked with the reinforcements and found that they would be brought in the next day by helicopter over the pass to block Joe's escape and hopefully trap him in a pincer movement. They all looked forward to having helicopter support once again.

The dawn came cold and early and they all rose to a warming fire, strong coffee, and fried bacon sandwiches. By mid-day, they had left the forest and entered the subalpine region of the uplands. Up ahead the mountains rose steeply, and they all felt the cold air cascading down from the surrounding ice fields. The going became quite rocky, and Manny had to rest frequently. They continually scanned the slopes up ahead for the fugitive.

The valley narrowed to a bottleneck, and the going became even tougher. It seemed loose rocks were always unstable underfoot. They hadn't been able to spot their quarry all morning, and presumed he had traveled some during the night, putting him far ahead of them by now. About two thousand feet above them, they could see the pass between two towering peaks.

A loud, echoing crack rang out. The sergeant screamed, falling backward. Paul just managed to keep his feet and hold on to him before he slid down the steep slope. A bullet had hit him in the left shoulder, and blood quickly soaked his jacket.

Everyone hit the rocky ground, scanning for where the shot had come from. All Paul could see was snow and ice interspersed with rock screes.

The sergeant groaned in pain. Paul tried to soothe him before they slowly backed down the slope for cover. Another bullet ricocheted from a rock near Paul.

"Quick, behind this rock bluff."

Richard helped him support the sergeant as they ducked behind their rocky cover.

"Damn, the guy's got us pinned down," Manny said.

Paul peered around the bluff. He saw the tell-tale signs of smoke from a campfire above them between some rocks. Joe Coyote had picked his position well. The forward path was steep and narrow, and there was no cover if they tried to move forward or back.

Paul reckoned their fugitive was positioned on a ridge outlined with a knife-edge of snow. The wind howled over its side, and tendrils of snow were swept off by the alpine winds, blocking their clear view. Up the steep slope, the snow lay in deep drifts.

"Radio the reinforcements up ahead; they must be pretty close by now." Paul asked Manny.

The garbled reply could hardly be heard; they must have been on the other side of the pass for the reception to be so poor.

Another shot rang out, and Paul felt the sting of rock chip on his cheek. He crept back behind cover. Every time Paul looked around the rocky bluff a shot rang out, and he decided it was just too dangerous to do again. They had no choice but to wait and see what happened.

Manny helped the sergeant with his wound, tearing his shirt to be used as a thick pad.

After what seemed like an hour of silence, Paul ventured another look. He couldn't see anything from the last position he had seen smoke. But about a quarter of a mile up the valley he saw the figure again. It was struggling through thick snow in a deep gulley.

Paul took a deep breath and walked into the open. His heart pounded in his ears, and his eyes bored into the fugitive's movements for the first sign he had been spotted. Richard and Manny quickly followed, ducking behind whatever cover they could find.

"Duck," Paul yelled when he saw the distant figure go into a crouch and take aim. The shot went high. Snow showered them from above the slope. More snow cascaded down over the shooter, momentarily obscuring him.

Paul tried to take advantage and make up some distance between them, only to have to duck, narrowly avoiding the wind of a passing bullet as Joe squeezed off some shots in quick succession.

Paul looked up and saw the thick overhang of snow and ice on the ridge quaver. More small clods of snow fell into the gulley. They landed in small puffs, but gathered more snow on their way down the very steep pass. Soon, a wider belt of snow began to pick up speed.

The distant figure looked up and immediately began to scramble as fast as he could when he saw the growing avalanche above him.

Soon, the whole width of the pass was a churning mass of snow and ice. Its frothing front hit a large boulder and it flew high into the air. It seemed the whole mountainside moved as a hundred-yard-stretch of snow bore down on the fleeing figure.

Paul ducked back with Manny and Richard, his heart in his throat. The snow above them was steady—for now—but they ducked back behind their overhang just in case. He began to feel for the fugitive, but then he remembered the look of terror on Wind Walker's face and set his jaw for the inevitable.

One minute there was a man, and the next just a mass of white cloud where the avalanche continued its way down the mountain.

It took over an hour for the air to clear. Richard and Paul moved forward slowly, since the snow was still loose underfoot. It was impossible to find Joe under the mass of snow, and rather than take any chances they called off the search and went back downslope to where they had left Manny and the sergeant. They radioed their team at the river and told them what had happened.

The helicopter arrived a couple hours later, landing on the flat sandbar on the inside bend of the creek. Paul's father ran out, checking him over for injuries despite Paul's reassurances.

They had radioed the reinforcements while they were in the air to call off the search. Then the helicopter took them and the sergeant to the hospital in Terrace.

Two days later, they were all at the Terrace RCMP station to give their accounts. Unfortunately, there had been no sign of Raven Eater, even after an extensive search of the area. They found a jet boat five days later hidden under some cut branches just beyond the mouth of Eagle Channel.

The only good thing to come out of the excursion was that Wolf Salmon had whole-heartedly given Paul his full support in his bid for the license. Paul and his father left Terrace the next day in time to finish their portfolio on the bid documents.

Chapter Seven
The Bid

Paul had Steve come over the night before the bid's preliminary hearing. All the participants had to have their bid in by 10 am the next morning. Starting at 11 am, each bidder had the opportunity to publicly state their objectives in front of a government-appointed jury of eleven men and women employed by the Forestry Council of British Columbia.

"Look, Paul, I'll be around at nine in the morning for a quick coffee, then we set off, okay?"

"Thanks buddy, and remember: if you're not in bed by eleven o'clock, then go home," Paul said in jest.

***

Michelle sat at her coffee table with Dean and Mary from the committee. They had been going over their group's bid one last time and felt satisfied with its content.

"Well gang, we can't do anything more, so let's call it quits," Michelle said. The other two left, leaving Michelle to bite her nails, pace the room, and drink more coffee before she had a restless night of sleep.

***

Meanwhile, in the corporate headquarters of West Skeena Timber in downtown Vancouver, Nick dismissed his army of advisors and went to the telephone.

"No, no: no violence. Yes, this is just to be an inconvenience. The first is a red Ford Mustang; the other is a white, E-Type Jaguar. They're at different addresses." He made sure his contact knew where to go.

"Don't fuck it up this time." He put the phone down sharply.

Nick sat back and sipped the last of his port. He felt confident about his company's bid, but was not going to take any chances. The bid had cost the company five million dollars so far in beautifully-prepared brochures and advertisements, all extolling the company's virtues. Also, two new luxury cars for certain members of the appointed jury.

Yes, he thought, *the bastards don't stand a chance.* He again picked up the telephone.

A woman answered.

"Yes, can I help you?"

"Yes, it's me, Nick. I'd like two girls to come over tonight." He ordered.

"Cost a bit more this time, dear. Say, two thousand."

"Yes, yes, but they had better be good, understand?"

"All right, but no monkey business this time, or you can entertain yourself, understood?"

"Just get them over here quick."

***

Paul grabbed the phone at ten past nine. "Where the hell are you, Steve? I said 9 am at my place."

"Hey sorry, Paul, but the damn car won't start. Don't wait for me."

"Shit, really?"

"Hold it—some bastard stole the distributor. Go check your car, buddy; I smell a fish here."

Paul felt the pit of his stomach go cold and ran for the door. He looked across at his car and saw two flat tires. It was too late to call a cab. He couldn't believe it: after all this effort, he may now miss the bid.

He grabbed his briefcase and ran two doors down. He knocked on the door. The time ticked slowly by. He was about to knock again when it opened.

"Hello, Paul. What a lovely morning it is. What seems to be amiss?"

He explained the issue to his elderly neighbor, who agreed to let him borrow his car; Paul had taken care of his driveway for him on their rare snowy days in the winter.

Paul anxiously looked at his watch. *Boy, I hope the Lions Gate Bridge isn't jammed.* He cursed himself for not starting off earlier.

Mr. Bradley's gleaming white 1966 Oldsmobile shone in the morning's light. It coughed once and the engine caught. Paul tried not to make the wheels spin as he quickly reversed out the driveway, but failed. He grinned sheepishly as he saw Mr. Bradley wince.

Once around the corner, he hit the gas. He was lucky: the lights were green, and by the time he hit the highway to the bridge he was doing over forty miles per hour. He glanced at his watch. *Good; I should be okay.*

He didn't see the big brown sedan until it was too late. It overtook him at speed and then abruptly slowed down in front of him. He laid on the horn, but to no avail. Paul couldn't get past: it started weaving in front of him whenever he attempted to overtake it. Paul could only see the black silhouette of a large man in the driving seat.

He saw a break, dropped the car a gear, and accelerated. He was virtually clear when he nearly had a heart attack.

With a vicious jerk, the big car side-swiped the Oldsmobile. Paul fought for control and missed oncoming traffic by inches. He tried to get back into his lane, but the big sedan had his rear quarter by its front bumper, and he felt the back end start to veer out. He touched the brakes and cleared the bumper of the sedan. In his rearview, he saw the grinning face of Raven Eater.

Shit, he thought.

He pushed his foot to the floor and then suddenly braked. Raven Eater had accelerated with him and reacted too late to the Oldsmobile's braking. Terrified other drivers watched as the sedan rear-ended Paul's vehicle. Then Paul took off while Raven Eater was in shock.

Paul saw the red light above the middle lane flick over to red and took a chance. He guessed the light was ready to accept traffic the other way; he may have five minutes before other cars came across the parkway. He pulled out into the middle lane and raced over the bridge at full throttle. In the rearview mirror, he saw the sedan following, but he slowly outpaced it.

A red Grand Am was heading straight for him, leaning on their horn. Just in time, Paul pulled back to the inside lane. He glanced at his watch. He still had fifteen minutes to go, and was now entering downtown. He bit his nails as he searched for a parking spot.

As usual, there were no parking places. Finally, he saw someone pulling away, and he leaped at his chance. He slammed on the brakes, turned off the ignition, grabbed his briefcase, and bolted across the street for the main entrance. He had less than 5 minutes when he hit the button for the twelfth floor.

He ran out of the elevator some many seconds later to stop at the reception desk, breathing hard.

"I'm Mr. Paul Whorton; here is my bid for TFL 41." He placed it smartly in front of the startled receptionist.

She looked at her watch and Paul's heart missed a beat. She looked up and gave him a beaming smile. "Yes sir; just in time. Please sign here."

He thanked her and excused himself. Paul walked back downstairs to inspect the damage to Mr. Bradley's car.

He felt the anger grow inside him as he thought about Raven Eater behind the wheel of the sedan. With a grim jaw and steely look in his eyes, he went up to the conference room, where the hearing was about to start.

The conference room was packed; even so, he was able to pick out Nick, who was surrounded by a barrage of his public relations men. Paul strode right through the clucking throng and approached Nick.

"Try that again, you bastard, and I'll personally tear your head off, you fucking moron."

A few people gasped and stepped back. Nick, however, didn't even blink; he just looked down his nose at Paul.

"What the hell are you talking about? It's time someone locked you up." He waved a disdainful hand at Paul.

"Now excuse me, but I have more important things to attend to." With that, Nick turned and gave instructions to one of his lackeys.

Paul was tempted to have another go, but his dad intervened with a tap on the shoulder.

"Not now, son; I'm sure your time will come. Where have you been? We were worried about you. Any problems?"

"Well, you could say that." He briefly told his dad of the recent events, and agreed to go with him to the station later and file a report, though Paul knew it wasn't likely to help—he hadn't been thinking clearly enough in-the-moment to get the license number of the sedan Raven Eater was driving.

Paul spotted Michelle by the windows. He walked up to her.

"Hi Michelle," he said.

He detected a faint blush in her lovely cheeks before she recovered and said, "Hi Paul. I heard you went on a little trip up to the Stikeen and had a spot of trouble."

"Yes." Paul sighed. "You can bet on who was behind it all, but of course I have no proof."

"Yes, I'm sorry."

Paul rubbed his neck. "Look, I do want to wish you good luck, but I still have to ask. You still have time to join me; it may be our only chance against him and his likes."

Michelle's gaze dropped away, looking out the window.

"I'm sorry, Paul, but we can't compromise our position. Sorry."

"Ah well, had to try again. But look, Michelle: no hard feelings, whichever way it goes, okay?"

Michelle acknowledged his touch of the arm with a return squeeze. Paul's heart missed a beat as he looked into her green eyes. He was relieved: he really wanted their relationship to continue, no matter the pressures that were on them at the moment.

"I'll call, okay?" And with that he turned away and joined everyone at their seats.

***

Michelle sat down as the eleven panelists filed in. An expectant hush fell on the room. Even the media people and their cameras were quiet.

"Ladies and gentlemen, the preliminary hearing for the acquisition of Tree Forest License 41 is now open."

An excited buzz echoed around the room. First, two southern coast forest companies were called upon, and both executives gave sound arguments as to why they should be granted the TFL.

Michelle's silently swore: all she heard was jobs, jobs, unused resources, and so on. No care for the land or the people that lived there.

179

It was West Skeena's turn next. Michelle was handed a brochure on the company and its plan for the license if successful. She glanced through the sleek brochure. One of their promises included a park area. That was a first for a Tree Forest License, even though the land was public in the first place.

Mr. Thomson, a man who introduced himself as the Vice President of Operations, took the stand and began.

"Our company, West Skeena Timber Ltd, has been part of the coast in question for over seventy years. We contribute over one-point-one billion dollars a year into the communities we serve and employ over five thousand people. Our commitment to our employees and their families is without question the best in the industry. With this acquisition, we would provide more secure, high-paying jobs for decades to come."

Michelle groaned softly and sat back. Just more of the same. She creased and folded the brochure in her lap. More of the same in shinier packaging.

"Our recently upgraded operations in Prince Rupert are ideally suited to get the best value from the resource and create four hundred jobs. There are some here who believe that this TFL should be preserved as a wilderness park—"

Michelle sat up indignantly at his tone. If that wasn't a pointed attack on her committee's bid, she didn't know what was.

"…but without road or communications, nobody but the wealthy could reach this remote wilderness. Yes, some areas of it are a natural treasure, and we have set aside ten million dollars for a world-class park covering some pristine forest and river. With new logging roads, the area will become accessible for all, not just the rich who can afford helicopters."

Mr. Thomson gave a smile that encompassed the room and allowed enough of a pause for the media photographers. It was a businessman's smile that didn't reach his eyes. "We aim to create jobs, have a working forest, and access for all. We want all the communities who rely on us to have a long and secure future. In the brochures we have outlined our proposal in detail, and welcome any comments or suggestions you may have."

There was a collective rustle as the room's attention was brought back to the glossy brochures.

"We sincerely hope the committee will award us TFL 41, and we look forward to the stewardship of this valuable resource. Thank you, ladies and gentlemen."

A flutter of applause broke out.

Next it was Michelle's group's turn and she took the stand as their spokesperson. Butterflies cavorted in her stomach. Quite a few eyebrows were raised at a woman taking the stand; it was still very much a man's industry. She thought she saw Nick lick his lips as he watched her walk up, and she tried to tell herself that he was just nervous about his company's presentation.

"Good morning, ladies and gentlemen. I represent the Western Wilderness Committee."

Michelle made eye contact with each of the panelists, making sure she had their complete attention.

"I'm here because, from space, there are only a few manmade objects that can be seen by the naked eye. One of them is the Great Wall of China; another is the Grand Coulee Dam. Here in British Columbia, we also have one. It is located just five hundred miles north of here, around the town of Prince George: a massive clear-cut the size of Kuwait."

She paused to let that sink in.

"This land has yet to be reforested, and there appears to be no plan to do so at the present time. It was supposedly a sustainable forest, which could be cut again in fifty years, but it was cut down in less than twenty. Logging trucks have to do round trips of two hundred miles a day."

Now she moved her glare to her fellow bidders.

"This is clearly a case of an industry that cannot manage its responsibility for the public lands they were entrusted with. And it's only getting worse. Fifty percent of all the trees harvested since Europeans landed here hundreds of years ago have been harvested in just the last fifty years. The world's media are now calling BC the 'Brazil of the North'. But in reality, this is unfair to Brazil: they have cut down only five percent of their forests."

Michelle had tried to keep any overt emotion from her voice, but at this point she couldn't help the awe that crept in.

"The Stikeen Valley, also known as TFL 41, is the largest temperate rainforest left in the world. It is an invaluable habitat for bears, wolves, cougars, deer, moose, and many other smaller species. In addition, all five species of salmon and the wonderful rainbow trout enter the river and its tributaries."

Michelle dropped a fist into her palm.

"This is our very last chance as wardens of this planet to save an ecologically-complete watershed for generations to follow. It would be a crime not to leave one out of hundreds of valleys to nature."

Before she lost the crowd, she concluded, "So that we don't end up with another object viewable from space by the naked eye, we propose a World Heritage Site of historic proportions. I hope that everyone here today has the vision—and guts—to take the bold step in preserving BC's last watershed for residents, tourists, and our children's children. Thank you, ladies and gentlemen."

Even louder applause enveloped the room. Michelle saw Nick glare at his Vice President of Operations, his face a deep shade of red. On the uplifting note of her speech, the hearing was adjourned for lunch.

* * *

Paul returned to a packed hearing room. The media had been busy interviewing the main contenders so far. Nick made a passionate plea, which would be no doubt heard on the evening news. *They say money talks*, Paul thought. *Guess I'll just have to make my voice heard on my own.*

Paul's mouth was dry, and the palms of his hands were sweaty as he walked up to the stand. He stood there looking at the faces, video cams, and cameras. He held eye contact with Nick, and gave him a smile as he made his address.

"Hi folks. My name is Paul Whorton, and I am a logger by birth and nature. What the Western Wilderness Committee said about TFL 41 is true and more. I have been there in person, and even so I can hardly describe it. There is a grove of mighty trees tucked away up a creek named after the color of its emerald waters. Some of them are over a thousand years old, and stand nearly as tall as this building, if you can believe it."

Paul noticed that he was getting some funny looks, and one of the panelists was looking back and forth between him and Michelle.

"But you're a logger, I hear you say. Yes, I am, and I want permission from you all to go in and do some logging in TFL 41. However, I propose to do it differently: I won't be building any logging roads."

Paul paused while his words produced a smattering of polite murmurs.

"My method of selective logging will have a minimal impact on the terrain by using a specialized blimp to retrieve those trees we have selected for optimized cutting. The sawmill I have proposed is a floating one, tied up at the head of the inlet. Workers will be mostly bi-monthly, and we will employ as many of the native Stikeen people as possible from the nearby village; who, by the way, have given us their full support on our bid for work on their land."

A few gazes dropped from his at this gentle reprimand. Paul continued past it.

"The most important aspect of my proposal is that, by selective cutting, I can sustain my cut forever. I believe the only way to save the valley is to use it wisely. With it, we can have the first sustainable forest in the history of British Columbia."

His audience still seemed to be a mix of interested and dubious looks.

"There are a few facts the others have neglected to tell you. If logged traditionally, the best estimates so far are that over two hundred miles of logging roads and dozens of bridges would have to be built. Creating such roads on the valley's steep sides would cause dozens of landslides."

"In addition, without government money to subsidize a full operating mill, it would be economically unviable. There's a good chance the logs will just be shipped directly to Japan without first turning them into lumber, which will really only lose jobs."

More confident now, Paul plowed ahead. "I plan to cut only fifty thousand meters cubed a year, an amount that can be sustained in that area in perpetuity. In addition, I would like to set aside the whole of Emerald Creek and its watershed as a world-class park."

This got some approving nods.

"My company will personally put up the money for the operation: no assistance is required from the government, or from those foreign investors who are only after the short-term gain."

He gestured to the room.

"This province relies heavily on the forestry industry. Some say that forty percent of our economy relies on it. I am a realist, and I can see the need for jobs and taxes generated by the forests. But we can't continue thinking in the short-term."

"We have raped and pillaged this fragile land for over two hundred years, but we have a chance to change that today. I would like to show my sons and daughters trees that can reach the heavens, and a land that supports a range of wildlife, from fish to packs of free-roaming wolves."

Paul took one last survey of the room. He had everyone's undivided attention.

"That, ladies and gentlemen, is my vision for a working forest of tomorrow. I hope this mill I propose will open up a new era in BC's forestry industry. Thank you for your attention."

Applause flooded the room, and cameras clicked away. His was a new vision, one that seemed to meet the interests of all.

The panelist members reminded everyone that the written proposals would be studied in detail, and their decision would be released within a month's time.

It was early yet, but Paul and his parents stepped out for a well-deserved drink. Paul downed three Bacardi and Cokes, letting the stress of the day flow out of him. Michelle's committee was there as well, and she came over and gave him her congratulations.

"Thank you, Michelle; and to you as well," he said. "Hey, may I call you after my parents have left town? Maybe we can go for supper, eh?"

"Okay, I would like that."

The four weeks dragged by slowly. But in that time, Paul was interviewed twice by the press and even a TV station. He published letters reiterating his proposal. Even some environmentalists started to take notice, and he began to feel more confident.

***

The committee had done all its homework, and the time for the final voting was at hand. Nick had been receiving updates from both of his committee members, and their news wasn't as promising as he'd expected: Mr.-Wholesome-Idealist, Paul fucking Whorton, had charmed the panelists with his pussyfooting around each of the camps in an attempt to make everybody happy. Most of the committee now debated between Nick's company and Paul's roughshod little start-up.

That wouldn't do. But Nick hadn't made it this far without learning the value of intelligence. Sometimes, all that was left was to let those who stood in your way know that you knew. Nick was confident that some of the panelists who were currently on the fence would soon see that choosing his company was simply the best choice for them, economically as well as personally.

The expected phone call came in July. The results, however, were not what he expected.

"What do you mean, we lost it?" Nick pounded his fist on the desk, wishing his VP of Operations were here in front of him instead of on the other end of the phone line. "I spent millions, and they gave it to some bastard with a hair-brained scheme. Clear your office; you're fired," he shouted.

He slammed the phone down, only to yank it back up again.

"Send the fucking pictures, now."

He barely held his composure. For him it was too little, too late.

Chapter Eight
The Mill

At Paul's parents' place, they celebrated the good news of the bid's acquisition with fresh Dungeness crab, followed by sizzling T-bone steaks done on the barbeque.

After the meal, Paul's dad took him aside to the study.

"Again, congratulations, son. I'm proud of you." For the first time in years, he engulfed Paul in a bear hug. He gruffly let him go and picked something up from his desk.

"Here, Paul. A check for six million dollars to start with."

"What, you haven't sold the mill yet?" Paul joked to hide his embarrassment.

"No: it was all subject to us getting the license. Now the deal is a go, but you should probably wait to cash it until we have the money in the bank from the first transfer—should be in about one week."

Just then, Steve knocked on the door—he had arranged to come by earlier. Paul showed him the check. After his friend got over the shock of seeing all those zeros, he asked, "How soon do you need the tanker?"

"Well, I reckon we may as well fly over to England next week when we have the check cleared; no point hanging around. That way, if we see the right one, we can jump on it." He turned to his father, who was leaning back on the desk. "And Dad, while we're away, can you go over the equipment list and start to hunt around?"

"Thought you might ask." His father heaved himself up, picking up a file folder along with him. It held information on all the auctions coming up in the next few months.

"Well, if you see anything, buy it. We can store everything at the mill until we get the tanker over here."

"I don't see a problem with that. There's a three-week period where we hand over the reins and the rest of the payments are transferred."

The next Friday the first check for the mill went through, and Paul and Steve caught a flight to Heathrow, London. Paul was excited: he had never been to London before. Steve had to drag him away from the sight of two Concordes next to the terminal. They passed through customs with their luggage and picked up a rental.

"Slow down, you mad bastard," Paul said as Steve wove in and out of traffic on the M25, a multi-lane divided highway that ran around London.

"Ah, don't worry. I've spent quite a bit of time here; you'll get used to the speed of the traffic."

"Hell, does everyone drive at eighty miles per hour here? I've never seen so many cars in one place."

Two hours later they arrived at Portsmouth, where the ship's agent was located. They checked into a hotel. Both were beat after the long flight and drive. But before retiring, they both went down to the hotel bar for a taste of the famous English staple of bitter ale.

"Err, it's like cold tea. Call this beer. Give me a cold Labatt Blue anytime," Paul said upon tasting the rather bitter brew for the first time.

"Eh, it's not that bad when you get used to it," Steve said. "In fact, it sort of grows on you."

Paul only had one, since he was very tired, but Steve stayed for "just one more."

The next morning, Steve joined him down for breakfast, looking like something the cat brought in.

As planned, they went down to the docks and met the shipping broker to go over the details of the ship they were interested in. The ship itself was berthed in the next county over, and despite the length of the drive, Paul was excited to see it in person. They drove down the winding lanes and rented a small fishing boat to get to where the tanker was berthed. On the way, they passed big, silent supertankers of another age. Now they lay at anchor, rust streaking their sides and seagull shit all over them.

"There she is. The *BP Endeavor* of London." Steve pointed.

Paul looked over and saw another tanker with rusty sides, just like the others. They climbed the ship's gangway onto the silent monster. The agent showed them the ship's maintenance log, which had been kept up-to-date since she had been decommissioned. Despite the rusty appearance, she seemed in fair condition.

After turning on the ship's emergency generator, they took a tour below. The engine shone in gleaming majesty and still dripped in oil. After another two hours scouring every nook and cranny, Paul and Steve asked for a meeting with the ship's owners.

They looked at a few more, but none were as good as the first tanker. Within two days, Paul signed a check for eight hundred thousand pounds: the tanker was his.

Steve arranged for a one-week overhaul of all systems in the local dry docks, which cost another sixty thousand pounds. Paul's account had already shrunk by one-point-one million dollars Canadian, but it was worth it: the tanker was the backbone of the mill.

During the overhaul, inspections showed only a few minor repairs, and sea trials went well with the newly hired skeleton crew.

They would depart as soon as the overhaul was completed at the beginning of August. Steve had his Chief Engineer's ticket and took on the position in return for a thousand shares in the company.

The captain was a young man about their age, and the second engineer proved to be very capable. Paul paid the biggest fuel bill of his life: forty thousand pounds for what amounted to fifteen thousand tons of diesel oil. The ship was ready.

It was a brilliant morning when the newly-named *Whorton Enterprise* set sail for British Columbia via Cape Horn; due to its size, the ship could not pass through the Panama Canal.

Two lazy weeks passed. The sea seemed endless to Paul. He kept busy writing the bid specifications required for the main mill equipment. At night, Paul and Steve pored over the plans to convert the tanker into a floating sawmill.

But on the twentieth day, they encountered their first problem: fuel contamination.

"You sure the temperatures never changed? Oil pressure remained steady the whole way?" Steve asked the second engineer.

"Yes, Chief: I checked it every hour, and still we had too much sludge going over the fuel evaporator," replied his second. "We must have had a bad load of diesel or something. I recommend we thin it down some more and reduce revs to two-thirds; otherwise we'll wear out the cylinder liners before we reach Chile."

It was a disappointing setback to encounter so early, but Paul figured it was one of the risks of business. He and Steve used the extra time on the ship's computer, where he had moved the mill's plans into a CAD drawing program. With the program's exactness of scale and ease of changing layouts, it was an invaluable tool. By the time they reached the northern approaches to the Horn, the major layouts were complete. Paul was ready for when they hit the shipyard in Victoria, where he had scheduled the work to be carried out.

Two days from the Horn, one of the generators blew. The resulting damage would require a complete rebuild of the crankcase when they reached Victoria. After Steve had inspected the damage and the maintenance logs, he concluded it had happened because of the contaminated fuel. They struggled onwards, the engine now running on only two generators without a back-up.

The southern Atlantic swells increased, and the nine-hundred-foot tanker rose and fell with the power of the sea. Walking up to the bow, Paul could feel the catwalk lift and flex. This was due to the ship actually bending along its length. Steve had assured Paul it was designed to do this, or the stress would become too much for the ship to take. It still made his stomach churn, although he had lost his seasickness weeks ago.

Paul consulted with the captain on the proposed route around the infamous Cape Horn. The captain had chosen to take an extra two-hundred-mile detour south around the Horn: considering their current fuel issues, he would take no chances near the deadly, rocky coastline; he wanted plenty of room in case of emergencies. Paul and Steve concurred, so they continued well out of sight of land.

The further south they went the colder it became. The sea began to break over the top deck, helped along by winds of up to forty knots. From the wheelhouse high above the main deck, Paul watched as the waves continually washed across the beam of the ship; only now and again could he see the distant forecastle between the crashing waves and spray.

Paul's reverie was broken by the blare of the engine room alarm. He dashed down into the bowels of the ship. Steve was already there, talking to the second engineer, who had acted just in time to shut off the main fuel pumps. He explained that they were overheating, and had thus clogged up.

"Right, switch to tank number four, and pray it isn't contaminated like the others," Steve ordered. "Surely one out of four should be okay." He scanned the myriad dials in the control room and shook his head in frustration.

Steam was put to the fuel oil separators and the new oil was cleaned. During this time, the stationary ship had turned broadside to the large swells, and the movement of the ship was now quite apparent, even in the depths of the engine room.

Steve and his second took oil samples. When the results were satisfactory, Steve pushed the air start. The compressed air kick-started the mighty engine. Paul felt it throb throughout the ship as the engine gathered momentum and they once again began to make headway in the cold, southern seas.

Steve ordered his second to constantly keep an eye on the fuel oil separators and take samples every fifteen minutes. If he spotted anything, then he was to call Steve back down straight away.

On the way back up to the bridge Steve told Paul, "Shit, we're going to have to put into southern Chile, probably Valdivia, and exchange the dirty fuel in tanks one, two, and three. I hope when we send the samples back to Falmouth you can get your money back."

"Steve, how many times in your career have you had so much contaminated fuel?" Paul could hardly think it was common.

"Oh, a few, but not this much. From the samples we took, I think the contaminant is coal dust; it's coagulated in the fuel and turned it all into a viscous mess."

At the look Paul gave him, Steve clapped him on the shoulder.

"But don't worry: the captain radioed ahead to Valdivia and told them we have a potential problem. They have a large tug there standing by in case we lose the engine altogether."

As they swung west across the Horn, the seas worsened and soon a full gale was in progress—it was winter in the southern oceans. The day's work plan was to clean the fuel in tank four, but the movement of the ship impeded the operation, so they could only clean the fuel going to the engine directly. Paul slept fitfully during the night as the seas continued to pound against the hull.

After two days of virtually no forward progress, the winds started to abate. The next day, they were enveloped in fog and drizzle.

Paul was up on the bridge with the second mate when a definite jarring ran up his feet. He looked over to the startled mate.

"What the fuck was that?"

The mate went flying out onto the bridge wing, gazing out into the impenetrable fog before returning to look at the radar for confirmation of position. He looked worried. He called the captain and Steve up to the bridge, but they were already on their way—they had felt the vibrations as well. Paul ordered the engines stopped.

The captain looked at the charts. The depth sounder showed them at five thousand feet, and they were about one hundred and forty miles off the coast.

"Look, I don't care what the instruments say: that sure felt like bottom to me," the captain said.

"It couldn't have been debris or a whale?" Steve asked.

"Bullshit. Let's see that radar again." He peered into the screen. It was all clear for a hundred miles. "Mate, get that standby radar on and tell me what you see."

While the radar was warming up, Paul went onto the flying bridge. The ship slowly drifted through the cold, thick fog, carried by its momentum. Moisture dripped from Paul's cap. He had just started to turn back to the bridge when the fog thinned. Paul couldn't believe his eyes. He ran to tell the captain of the dark shape ahead of them.

He entered just in time to see the captain take one look at the now-functioning backup radar and dash to the engine controls. With a shout, he put them into full reverse and swung the wheel hard to port.

Paul rushed over to the spare radar as he felt the engine start up again. Through it, he could see the jagged outline of the coast, which reared its hungry talons toward the ship not two miles ahead. The general alarm was sounded, and soon ten out of eleven members of the crew were assembled on the bridge. Steve and his second engineer had returned to the engine room.

"Quiet, everyone," the captain ordered. "All life jackets on, and be prepared to go to emergency stations. You"—he pointed to one of the navigators—"get our engineers up here and leave us on bridge control for the engines. How far now, mate?"

"A thousand yards, and still closing."

The ship had slowed with their reverse thrust, the propeller clawing into the churning sea, but not enough yet.

"Four hundred yards."

Everyone peered nervously ahead into the fog. Paul could hear the booming of surf ahead, even through the doors of the bridge. He gripped the stanchion hard, expecting a loud crunch at any moment that would rip the bottom out of the tanker.

It didn't take long. Out of the starboard quarter, the fog turned black and the scream of thousands of seabirds shook the air. The craggy cliff looked close enough to touch, and the depth sounder showed only sixty feet: the ship's draft was fifty feet. Still the ship moved forward, slowly turning to port.

A jar hit the deck. A sickening vibration ran under them, which became worse as the ship tore into the rising bottom. The rocks burst through the steel plates under the bow before continuing into hold number one. The gash widened to ten feet and grew longer as the ship carried on.

"Emergency power, full ahead," the captain shouted. Paul knew he was taking a risk, but they needed to get off the rocks as fast as possible in case they became stuck over them.

The ship vibrated to her every weld at the sudden reversal of torque. The ship shuddered as the rocky reef continued to rip the bowels out of her.

In the end, the ship's two hundred and fifty thousand tons of momentum saved her: the jagged rocks broke off under the pressure of the steel. The ship was free, and they were now in open water. However, they were listing, and the bow was nearly submerged.

Steve and his second had joined them on the bridge. "Paul, come with me," Steve ordered, and they rushed along the catwalk to the bow. Breathless, Steve pointed to the large valve wheels. "Open that one and that one."

They ran back to the engine room and started the pumps. Soon, both pumps were gushing a thousand gallons per minute out of the flooded forward tanks and back into the ocean.

The captain had sent a distress call. However, the nearest port was over seven hundred miles to the north, so they were basically on their own. The tug from Valdivia had been dispatched, but wouldn't reach them for two days.

The pumps made some headway, and by purposefully flooding some of the middle tanks, the ship's trim eased. Luckily, the rocks had only ripped into the front third of the tanker, but cracks had appeared in the decks due to the pressure. They limped on at quarter speed, heading due north toward Chile and hoping the tank walls would keep up.

Paul and Steve talked in the confines of their cabin. They were now sure they had a saboteur on board, but had no indication of who it may be.

The next day they met the tug. A line was attached just in case, but they kept on under their own power.

On the third morning after hitting the reef, they sailed directly into the empty dry dock. Two weeks and two hundred thousand dollars later, they headed north again: this time, minus one second engineer. He had failed to show up on the morning of sailing. Paul kicked himself for not thinking to look into their skeleton crew more carefully before they had left England.

Steve and the third engineer now alternated in six-hour shifts, since Paul hadn't wanted to take the chance of employing an unknown engineer last-minute.

Ten days later, in late September, they arrived in Victoria and headed for the dry dock where all the mill modifications were to be performed.

Paul's dad greeted them at the dock with more bad news. The second payment for his mill had been put on hold, and he hadn't been given any reason why. Paul went with his father to Vancouver to find out what they could. The lawyers for the company buyer told them that the company itself had just been sold: to West Skeena Timber Ltd. Paul feared the worst.

Paul and his dad entered the lion's den unannounced. They brushed past the startled secretary and into Nick Barrett's glass-and-metal office.

"I didn't know you had an appointment," Nick said in false surprise. "But please, be seated." He gestured to a pair of chairs across from him, a smug smile on his face.

Paul ignored the chairs and stalked up to the desk, leaning across it to stare the conniving businessman in the face.

"You now own Canadian Pacific Forest Products. So why the delay in our second payment? That four million was supposed to have been transferred to us by now." Paul said.

Nick looked shocked.

"You mean you haven't received it yet? I authorized it only last week." He laid a hand over his heart. "I'm sure it won't be long and, in the meantime, I will personally look into the matter for you."

"Well, it better be damned quick, or I will see you in court for breach of contract," Paul's dad replied.

"No need for that, I assure you. As I said, I will look into it immediately," Nick said with a placating gesture.

Paul and his dad left, receiving concerned looks for their outburst. Paul seethed. Nick had them by the balls. Even if he did renege and they received a settlement, his newly-started company wouldn't survive any delays.

The next morning, on the ferry back to Victoria, they received a phone call from Matt, the old mill manager.

"Sorry, Mr. Whorton, but we've had a fire at the mill."

"What? Where?"

"In the basement, by the chipper. It must have started in the early hours of the morning. We managed to contain it but…there's been quite a lot of damage. I'd say we've lost a quarter of the mill."

"Anyone hurt, Matt?"

"Everyone is okay, except for smoky eyes and a few scratches."

Paul swore viciously after his father hung up.

"You know who was behind this, don't you?"

"The timing is certainly suspicious. But we don't have proof—yet."

The ferry couldn't reach the dock fast enough. Paul drove his Mustang north along the Island Highway as fast as he dared. As they entered the sawmill gates, they saw a thin tendril of smoke rising. Paul stopped the car just short of the charred remains of the back quarter of the mill.

Paul stepped out of the vehicle just as his father's mill manager jogged up to meet them. "Any idea how it started, Matt?" Paul slammed the car door.

"No, but the fire department is investigating. They don't seem particularly hopeful: the fire was so intense; all they can tell is it started by one of the waste chippers."

The next day the whole crew, including loggers, came to the mill to be split into work groups. They salvaged as much equipment as possible. A camera crew arrived, and the scene of the charred mill was shown on the evening news.

Paul's dad came over to him.

"I received a call from the lawyers. The second payment is now officially on hold, since our agreement was for a mill in good working order. We don't have a leg to stand on, and they have us by the short and curlies."

"Damn," Paul swore, "that bastard is out to stop us for sure. First the tanker and now this? It can't be pure coincidence."

The next few days dealing with the insurance company were nerve-wracking. Insurance needed to make their own investigation of the fire, and only then could they start to get estimates from construction firms to rebuild.

They wouldn't see the next payment from West Skeena until the mill was back in working order, and that would take too long. Paul needed the security of another four million in the meantime: the bills at the shipyard were due, and they had to finish buying the equipment they needed in order to meet the shipyard schedule.

And so, armed with the insurance company statement and the information on their upcoming payment, Paul and his father went to the bank to get a short-term loan. However, the interest would cost them dearly: an extra three million dollars by the time the loan was paid.

With the money from the loan, their floating mill could be completed. Manny came down to Victoria to help supervise the installation of the new machinery.

The ship looked a mess of odd bits of steel and big, gaping holes in the deck where machinery was to be placed. Manny worked the men hard, and now they were always on the lookout for another saboteur. Manny brought in three of his own men from Terrace, and the first pieces of mill machinery were swung into place and lowered onto their supports. Paul was pleased with the progress to date. He could taste the finished mill and envisioned it with logs and lumber on its decks.

Within weeks, the outline of the mill began to take shape. It hardly looked like an old oil tanker now: there was plenty of new equipment, and the top deck boasted a forty-ton revolving crane at the bow. This would lift single or small bundles of logs from land or sea and place them on one of the six-inch parallel chains that formed the storage and feed deck. The chain conveyors led into the usual sequence of debarkers, cutters, and edgers that made up the bulk of the mill. Their hog would run beneath it all on the lower decks, mulching up the bark and any of the waste wood.

They even had a whole log chipper to take care of any rotten logs or sections: in a first growth forest, nearly twenty percent of all trees were rotten inside, and there was no way of telling before it was cut down. But all the wood that went through the hog and the chipper was sold to the pulp mills, such as the one in Prince Rupert, to make pulp for paper and cardboard so that none was wasted.

Paul had arranged for barges to be continuously tied up to the ship so that residual pulp wood could be loaded onto them. Once full, tugs would take them from the ship and another empty one put in its place. The sawdust would go to a particle board plant in Vancouver. Meanwhile, the finished bundles of wood could be stored on land or loaded directly onto a ship by the revolving crane.

Paul had designed the mill to target the lucrative overseas market for custom-cut lumber. Buyers could choose their own logs and then ask for whatever dimensions they needed. Most of the lumber produced would be large pieces clear of knots, especially the beautiful cedar which was used decoratively in upper class houses or handmade furniture. In this way, the maximum value of every log could be extracted for a relatively small production.

With the bulk of the conversions completed, Paul was finally given a chance to breathe. That week, he called Michelle and they arranged a date for Saturday in Vancouver. All week Paul thought of her. He met her at the Salmon House on the Hill, which overlooked the sparkling lights of Vancouver and the ships in the harbor.

Paul ordered Pacific halibut in cream sauce, while Michelle had the stuffed baby Pacific salmon. The white Californian wine accompanied both dishes well, and they relaxed while they caught up on events since they'd last had dinner. Michelle was still working for the Western Wilderness Committee, and Paul broached the subject of the park he had visions of in the Big Fir valley.

Michelle agreed that the plan was something the committee could accept, and Paul couldn't have felt happier. Michelle's foot tickled his from underneath the table, and Paul reciprocated. Soon they were giggling like school kids, although the undertones of physical contact made them both breathless. Paul paid the bill and they arranged to meet at her apartment downtown.

***

Michelle opened the front door for Paul and smiled when she saw the outline of his swelling manhood under his jeans. It had been months since they had last met, and neither of them made a move for a good hour while they drank their coffee.

Michelle turned over the tape she had playing Van Morrison, which seemed to prompt Paul into action.

"Care to dance?" he asked.

Michelle melted into his arms. She felt his hardness grow, and soon they were kissing each other's necks as their groins ground into each other.

Michelle's blouse was the first thing to come off, then her bra. Paul bent down and gently sucked on her hard nipple. Her hand, in the meantime, struggled with his jeans, and she grasped him firmly in her hand.

Paul slid his hand over her skirt and slowly worked his way to her womanness. She felt the warmth of his hand as he slipped his fingers under her sheer panties and groaned deeply. She lifted her leg slightly to allow him further in as her desire increased.

He took the hint and moved them both slowly toward the couch, gently laying her down. Kneeling, he withdrew her panties before caressing her stomach with delicate kisses, ever-so-slowly moving down her stomach.

Michelle moaned and opened her legs for him, allowing him to use his tongue to explore her inner depths.

He pulled away and she grabbed his throbbing member to guide him into her. He sank in deep. Neither of them lasted long; as the tape ended, they were both shook by delicious waves of orgasm. They made love again before falling into a deep and satisfying sleep in each other's arms.

***

Paul and Michelle spent the next day lazing about and talking about their plans for the park. The Wilderness Committee had agreed to donate five hundred thousand dollars to help set the park up as a wilderness habitat, and Michelle was considering taking on the job of Warden of Operations. They needed to go visit the valley to set the boundaries for the park with Chief Wolf Salmon and go over logistics.

The next Monday, both Paul and Michelle took the early morning flight up to Terrace, and then a chartered helicopter to reach the Stikeen Valley. Wolf Salmon greeted them warmly, and Wind Walker gave them a bouquet of wildflowers in appreciation for Paul's and Manny's efforts earlier in the year.

Paul and Michelle met with some of the elders, and Paul suggested that ten of the younger men be sent to the technical college in Terrace to receive some training before the mill was functional later that fall. The people were enthusiastic when Paul passed photographs of the tanker and its progress.

The next day, they went downstream in Wolf Salmon's jet boat to the site chosen to berth the *Whorton Enterprise*. Just feet from shore, the water dropped off to over one hundred and fifty feet deep. Behind it lay a large, flat, wooded area. Once cleared of trees, it would act as a storage yard and maintenance shed. The site was protected from any windstorms that might blow up during the winter. Paul planned to send up a civil engineer to lay out the area.

After breakfast the next day, Paul and Michelle made their way upstream to Emerald Creek in Wolf Salmon's jet boat.

"Oh Paul, just look at those trees: aren't they magnificent? We can have a small lodge at the entrance to the creek so that visitors can come up and take trips up the valley."

They decided to have lunch under the sweeping branches of the Big Fir. It was a simple meal of bread and cheese with a bottle of white wine that Paul had brought up with him for just this occasion.

Paul's hand touched Michelle's. No words were spoken as they slowly reached for each other. They made slow and languid love under the tree and savored the peace of Mother Nature in the raw. Only the soft burble of the creek and the occasional crow could be heard.

After taking a cold but refreshing dip in the creek, they rode another five miles upstream to the junction of a small tributary. Here they made camp, and soon Paul had a warm, glowing fire ready. They explored the area until their appetites called them back to the fire. Michelle prepared shish kebabs of steak, onion, and tomatoes, accompanied by linguine that they boiled over the fire. They ate the delicious meal, burned bits and all, licking their fingers clean afterward.

The fire crackled in the night, and a lone wolf howled further up the valley. Michelle sprawled out on her back; her head tilted up to the sky.

"Paul, do you ever wonder if there is life up there?"

"Yeah, I know what you mean." He sat back and gazed up as well. The stars shone brightly in the inky blackness of the sky.

"I mean out of the billions of billions of stars out there, there must be some planets with life similar to ours. Think of it—there may be a planet with two life forms just like us looking up at the stars and thinking the same thing."

Both remained silent for a while, taking in the splendid heavens and the sounds of the wild. The moon rose over the mountains, and huge, black shadows from the big trees surrounded them. They kissed by the firelight, and soon their clothes were coming off despite the night chill.

Michelle stood naked by the fire, shadows flickering around her perfect curves and dancing over her full thighs and swollen breasts. Paul's rock-hard penis throbbed in the starry light. Both moved in unison until their moans of rapture came together as a wolf howled in the darkness.

They set up their shared sleeping bag in the bottom of the boat and fell asleep to the wash and ripple of the creek.

In the morning, they wolfed down a plate of bacon, eggs, mushrooms, and a steaming cup of black coffee. The jet boat made fast progress up the creek. They surprised a grizzly bear and her cub looking for washed-up salmon down by the water's edge, and Paul pointed out the spot where he and Manny had smashed into the bank and the cut stump of the tree Nick had blocked their passage with.

The valley opened up ahead of them, with the creek meandering through. The towering mountains were topped with snow, each shining in the brilliant sun.

They reached the lake after another hour. The wind only gently rippled its surface, distorting the reflection of the brilliant white glacier at the lake's head, but not obscuring it. Paul took the jet boat to the middle of the lake and cut the engine. The silence was deafening, and their ears took time to adjust to its completeness.

The sun was high in the sky, and they both took their shirts off to let the sun soak in. Eagles and ravens soared in the sky above. So deep was the emerald color of the lake that, if painted, it would have appeared false.

They pulled the boat up to shore, intent on hiking up to the higher alpine meadows in the distance.

Two sweaty hours later they reached the first meadow slightly out of breath. The flowers were a thick carpet of red, green, yellow, and violet, with bees darting eagerly from one flower to another. Paul pointed out some distant white specs on the craggy mountain slopes high above them, and Michelle squealed in delight when she saw them move. The mountain goats stuck to the precarious slopes to avoid the danger of predators like bears and cougars.

"Michelle, with all I am I want to keep this valley as pristine as this." He needed her to understand that.

"We can selectively log some of the smaller valleys, and with the Cyclotron doing the work you wouldn't see where we had logged from the main creek."

Michelle looked up at him with trusting eyes. "It's a small price to pay for the whole valley."

She picked out a small point down on the lake for a weekend cabin for the park's guests. Paul was excited for her. Here in the wild north, they would create one of the most spectacular parks in the world.

They went back to their camp and ate ravenously, gazing into the firelight. They were so in tune with each other and their surroundings; Paul didn't want it to end.

"Michelle, would you consider moving up here, permanently?"

"Of course; as Park Warden I would be up here most of the time in the summer and partly in the winter."

He looked down at their clasped hands. "No, I mean with me."

"Yes, we'll see each other a lot."

Oh, what the hell, he thought. He shifted onto one knee and looked into her emerald green eyes.

"Michelle, you would give me the honor of being my wife?"

Michelle was silent for a while, and Paul didn't breathe until she mouthed the word "Yes."

She pulled his face up to hers and gently kissed him.

The sun rose early the next morning and they made their start. On their way down the creek, they stopped for a small hike to one of the hot springs Wolf Salmon had told them about. The hot water bubbled up from deep within the earth's crust, and the air around them smelled of sulfur and salt. The hot water soaked into their young bodies.

Michelle told Paul how she thought the visitors should be kept to a reasonable number to avoid the area becoming like Yellowstone, where too many people spoiled the wilderness experience. He agreed wholeheartedly and found himself glad it was her working on this project with him.

After the hot pool, they got out the small gold pans that Wolf Salmon had lent them. Michelle once again squealed with delight when she saw the first tiny specks of gold in the small creek they panned.

"Sorry, Michelle: that's mica. But at least we're in the right type of sand."

An hour later they had some real gold flakes: not a fortune by any means, but another memory of the splendid valley and its resources. They both reluctantly headed downstream. At the Big Fir, they made their farewells to the valley for a while.

***

Nick paced up and down the thick carpet in his penthouse suite at West Skeena Timber headquarters. He held a report in his hand, and it didn't look good. Haulage rates for chips had increased over fifty dollars per ton, since the chip trucks and barges had to travel further and further from the distant lumber mills. Now, even some of their main log supply trucks only made one trip per day.

Raven Eater walked in the door and took a seat before Nick.

"Got anyone for the mill yet?" Nick asked.

"Yes, two; but they don't come cheap."

"How much?"

"Fifty thousand. Each."

Nick winced.

"Okay, but they only get paid if I see results fast—be sure to make that perfectly clear."

With that, Raven Eater left. Nick watched from the penthouse window until he saw Raven Eater exit the front doors and become swallowed up in the large metropolis of Vancouver.

For a brief time, he'd thought there was a silver lining to losing the bid for the Tree Forest License: he'd gotten to meet Michelle again. But that hope was short-lived. She was involved with Paul. *Again.* Did that man have to take everything from him? It crept in on his thoughts constantly, like a cancer in his brain.

Nick's eyes narrowed at his own reflection in the window as the light faded outside. Maybe it was time for positive action; he would take something from Paul Whorton. And maybe, just maybe, Michelle could be his again.

***

Manny met Paul at the airport in Victoria and gave him the skinny on the progress of the mill tanker. All had gone well while he had been away, with only one small mishap. A small fire had broken out late one night, but the night watchman had put it out quickly before it had a chance to spread.

They had remained diligent, not knowing what was accidental and what might be the work of a saboteur. Most of the mill machinery was now in place, with only the minor conveyors and decks to be finished.

The official launching of the mill was set for Friday. The whole shipyard turned out to see the odd creation in dry dock. Even Paul had to admit the tanker looked funny with a roof outlined for half its length. At the bow, the big debarkers waited hungrily for their first taste of logs. The Cyclotron hovered overhead.

Paul's mother broke the ceremonial bottle of champagne on the blunt bow and the dock gates opened. The massive tanker was pulled out by tugs, and a number of pleasure craft in the harbor honked their horns as the *Whorton Enterprise* fired up its main engines for the first time.

Soon she was sailing west up the Strait of Juan de Fuca out into the open Pacific, where she would follow the rugged coastline up to Eagle Channel.

Meanwhile, Paul flew up ahead to direct the installation of the huge anchor cables and the clearing of the level land on shore for log storage. Most of the labor came from the Stikeen people, and Paul found them very dedicated. Wolf Salmon was pleased, since his people could now start to earn some decent wages and not be solely dependent on government assistance.

A few portable trailers brought by a tug and barge housed the workforce until the ship arrived. After that, the *Whorton Enterprise* could accommodate its crew in the spacious rooms they had made in its huge hull.

The Cyclotron had also come up from Victoria, and it transported concrete and other supplies to designated spots in the valley where it could be refueled and maintained if required. It proved invaluable in helping to clear the coming mill's storage site, and Paul was glad he had ordered a second one built.

He had been in touch with Michelle, who was also busy arranging the park's headquarters: a small log cabin being built at the junction of the Stikeen and Emerald creeks. It was a modest building which could house up to twelve guests at a time, including an office.

It also had a small landing dock where they would berth the lodge's jet boat for explorations up the river. Another smaller cabin was built up at Emerald Creek for overnight stays.

Michelle had spent the week talking to travel agents about the valley. Travel magazines for the adventurous soon had beautiful articles showcasing the spectacular valley. Booking inquiries had already come in from all parts of the world for next spring.

Despite the communication, Michelle and Paul hadn't seen each other for a couple of weeks, and both eagerly awaited the arrival of the *Whorton Enterprise*.

Michelle left the lodge and came over to celebrate its arrival. There was even a lower mainland TV crew to advertise the event. Paul had been dropped off at the tanker by the Cyclotron just five miles out of the inlet. He now stood on the bridge, incredulous that his dream was just about to become reality after nearly a year of hard work.

Paul felt his nose tingle as the tugs finished their job. Once the ship lay snugly against the wharf, the order for 'finished with engines' was given. The whole crew came out on the bridge wings, and the villagers on shore gave the ship a tremendous welcome to the beat of traditional drums and colorful dancers. The village shaman christened the bow with fresh salmon roe, as was the tradition.

Michelle was the first to rush up the covered stairway that served as the ship's gangplank. She and Paul embraced and received catcalls from the crew when they kissed passionately. Paul's dad gave him a rather gruff hug once Michelle had finished with him.

Paul led Wolf Salmon around the floating mill and answered a dozen questions the man had. The crew quarters on board were rather spacious, as occasionally the millworkers would have to stay for double shifts. They had a full gymnasium, a games room, and a large 15-foot dish installed atop the bridge for satellite TV.

As the afternoon progressed, the villagers made their way back to the village to the sound of the hum of the diesel generators. The running ship lit the land around them, shadowing the logs that lay ready to feed the mill.

Paul took Michelle up in his arms once they reached the privacy of his cabin.

Michelle broke the embrace and looked into Paul's eyes.

"Paul, I think you should sit down." Once he was settled, she answered his inquisitive glance with a smile.

"I know you have a lot going on right now, but I wanted you to know right away: I think you're going to be a father."

Paul sat back, taking it in. There was so much to say. In the end, he boiled it down to, "Wow. That's great, my love." He hugged her a bit less hard this time.

"Shit, it's a lot to think about. It certainly speeds things up a bit, eh? For instance, when do we get married?"

Michelle gave him a sly grin. "Oh, I don't know—how about tomorrow?"

"Come on, you can't be serious."

With that, Michelle pushed Paul toward the bed.

The next day, Michelle went back to her nearly-built headquarters. Paul insisted she take the Cyclotron instead of the jet boat up the gorge.

"Oh, don't fuss so," she said with a smile that told him she didn't mind all that much.

In the morning, the tugs brought in the barges for sawdust and chips, and the mill was ready for its first production.

Chapter Nine
The Big Fir, Part Two

The crew assembled on deck Monday morning. All were eager to start. Each operator was given a small team and work area in case modifications were needed when the logs started to enter the machinery areas. The crew went to their stations, and Paul blew the ship's horn for the first shift.

The crane operator swung the huge boom and lowered the large grapple into a bunk full of logs that lay on the dockside. The forty-ton crane easily lifted the bundle and swung them onto the chain deck.

Paul snapped a couple Polaroids as the first log rolled onto the infeed conveyor. After passing through the debarker, the first log's skin lay open to the sun, the sap shining brightly.

Production started in earnest, and so far, everything was going smoothly, albeit at a slower speed than design. The wood would get hung up at various spots and Paul and Manny sent in the crews to make adjustments. The mill began to fill up with logs and lumber. These logs had already been carefully selected by Japanese buyers, and they looked anxiously at their lumber being produced before their very eyes. They had given Paul an order of up to twenty different cut specifications.

As the first stacks were being sent to storage, ready for an overseas ship to take them to Japan, the first break whistle went off. The crew and operators went to the conference room and highlighted any problem areas they had encountered over coffee and hot buns. Manny took notes for the night shift's modifications, prioritizing them in order of importance.

Paul's dad and Steve went through the list, and that night a team of mechanics, electricians, and programmers went to work to hit each item. After a week of late nights like this, all of the bugs were taken out of the system.

Once that was settled, Paul decided to see how the logging itself was going. Roger, the pilot of the Cyclotron, woke him up just as the light was rising over the mountain tops. They walked across the silent yard to where the luminous Cyclotron hung nose-first from a steel tower.

They climbed the steel stairs up to the access platform. The Cyclotron, not unlike a weather vane, was free to swing in the wind. The circular platform around the top of the tower gave them access to the under-slung, six-man cockpit. They climbed in and Roger pressed a button on the console. All the instruments glowed in the dim light.

"Have to give her a shot of helium," Roger said, gesturing to one of the panel's levers.

"Otherwise, we don't have as much lift in the morning, since the helium is denser when it's cold." With a muffled hiss, the gas tanks under their feet let more helium into the big air bags above them.

"Okay, and we're off." Roger switched on the pivoting engines on either side. Paul felt the Cyclotron take up the strain against its nose tether before Roger released it and they were free.

The Cyclotron glided backward, and Paul checked his harness: he knew what was coming. The nose of the machine rose, and then slowly gained in altitude into the morning sky. The bag around them revolved, which, in conjunction with the main engines, provided forward thrust. Soon, the ship below them looked quite small, and the few people just minute.

"Super view from up here, eh Roger?"

"Yes, the best. This part of the day is my favorite: the air is so still and crisp."

The gorge lay beneath them, and Paul could see the twists and rapids of the river's deep interior. Paul asked Roger a series of technical questions, to which he replied to knowledgeably.

"Can I take her for while?" Paul asked.

"Sure. That pedal is for up and down, this left and right, and this throttle controls the pitch of the blades for speed. Here, you have a go; I'll keep an eye on things."

"Hey, this is great," Paul said as he effortlessly controlled the big machine over the gorge, heading inland. He was heading straight into the early-morning sun, and had to put on his polarized sunglasses to block the direct light.

Beneath them, on the north side of the river, Paul saw the First Nations village, everyone still asleep.

Roger took back the controls and headed up Emerald Creek. As they passed the valley below, Paul easily spotted the Big Fir, reaching up closer to them than the rest. At the head of the valley, they had an unparalleled view of the glacier's bluish ice as it slowly carved its way down the steep mountain. They hovered over impossible rugged peaks which threatened to crack and fall thousands of feet into the still, flat lake below.

"Thanks, Roger, but I suppose now we have to move on to the logging site. Enough sightseeing for a day," Paul said.

Roger made a smooth bank back down the valley. They passed over the new lodge at Emerald Creek, and Paul promised himself to go and see Michelle soon. They hadn't seen each other since opening day, since Michelle already had her first party of tourists to look after.

They headed east along the valley, following the river's course. They had decided to log the upper reaches first, which would give them the longest possible time to re-grow before they had to come back to log again—Paul estimated that would be in another hundred and fifty years.

Roger radioed ahead so that the men on the ground were ready. Roger lowered the Cyclotron into a small clearing. Here, lying on the ground, were about ten large logs which the men had strapped together, ready for hoisting. Roger let the heavy steel hook and cable down, and the men on the ground affixed it to the waiting bundle.

Roger blew a siren, and the men cleared the area while the Cyclotron rose in the air. The machine creaked as it took on the strain of sixty tons of logs. The steel hawser sang as all the slack was suddenly taken up and the logs slowly lifted off the ground. They continued to rise to six hundred feet, and then moved west back down the river. The slight morning's breeze didn't have an effect on their load.

Soon the ship came into view, and Roger asked the mill if they could deliver the load directly to the mill decks, saving the ones in storage for a later date. They lowered the suspended bundle down, and the crane operator deftly unhooked the strap. The logs rolled evenly across the deck.

For the rest of the day, the Cyclotron was used to pick up single logs out of the forest into the loading area, and they made a further six trips back to the mill. Some of the logs they collected went into storage and some straight onto the decks again.

"Well, thanks, Roger; I really enjoyed that."

"Anytime, Paul. I'm sure glad you saw the possibilities of using this baby instead of it just being used as a tourist attraction."

"Well, time will tell, but I think both machines can easily keep up with the mill. Perhaps in any spare time we can do a bit of both: there will be the tourists from the lodge."

The following day, Paul was dropped off on the ground with the six-man logging crew, headed by the foreman, Jake. Paul took up one of the four-foot chainsaws and followed Jake into the woods. Here, they selectively marked certain trees for felling. The resulting opening was large enough for the young trees they would plant to grow. This way, there would be no ugly cleared areas.

"She's all yours, Paul," Jake said after they had discussed what angle to take down the first tree. The idea was for it to fall between the uncut trees unimpeded.

Paul pulled the cord and the chainsaw buzzed to life. He lined up to the spot they had chosen, around four feet above the base, and the saw entered the bark, sending streams of fragments behind him. The chainsaw's note took on a deeper sound as it came under load. Fine, yellow sawdust filled the air behind him.

Paul finished the initial cut. The next one, angled slightly upward, took out a slice like a piece of triangular cheese. The two-hundred-foot balsam shuddered as her base was nearly severed. Dead fir needles coated Paul's back and hair as he walked to the opposite side. Here, he made a thirty-degree cut meant to meet the cut-out wedge on the opposite side. As he neared the center, he felt the tree tremble deep inside to her roots. The towering top swayed a bit more: Paul had less than two inches to cut all the way through the base. He pulled the chainsaw out.

"Timbeeeer," he yelled. He heard the death crack of the last strands that held the tree aloft. Paul ran back, and watched the tree begin to fall away from him. The top whipped back as its main bulk accelerated, the side branches snapping like twigs.

The trunk hit the ground with a tremendous roar. The ground beneath their feet shook, and the air was a haze of dust and needles. Silence settled in, and the four-hundred-year-old tree lay deathly still. It was always amazing to Paul how, in little under a half-hour, a tree that took so long to grow could be felled with a few choice chainsaw cuts.

In just a few short weeks, this tree could be in one of a dozen countries around the world to be turned into housing.

Paul restarted the chainsaw and approached the fallen giant. Like a tight rope walker, he walked the four-foot trunk and began to saw through the branches left after the fall.

After three sweaty hours of work, the tree was as clear as a telegraph pole and ready for the Cyclotron. Some of the lower limbs were also of a good enough size to be used for lumber. He called Roger on the radio to tell him he could take the log to the bundling station anytime.

Two helping hands positioned the trunk and attached it to the Cyclotron's chain. Paul was a few paces away when it happened: the tree started to rise, but then he heard a crack like a rifle, and the trunk crashed back to the ground. The Cyclotron, now suddenly devoid of its load, shot into the air, where Roger fought for control.

One of the ground crew was hit with a branch that snapped in the log's passing and was thrown to the ground. The tree rolled dangerously downslope before coming to rest at a stump on an early-felled tree.

All was silent except for the Cyclotron's motors. Paul rushed over to the fallen logger and was relieved to find him conscious. He was heavily winded and sucked in deep breaths. Luckily, he had been hit in the stomach, and he didn't appear to have any broken bones or serious injury.

"What the fuck happened there?" the logger asked when he got his breath back.

"That's what we're going to find out," Paul said. "Come on, up you get. I'll get Roger to take you back to the mill and let the medic take a look at you."

A couple of his coworkers helped the logger up and over to where Roger was landing the Cyclotron on its under-slung landing assembly.

"Jake, bring all the slings over and let's have a closer look, shall we?" A wire sling with a safety factor of ten-to-one should never snap, especially when new.

After examining the sling in question, Jake pointed to one of the tie wires.

"Paul, look: someone has tampered with this one." The break could clearly be seen: half of the thirty-six metal strands had been pulled to fine points, but the other side was cleanly cut, not stretched.

"Right, Jake: let's check all the others carefully. Load this one on the Cyclotron and take it back to the ship for further examination."

An hour later another sling was found to have been nearly cut in half and Paul raged. This was paramount to murder. He racked his brains to think if any of the crew had looked suspicious, but no one stood out.

When they got back to the mill, Paul got on the ship's address system. "I want everyone onboard in the conference room in five minutes. Shut down the machines and please assemble."

The machines died down one by one, and the men assembled in the conference room, looking to each other for the reason for the meeting.

Paul took a section of the severed cable and addressed the men. "I want you all to take a close look at this." He handed it to the nearest worker to be passed around.

"You will see it has been hacksawed in half. Charlie, here, nearly lost his life when it snapped while carrying a full-size log. That is tantamount to attempted murder. This cable, like all the others, was stored in the yard in the maintenance shop."

Paul paused to let that sink in.

"Not many people have access to this site. We either have an intruder or a saboteur. If anyone thinks they know anything about this incident, even if it seems trivial, please inform me or Steve immediately. From now on, I want everyone to be on guard. Inspect your machines and workstations before working, and if in doubt, double-check."

Paul ran a hand over his face and took a deep breath to calm down.

"The RCMP have been advised of the incident. I will not stand for anyone who risks the safety of this crew. Do I make myself clear?"

The crew looked around at each other before nodding in agreement. When the shift started again, Steve and Manny stayed behind with Paul.

"Damn. We have at least one bastard on board who wants to fuck us up. Any ideas?"

Both replied negatively. All of the crew were new, and as of yet no one had acted suspiciously.

"I bet that bastard Nick Barrett is behind all of this. Once I get proof, he's a dead man," Paul said.

The next week passed. No one trusted any one on the site anymore, and the mood was sullen. However, production went up, and more minor bugs were taken out of the system. The two barges full of chips were shipped north for sale to the pulp mill. It would be the first money the mill had made, and Paul radioed Michelle to tell her the good and bad news.

On Saturday, he went up to visit her. The lodge's last guest had left the day before, and none were due until the following Wednesday. They had all been mightily impressed with the valley and vowed to come again.

The two of them spent a lazy day together, and Paul showed her his Polaroids of the growing pile of high-quality, finished timber that would soon be shipped to Japan at premium prices. He told her about his idea to rent out the other Cyclotron to tourists. Soon they worked out a reasonable rate and a tentative schedule that would fit the mill and the lodge for next spring.

As soon as he returned to the ship, he found a message from Roger, the pilot, to see him.

When Roger came in with the next load, Paul flagged him down.

"What's up, Roger?" Paul pitched his voice over the engine of the Cyclotron, which was just powering down.

"Didn't like to say anything over the radio, but we have some log poaching going on in the northeast segment. I saw a Sikorsky helicopter in the distance, and at dusk I went up there to take a look. They've cleared about twenty acres so far in the lower part of Bear Creek."

"How many men, do you figure?"

"I reckon it's gotta be about the same size crew as ours: six or seven. Why?"

Paul crossed his arms. "Well, tomorrow we'll pay them a visit with some of our own men."

They took off the next morning. Steve and Manny joined them, together with three of the logging crew. After about an hour, they came to the northeast section of the TFL. From high above the bare patch of forest looked like an ugly sore. The Sikorsky was nowhere to be seen, but a few figures walked along the ground.

"Right, Roger, take her down. Just let us off at the edge of the clearing," Paul ordered. "And keep your radio on."

They alighted and walked toward the knot of men in the clearing as a group.

"Hey, who's in charge here?" Paul asked.

A big burly Italian spoke up.

"Me. What's it to you?"

"You are trespassing on my TFL. I want all your equipment and gear out of here in one hour. Do you understand?"

"This is not your forest, man. Fuck off, pretty boy." The Italian spat on the ground between Paul's feet.

Paul advanced on him and the Italian took a swing. Paul had anticipated it and swayed to his left. As he did, he drove his fist into the Italian's fat gut, followed by another to the side of his head. The Italian grunted and lowered his head to charge Paul.

At the first swing, the others had raced toward each other. Fists between the two crews flew heavy and fast. Paul could see Steve deftly boxing his opponent, and Manny was like a Wolverine, forcing his opponent to retreat under his barrage of punches and kicks. Jake wasn't doing so well: the giant of a man before him took all of his punches in stride.

Meanwhile, Paul met the Italian head-on and soon was clinched in a bear hug. Huge, hairy arms knotted, and Paul felt the breath drawn out of him. He pummeled the Italian in the face as hard as he could, but the pincers grew tighter and tighter. He felt the blood drain from his face, and his ribs groaned from the onslaught.

Paul drove his forehead down square into the Italian's nose. He heard a crack, and twin showers of blood spurted down the man's face. The Italian let go and clutched his nose.

Paul took some deep breaths to recover and kicked the man hard in the groin. The Italian dropped like a tree and lay on the ground, moaning.

Paul looked around and saw Jake, now on the ground and being kicked by the giant. He ran over and jumped on the giant's back, getting his arm around his neck.

The man stopped kicking Jake and tried to shake Paul off. The giant whipped forward, and Paul was catapulted to the ground.

Paul rolled over and felt the breeze of a steel-toe cap miss his face by inches. He rose quickly, took aim at the ugly face, and smashed his right fist into it with all his might.

The guy just smiled and came at him.

Paul took the first blow to his ribs, and felt one crack like a twig. Sharp pain racked him. He hit the giant twice more, but it felt like hitting stone. He retreated while jabbing away at the man's face, which slowly showed signs of his expert blows. The giant stopped and grabbed a chainsaw. Blood dripped from his gashed mouth and he smiled it as he started it.

"Hey man, enough is enough," Paul said as the man advanced in a rage.

Paul bent down and grabbed a solid branch, swinging it at the man's head. The chainsaw changed note as it bit into the wood. The force of it yanked the makeshift weapon from Paul's hands.

Paul backed off. His ankle caught a branch, and he fell backward.

As Paul rolled away, he saw Manny come up behind the giant unnoticed. He had somehow found a chain, which he swung around his head and let fly. It hit the giant's head with a muffled crack.

The giant dropped the saw, staggered, and fell to the ground. Blood oozed out of his ear. He started to rise, and Paul saw his chance: he kicked the man hard in the stomach. The giant fell and didn't rise again.

The other men stopped fighting when they saw two of their best men down and backed off. Everyone heard the Sikorsky approach. The helicopter landed in a maelstrom of dust and debris. Paul and Manny dragged the giant over to the craft—none too gently.

"Get. Out," Paul said through gritted teeth. "Now. Or more blood will be spilled today."

They glowered at Paul, but all the fight had left them and they did as they were told. The helicopter rose and Paul and his men all covered their eyes from the dust.

"Well done, guys," Steve said tiredly. "Don't reckon they'll be back for a while. Now come on: let's clean up this mess." They all moved rather slowly, still feeling the cuts, bruises, and, in Paul and Jake's case, broken bones.

By late afternoon, they had gathered two bundles of logs for the mill, and Paul called it a day. They all piled into the Cyclotron for the trip home.

All had gone well at the mill while they were gone, although at dinner they noticed that two of the crew weren't to be found. The last anyone had remembered seeing them was that morning, when Paul and the others were off the ship.

They searched, and only found that one of the jet boats had disappeared. Paul called the Terrace RCMP to tell them about the log poaching and the stolen jet boat.

Two days later, the RCMP radioed them from Kitimat to say they had found the boat abandoned, but no men could be found.

The storage yard was now nearly full of stacked lumber, and Paul hoped the transport ship wouldn't be late. It was on a regular route from Japan, and went to the pulp mill in Prince Rupert for a load of paper every time it came across. Paul had arranged for it to come to the mill to pick up the first big load of lumber.

Paul's customers were delighted with the quality, and they promptly gave Paul another large order to be completed by next month. Paul was pleased, and now after two months of operations, felt sure the mill would be a success.

***

Raven Eater peered through the evening gloom. He crept closer to shore, clutching the sports bag tightly to him. It was near the end of the day shift on Paul Whorton's floating mill.

After waiting a half hour in the cold, he saw his chance: the deck was clear. He dashed up the gangplank. Sweating heavily, he opened the basement stairwell door. The dull glow of lights led him down into the bowels of the ship.

Raven Eater walked between the moving chain and belt conveyors, then passed the rumbling chipper. Whole chunks of wood cut from the trim saws and head rig rippled along the vibrating conveyor, feeding the revolving knives of the chipper.

Raven Eater crept into the gloom on the starboard side. He set down the sports bag and opened it. The explosive was a dull gray putty at the bottom of the bag. It felt a bit warm to the touch.

He took out one of the detonators he had in his pocket, then froze when he heard something above the noise of the machinery.

Slowly, he slipped the detonator into the explosives bag and pressed closer to the shadows behind one of the chip screens. Here, he grabbed a pick-a-roon, a tool used to take trapped pieces of wood out of the chipper. It was not unlike a climber's axe, but was thicker at the point. It would serve his purposes just fine.

***

On his closing rounds, Manny circled the chipper and put his hand on the bearing to check for overdue heat. The last one had been faulty, and they had changed it just yesterday. The new one seemed to be performing fine, so he gave it a pat and moved on.

As Manny was leaving, he caught a bit of movement out of the corner of his eye. Maybe a piece of wood had come out of the conveyor. Sure enough, he saw a bit of wood on the floor and bent down to pick it up. A shadow moved behind him.

Startled, he turned. A man—Raven Eater, he realized belatedly—stood behind him, swinging a pick-a-roon high in an overhand arc.

Manny threw up his hands to defend himself, but he was too late. All he managed to do was knock a sports bag off of Raven Eater's arm and onto the vibrating conveyor. The pick-a-roon came down unimpeded, and the point hit him squarely in his upper shoulder blade. Manny opened his mouth to scream, but the pain was too intense: no sound came.

He crumpled to his knees. He grunted as Raven Eater shook him, trying to get the curved point out for another blow, but it was stuck in too deeply. Manny desperately tried to reach back and grab the handle, but a wave of dizziness spread over him and he couldn't get a grip.

Raven Eater pulled back on the pick-a-roon and dragged Manny toward the conveyor. Manny strained against the movement and felt a shoulder muscle rip. Despite his efforts, he was being dragged along. Raven Eater pushed Manny against the side of the vibrating conveyor.

Manny tried to weakly kick out at him, but Raven Eater caught his leg and hoisted it over the side. Manny moaned in pain as the pick-a-roon was finally yanked free from the motion. He tried to rise, but a fist slammed into his face and he fell back heavily onto the conveyor.

He was jarred up and down among the pieces of wood destined to be chipped up. Manny grabbed the sides of the conveyor to slow his progress toward the approaching chipper.

The pick-a-roon came down heavily on his fingers, and blood gushed from the one it hit. He fell back. Raven Eater followed him closely as he got nearer to the chipper's hungry mouth.

A steel bar passed over the conveyor near the mouth of the chipper. Manny desperately grabbed it with bleeding hands. He felt the pull of the conveyor beneath him and the pieces that passed him as he clung to the bar. The noise of the chipper behind him was deafening, and it slashed only inches from his feet. He started to heave himself away from the chipper's gaping mouth.

Raven Eater swung again and broke Manny's thumb in half.

Manny gasped in pain. He looked up pleadingly to Raven Eater's face, but only saw him raise his weapon again with an evil grin. He didn't seem to notice the sports bag coming down the line toward them.

Manny's shoulder felt like it was being ripped apart, and he screamed as the pick-a-roon dug into his remaining fingers. He was going to fall.

Raven Eater raised the pick-a-roon again and Manny said a prayer. The only regret that flashed through his mind was that he wouldn't get to see his son's first upcoming birthday.

The sports bag passed under Raven Eater's arm at the same time he severed Manny's grip on the steel bar. Manny made a grab for it. His three remaining good fingers hooked onto the shoulder strap just as he felt himself being sucked backward. He drew the bag toward him and for the first time saw fear touch the face of Raven Eater.

Manny didn't feel his feet, calves, knees, or thighs go; it was all too fast. But when the knives hit his pelvic bone, he felt a sharp, searing pain and unbelievable pressure as the knives sliced up large bone and guts.

Raven Eater leaned dangerously over the vibrating conveyor and tried to wrestle the bag from Manny. Seeing Raven Eater's desperation, Manny held the bag securely under his chest as the chipper continued to carve up his insides.

Raven Eater let go of the bag and ran behind the nearby chip screen as Manny slowly disappeared into the chipper.

***

Paul felt the thud of the explosion high up in the control room and quickly ran for the door. He nearly bumped into Steve, and they exchanged alarmed looks.

"I think it came from the basement; let's go." Paul rushed down the stairwell, Steve following close behind. Paul's feet hardly touched the basement steps as he frantically raced down them. *Please, not another saboteur,* he thought.

He reached the steel deck and looked down the length of the basement, which was shrouded in smoke. Both men ran toward the back and saw what remained of the chipper. The motor still sparked: the twisted, two-foot-thick disc had taken nearly all of the impact of the explosive.

The plates beneath were slightly buckled, but had held. The explosion had hurled back pieces of wood, and the body on the floor was unrecognizable as a human being. The wood had splintered and ripped his upper body into a bloody mess; only his legs remained unscathed.

Paul lunged for the motor control center and pulled the off switch so that the chipper wound down and stopped sparking.

Paul sounded the general alarm, and slowly all machines stopped; only the hum of the generators could be heard. They left the body where it lay and climbed back to the muster point to do a roll call.

"Okay, where is Manny. Anyone seen him?" Silence followed as all the men looked around. "Right, spread out and find him," Paul ordered, and two dozen men each took a different direction. The only relief Paul felt was that the body by the chipper belonged to a young native man—not a match for Manny.

After two hours, Paul called off the search—the RCMP helicopter had arrived from Terrace. Paul showed the officer the body and explained it wasn't one of his crew, although they did have a man missing. The officer had the body sealed in a body bag to be ready for flying out in the morning.

The officer looked at the damaged chipper and noted that the signs pointed to a plastic explosive. They also found some splattered blood on the chipper disc.

"You say Mr. Raposa left about six o' clock, headed for the basement to inspect the chipper?"

"Yes. Around half an hour later we heard the thud of an explosion, but there's been no sign of Manny anywhere, even after an extensive search." Paul felt a growing sense of unease as the possible scenario began to form in his mind.

"Where do the chips go after the chipper, Mr. Whorton?"

"They're carried by conveyor to the chip barge outside."

"How long did the conveyor run after the explosion?"

"Ur, about five minutes? Turning off the chipper turns off all the conveyors in the basement."

"I think we had better go and look at the chip barge," the officer said. He followed Paul outside.

Paul asked a crew member to turn on the outside floodlights and shine them on the top of the chip pile. Paul, Steve, and the officer climbed up the steep pile of chips and started to sift through them.

Steve was the first to find chips that were pinkish in color; others with definite signs of blood soon followed. Within a few moments, some cloth and bone fragments were found. Paul nearly lost his stomach when he realized what had happened to Manny.

The officer took plenty of samples to send to a lab in Vancouver as forensic evidence. He also accepted Paul's offer of accommodation for the night. Paul showed him and the pilot to their quarters. Paul returned to his own cabin with a heavy heart.

The next day, Paul halted operations. Somehow, he found the strength to tell the crew about the explosion and what had likely happened to Manny. The mood was somber as the men pitched in to dismantle the ruined chipper.

Paul radioed his dad so that he could find a replacement chipper. Paul was glad his father was able to look after the logistics; he didn't think he could handle it right now. Steve had gone with him for the hardest conversation of his life: telling Manny's wife their suspicions with him missing and remains found.

Five days later, Paul received confirmation that the body found was Daniel Raven Eater, and the bones and remains on the chips were Manny's. After everything they had gone through with Raven Eater, Paul couldn't mourn the man, and the look on Wolf Salmon's face when he passed on the news told him the chief felt the same. But now he faced the onerous task of confirming with Manny's wife that he was dead. This time, he went alone.

Before the first shift started, Paul addressed the crew.

"Hello, everyone. I…I am sorry to say that our fears have been confirmed: Manny Raposa is dead, in the same incident which caused the chipper explosion."

He took a deep breath. "Don't let the bastards who did this to break us. We all know that's what they want. Before you know it, this valley would be stripped for chips and precious little lumber. We have one chance to prove to the world there is a better way."

Paul broke off and cleared his throat of the tears that threatened to choke him.

"He would have wanted this place to buzz, not be stifled like a morgue. So, if you really want to make him smile, then go out there and make those logs into the best lumber you can. As Manny would have said, 'Move your asses and let's cut wood.' Thank you."

That first shift went smoothly, and two weeks later Paul went to the inquiry in Terrace, where it was officially declared an attempted sabotage and the murder of Manny Raposa by Daniel Raven Eater, who was wanted for assault and kidnapping. Raven Eater had died at the scene when the explosion went off, and the case was closed; no links could be found to other parties. Paul felt frustrated that there wasn't anything found to implicate West Skeena Timber and Nick Barrett.

***

Nick brooded in his office. All his plans so far had been thwarted, and now he had lost his good fix-it man, Raven Eater. Worse, the police had been asking probing questions about his death, which, of course, he claimed to have no knowledge of.

Pulp prices were down, operating costs were up, and, to make matters worse, the directors were in near-open rebellion after his failure to obtain the Tree Forest License and all the chips it contained for his pulp mills. The loss angered him greatly. He wished he could get back at Paul, the man who had taken so much from him. Paul had ruined his operation, but he couldn't manage to do the same to Paul, not even enough to take the license over.

His loins still tingled when he thought of Michelle, and the thought of her and Paul together in what should have been his valley obsessed him until it absorbed most of his waking thoughts. Lately he had been drinking more and more at night, along with his sleeping tablets: he could hardly sleep without getting drugged up.

He slammed his fist down hard on the table. No. He wasn't going to let this consume him. He collected his briefcase and decided to go hunting. That would distract him. It was goat season, and last year he had failed to get a set of trophy horns from the hills north of Emerald Lake. This year, he promised himself, they would be his.

***

Michelle checked the jet boat and was satisfied. She was going up to the overnight Emerald Lake cabin to tidy things up a bit and take a list of stock they would need before winter set in. Paul had forbidden her to use the jet boat in her present condition, but she ignored him. She was only three months pregnant, and besides: it was tremendous fun.

She tapped her slightly swollen belly and smiled. She had proved to be a very able pilot, and had done the trip so many times she knew the creek like the back of her hand. Even so, maybe this should be the last time for now.

***

"Swing over to the floating mill at the head of the inlet; there's something I have to see," Nick ordered his pilot. He'd hired a new helicopter pilot since last year, one who was better at taking orders. The man dutifully altered course for the mill.

Nick quickly assessed the operation. He couldn't help but admire the compactness of the set-up, and what a seemingly smooth operation they had achieved so far despite his attempts at disruption.

"Go: I've seen enough."

The pilot swung east up the gorge. The helicopter rose higher and higher until it just skimmed over the tops of the mountain range and entered the watershed of Emerald Creek. It was only ten in the morning, and they saw no activity below.

The helicopter landed in a field by the park's overnight cabin on Emerald Lake. Nick was curious, so he opened the unlocked door and walked in. The pleasant musk of new cedar logs filled the room, and all was neat and tidy. Sleeping bags lay on the cots, and the fireplace already had fresh logs ready to go.

How thoughtful of them to provide such ready-made facilities, he thought. He vowed to spend the night there if it still proved to be empty later in the day.

They took off and followed a large cleft at the valley's head to the bottom of the ice fields. Nick saw a quite a few mountain goats, but none with a set of horns like he was after.

Half an hour later he spotted one. He ordered the pilot to land clear above it, near the toe of the glacier. Here, he could cross a small spur and look down on the meadow where the goat and his harem peacefully grazed.

"When I radio you, you come back and pick me up; but keep out of sight in the meanwhile, just in case someone comes up the lake with a group of fucking tourists or something. I should be about two hours if all goes well, so don't drop off to sleep, okay?"

"Yes sir," he replied. The pilot, Curtis, had been on a few of these trips before, and was paid well enough to keep his mouth shut. Unlike Nick's last pilot, Curtis didn't second-guess him with a hundred and one questions.

Nick scrambled over the toe of the glacier and buttoned up his jacket against the cold air that wafted down from the millions of tons of ice above.

An hour later he reached the top of the spur and looked down on the meadow below. There it was, and what a beauty. He crept forward for a better shooting angle.

At two hundred yards away, he stopped and regained his breath. He raised the 303-hunting rifle and looked down the scope, eyeing up the ram. It raised its head now and again to check its harem before resuming to feed. It had lived as king on these slopes for over twenty years, and it was a magnificent specimen: no other ram was able to challenge it in the mating season when the clash of horns echoed in the valley.

Nick lowered the rifle from its head and went for a heart shot. He adjusted slightly for the downward angle and pressed the trigger.

The hammer blow of the bullet's impact bowled the ram over. Nick had missed the heart, and it staggered to its feet and ran. At each step, its big heart pumped bright arterial blood in a spreading stain down its side. It slowed down, and when its heart finally burst it fell, stone dead.

"Yahoo!" Nick fired off some more shots at the fleeing ewes and kids. One of his shots hit a small kid in the lower leg. It bleated as it continued, crippled on three legs. It managed to reach the safety of a rock cliff and ran around a boulder to lie down in shock and bleed to death.

Nick ran down the slope as fast as he could and stopped, panting, by the side of the ram. It was a beauty all right, and he gave a cat-like smile at his achievement. He took out his hunting knife and, after admiring the gaping wound, expertly began to skin his trophy.

Half an hour later the skin, complete with legs and head, lay stretched out on the grass. The grotesque bloody body of the ram lay on its side. Already it had attracted dozens of flies, which sucked up the blood greedily. Nick wiped the back of his hand across his forehead, leaving a bloody streak behind.

Nick flicked on his radio and called up Curtis. Soon, he saw the helicopter lift over the spur and come to land in the meadow beside him. He ordered Curtis to help him with the day's prize.

***

Michelle set off in the early morning. The day was bright and new life stirred in the air. It felt good. She took her time up the creek and took some photos to use in the updated brochure they were planning. She snapped a great shot of a black bear that had run up a sandbar when it saw the jet boat come into view.

She took yet another shot of the grove and the Big Fir. She never tired of staring at the grandeur of the grove. Its massive inhabitants were like the spires of an ancient and regal castle.

At midday, she entered the lake. The wind was picking up, and the 'V' of the jet boat's wake was soon lost among the chop.

Michelle heard a couple gunshots echo down from the mountains. *Who could be up here?* No one was allowed to hunt on park grounds. Or was it noise from the loggers? Perhaps they had to scare away a cougar.

After those first couple, she didn't hear any shots repeated. Her concern vanished when she entered the Emerald Lake cabin and noticed some muddy footprints in the entryway.

Damn, she thought. *Thought I had cleaned up last time.* It looked like she was going to be there a little longer than she thought.

***

After the last couple weeks he'd had, Paul needed a day off. He figured he would pack up his fishing gear and go up to the Emerald Lake cabin, maybe surprise Michelle.

He told Steve what he was doing and loaded up the jet boat to make the run up to the wilderness lodge. Late in the afternoon, he passed the Big Fir and made a couple casts in the long gliding run. He landed two beautiful steelhead and thanked his lucky stars for where he lived and worked.

***

Michelle had just finished transporting some books on wildlife for the cabin when she heard the helicopter. She scanned the horizon and saw a tiny speck approaching from the glacier at the head of the lake.

Funny, she thought, *no one called up about visitors.* She waited in front of the cabin as the helicopter neared. It landed in a swelter of swirling air and noise. She clasped her ears against the intrusion. She looked up and took one step back.

"Hello, Michelle, fancy seeing you up here," Nick said as he jumped down from the helicopter while the blades were still slowing down. Michelle looked at his blood-stained forehead and guessed now who had been shooting.

Nick looked around. "Are you really here all on your lonesome?"

Michelle sidestepped the question. "I just had to come up to restock a bit before the next visitors."

The faint gleam of a smile lit Nick's face. "Well then, mind if we bivouac here for the night?"

"Yes, I do, in fact. You really should have called the lodge first for permission." She noticed the bloody skin tied to the rails of the helicopter and felt the first feeling of anger rise.

"Did you shoot that here in the valley? Hunting is not allowed in the park boundaries."

"No, we shot it in the valley just south of here." Nick pointed a thumb back to the helicopter. "I can show you my hunting tag, if you want."

"No, that's okay. You should leave now, anyway."

"Oh, come on, Michelle. We're thirsty and tired. Can I just grab some water from your well, then?"

Michelle couldn't think of good enough reason to refuse his request. She nodded her consent.

"Look, don't even worry about me; I'll just let my pilot know what's going on." He turned back to the helicopter, where his pilot was inspecting the skid rails and goat skin.

223

A little wary, Michelle took a casual step closer to overhear what they were saying.

"Just for a bit, okay?" She heard from Nick. "I think she's nervous with an unfamiliar face around."

"Sure, Mr. Barrett," the pilot said. "I'll be on the same channel. You know her?"

"Yes, she was an…old flame of mine." Michelle didn't like the emphasis Nick put on that. She quickly turned on her heel and walked back into the cabin, clutching her tummy protectively. He'd get his water and then be gone.

"Can I do anything to help, Michelle?"

Michelle jumped. He had followed her inside. "No thanks; I've done everything now. I have just to dust the place and all finished." She turned her back on him sharply to get her point across.

She wasn't worried when she heard the helicopter start up, but spun around when she realized it was taking off.

"Where's he going?" she demanded.

"Oh, I told him to get the tents we set up earlier, since you told me we couldn't stay here. He won't be long."

Michelle wished she had worn a bra as she caught Nick's eyes on her breasts. They had already begun to swell with her pregnancy, and she hadn't gotten the chance to fly out and get maternity ones that wouldn't pinch. Usually out in the wilderness, there wasn't a need.

They pretty well avoided each other in the cabin as Michelle dusted and arranged the books in the library while Nick helped himself to a glass of water.

Michelle started to feel uneasy, and kept flicking her gaze to the window to watch for the helicopter's return.

Nick had finished his water and approached her slowly. "Well, Michelle, how about we finish that date you promised me long ago?" he said huskily.

Michelle backed up. "I don't think so. You know I'm engaged now, right?"

"No—who's the lucky fellow?"

"Paul. I think you know that."

"Ah, mister clever-dick Whorton, no less. We share a lot in this business, he and I. I'm sure he wouldn't mind." He took another step closer.

Michelle backed up until she bumped the edge of the fireplace. She noticed the straining outline of Nick's pants and gulped hard.

Nick followed her gaze and smiled.

"Yes, you know, I really admire you. If you like, I can show you what a real man has in his pants. It'll be really easy for you." He chuckled. "Or hard, as the case may be. Your choice."

"Keep away, Nick. You know Paul would kill you for this?"

"Bullshit. In fact, I think I'll compare notes with him." He lunged forward and blocked her sideways retreat with one arm, roughly pressing his other hand over one of her firm breasts.

Michelle recoiled the other way and grabbed the fireplace poker. "Get back, you bastard, now. I mean it!" she shouted.

But Nick just smiled and advanced more cautiously. Beads of sweat made the blood slide down in red streaks across his forehead. For the first time, Michelle noticed that his fingers were dark red under the nails.

"Oh, it's 'bastard' now, is it?" he said. "I'll have you screaming for more in a minute, you little stuck-up tart." He pounced like a coiled cat.

Michelle swung the poker, and Nick clearly didn't anticipate her speed. It caught him above the eyebrow, and his skin split like a plump pear. He stumbled into a chair.

"You fucking bitch!" He feigned a lunge to the left.

Michelle threw the poker like a javelin. Nick ducked just in time, but it gave her time to run for the door. Nick clutched out blindly and grabbed her T-shirt. She didn't stop, and it ripped in his grasp as she passed him.

Michelle headed out the door full pelt, but Nick quickly followed.

She would have made it to the jet boat if it hadn't been for the marmots. They had made holes all over the place, and her foot rolled into one of them. She fell heavily at the sharp pain in her ankle.

She tasted blood as she rose. She nearly fell over again when she put weight on her injured ankle but fear overcame her pain. She carried on to the jet boat among the trees by the lake.

Nick was behind her at a full run and caught her by her flowing hair, which he tugged viciously as he came to a stop. Michelle screamed in pain and fell backward. It felt like her scalp was coming off.

Nick released her hair and kicked her in the side. Michelle sucked in air deeply as her insides took the brunt. He was on top of her in a flash. Blood from his wound dripped on her. Michelle shuddered and lay still, unwilling to risk hurting her baby more. She would wait for her chance.

Nick mistook her actions. "That's better, you horny thing you," he said with a deep, shuddering breath. He bent down and kissed her hard while his big hands squeezed her nipple where it was exposed from the rip in her shirt.

Michelle bit her lip against the pressure. She shifted slightly and opened her knees apart a little. She felt him move his legs in anticipation.

Her timing was perfect. She jerked up hard and Nick crumpled in agony as her knee slammed into his crotch.

She tried to scramble up, but he still had a grip on her hair. She tugged away hard and felt her scalp tear. All he was left with was a handful of hair and roots. She was up and limping, but free of his grasp.

Nick got up and painfully followed in a crouch.

They had not gone twenty feet when Nick lunged, his shoulder catching her in her lower back in a fierce tackle. Michelle felt something tear deep inside, and she screamed in pain.

This time Nick rolled her over and slapped her hard once, twice, then three times. Her lip burst, and he tore at her T-shirt. He sat astride her, and all she could do was moan softly beneath his weight.

Nick dug his hands harshly into her breasts; his fingernails left deep, red marks. He tore at his zipper and his swollen, throbbing member sprang free. He grabbed one of Michelle's hands and she recoiled as she was forced to grab him.

Nick stopped kneading her breast and roughly forced her jeans and panties down to her ankles. When she tried to rise, he struck her with his fist. His knees forced her legs open, then he roughly probed her vaginal opening. He jabbed three fingers up hard, and she cried in pain at the rough intrusion.

Nick withdrew his now-bloodied fingers and guided his penis into her. Michelle was hardly conscious now, and he drove hard and fast. A sharp rock cut into Michelle's back as his two-hundred-pound weight pounded on top of her.

Nick bent down and took her nipple in his mouth, and she cried out when he bit down hard, pulled back to full consciousness. With a violent lunge, he spurted deep inside her. Nick lay still for a while, then started to grind against her again slowly.

Through misted eyes, Michelle saw the wicked grimace on Nick's face as he despoiled her again. She tried to move out from under him and groaned at the effort. She couldn't move.

***

Paul cut the engine when he heard a distant, female scream. His heart pounded. *Michelle.* In a second, he gunned the engine toward the nearby shore.

The jet boat skidded up the beach before the engine died and he bounded ashore toward the cabin.

Paul ran up the slope. He would have missed them except he heard Michelle groaning. He saw the sole of a boot poking out from a thicket beside the path.

"Michelle, Michelle," he screamed as he raced toward it.

A man bolted upright and pulled up his jeans fast at his voice. A twist of fear and surprise hit Paul as he recognized Nick Barrett.

But only for a moment. His fist hit Nick full in the teeth. Nick bowled over backward and lay still.

"Michelle, can you hear me? It's Paul." Paul bent over the now-curled up Michelle. Michelle opened a bruised eye and whimpered.

Whack! A branch connected solidly with Paul's shoulder, and he fell over sideways. Before he could get up, a boot hit him in the stomach. He gasped for breath. He tried to get up, but another kick kept him down.

He rolled over in time to see the next one coming. He managed to catch it with both hands and yank. Surprised, Nick fell over backward. Before he could get up, Paul was on top of him. He looked into Nick's ugly face and put all his might into the punch.

It hit Nick square on the nose, and he felt it break as it had all those years ago. Nick howled in pain, and Paul ran back to where Michelle lay. He bent over her, but this time kept one eye on Nick where he groaned on the ground nearby.

Nick staggered to his feet and ran toward the boat.

Paul started to rise, but Michelle hung onto him and whimpered softly. He picked her up and she fainted.

Paul half-ran and half-staggered up to the cabin. He laid Michelle down on one of the beds. He spotted her radio and called for help on the emergency channel.

"Hello, this is Curtis Simons, go ahead. Where are you?"

Paul didn't know any Curtis but carried on. "I'm at the tourist cabin at Emerald Lake and have a badly injured woman here."

The radio crackled. "Okay, I know where you are. Where is Mr. Barrett? He was there not long ago."

"How do you know that?" Paul demanded.

"I'm his pilot. I dropped him off there."

"Well, your boss has nearly killed my fiancée, so get your ass down here," Paul snapped. "We need your helicopter to get her to the hospital in Terrace."

There was a shocked pause, then a quick, "Be there in a few minutes. Over and out."

When Paul heard the chopper approach, he wrapped Michelle in a sleeping bag and carried her outside to the helicopter. He was disappointed to see that it was only a small pleasure craft.

"Right, get her to Terrace hospital straight away. Radio, Roger, my Cyclotron pilot, and tell him to meet me at the tourist lodge."

"Hey man, I'm sorry; I had no idea this would happen," Curtis said as he looked down at Michelle, fastening her securely into the only other seat.

"Look, just get going: she's hurt bad and needs help. Can you manage alone?"

"Yes. I'd fit you if we could." At which point, he closed the door and waved Paul away.

Paul ran back. He didn't bother to wipe away the tears in his eyes. He got one last glimpse of Michelle's bruised face through the glass doors.

Paul ran down to the water's edge and noticed Michelle's boat was gone. He jumped into his and roared down the lake at full throttle, the wind smarting his eyes. He knew the river intimately, and had no doubt he could catch Nick before he left the valley.

***

Nick rounded the corner to where the Big Fir spread its mighty boughs. Nick ran the boat onto the shore just in front of the log jam and cut the engine.

Nick spat a globule of blood on the jet boat's floor and picked up an emergency axe from where it was tucked under the seat. He doggedly ran over the grassy slopes toward the massive tree, his rage blinding him. He cursed for not having his rifle with him. Still, his revenge would be complete.

He stopped at the base of the Big Fir and carefully viewed its ten-foot diameter.

"Well, you bastard, if I can't have it neither can you." He started hacking away at the thick bark, intent on exposing the fragile skin beneath. He wouldn't be able to make it through the trunk's massive girth, but if he could cut away even a thin strip of bark all the way around the tree it would wither and die.

A black squirrel ran up the trunk, frightened by the sound. One thousand years of history trembled, and loose fir needles cascaded down. Nick had to stop often to wipe them from his brow.

***

Paul came swooping around the corner and nearly hit the parked jet boat. He turned the wheel hard and at the same time cut the throttles. The boat did a complete circle and came to rest in a welter of spray.

Paul pushed the boat up into the shallows and ran up the log jam toward the figure of Nick, whose back was to the creek. He didn't seem to notice, or care, about Paul's presence.

"Nick!" Paul shouted.

That got his attention. Nick spun from his grisly work at the tree—he had carved almost a two-foot length of bark off it. Tears ran down his cheeks.

"You!" he shouted. Spittle flew from his mouth. "You've taken everything from me. Everything!"

Paul took a step back as Nick came running, swinging the axe. Paul hurled himself sideways, then rolled to crash into the Big Fir. He stumbled and stood.

Nick had spun and was ready for another blow. Paul threw up a protective arm, catching the shaft of the axe. His arm took the full impact of a blow. He dove instinctively into Nick's belly and tried to knock him over.

Nick back stepped quickly, but Paul screamed in rage and barreled forward faster. Their momentum was too much, and both fell heavily to the soft ground. The axe flew from Nick's grasp.

Remembering how hard it was to fight without air, Paul locked the bigger man in a bear hug and squeezed as hard as he could. All his years of hard work went into his knotted arms until the vein popped out in stark relief. He closed his eyes and continued to squeeze.

Nick tried to force Paul's head back, but it wasn't enough. So, with a quick whip lash motion of his head, he hit Paul squarely in the nose. Paul's nose broke cleanly. He relaxed his grip a bit at the sharp pain, but held on.

Nick repeated the action, and Paul felt the cartilage get mashed to a pulp. The pain became unbearable and he let go, involuntarily clutching his bleeding nose.

Nick drove an undercut into Paul's midriff. Paul doubled up, and Nick sent a knee crashing into his face. Paul screamed in pain and lashed out like a wounded animal. Nick ignored him and rained blows down on his head.

Through misted vision, Paul saw a branch from the Big Fir on the ground nearby. He grasped at it blindly.

Another blow from Nick, and he almost lost consciousness. He hung on, and swung the branch hard up at the wild man above him. The blow dazed Nick for a moment: just enough for Paul to get another hit with the branch up and under his chin. Nick slumped over sideways and lay still.

Paul lay on his back for a while, gasping. Blood pumped from his nose every time he breathed and blew out a mist of red.

Eventually, he stumbled to his feet. He looked down at Nick in the fading light that filtered down through the massive branches above them. He was still breathing.

Paul clenched his trembling fists. He stared down at Nick for a time, breathing in and out hard. He raised his knotted hands slowly.

The wind picked up, rustling the great branches of the Big Fir above him. Paul looked up at it, standing stoic sentinel over the grove. His hands slowly lowered, and his shaking eased.

Abruptly, he turned on his heel and strode for his jet boat without looking back.

***

Roger was clearly shaken at the sight of Paul when he stepped into the Cyclotron. "Shit, what happened, Paul?"

"It's a long story. Just boot it to Terrace hospital; Michelle should be there."

Steve was at the hospital when he arrived, and Paul related the earlier events to him. "We'd better get the RCMP and some paramedics out there to pick him up," Paul concluded. "I moved Michelle's boat to the opposite shore, so he'll have a tough time getting away if he regains consciousness before they get there."

"Hell, the bastard deserves what's coming to him," Steve said.

Paul shook his head as Steve went to use the hospital's phone, but stopped when even that hurt. He went to find the doctor.

"How's Michelle?" Paul leaned against the wall. His knees felt rubbery as the adrenaline wore off.

"You look as though you need some attention as well, son. Come with me."

Paul brushed him off. "No, later; how's Michelle?"

"Are you her husband?"

"No, fiancé." Paul shook his head to clear his vision.

The doctor hesitated.

"How is she?" Paul heard his voice crack and didn't care.

"Well, she will recover. But I am afraid we could not save the baby. I presume you knew she was three months pregnant?"

Paul felt his heart wrench for her. "Yes. How is she otherwise? Can I see her now?"

"Okay, follow me. But you can't be long." The doctor grabbed some gauze from a tray as they passed. "Here, you can clean up some of the blood from your face: she's had enough shocks for the day."

Paul painfully wiped away some of the blood from his dried lips and shattered nose with the gauze and followed the doctor.

He entered the room. There lay Michelle, under a stark white cotton sheet and blanket. A tube rose out of her arm to a drip bag. Her face was black and blue, with a deep gash on her lower lip.

"Oh, honey, I'm so sorry. So sorry." He dropped to his knees by her bedside. Tears streamed down his battered face. Belatedly, he felt something tug gently on his hair.

Michelle whispered through her cracked lips, "Paul. Paul, I'm okay. Look at me."

Paul lifted his head at the sound of her voice.

"Paul, are you all right?" she said when she saw his face.

"Yes, just a bit sore, that's all," he lied. His mouth trembled at the sight of her. He stroked her fine, black hair away from her face.

"It's okay, we'll have another. I promise you that." She smiled weakly.

Paul's heart nearly broke. He wanted to hug her so badly it hurt.

"Just…" Michelle's eyes fluttered as the drugs took effect again. "Just promise me…is it safe now?" Her eyes closed.

"Yes, my darling, my love," Paul murmured. "It's over. We're safe now. It's all over."

A nurse stepped up beside him. "Come on, Mr. Whorton; she needs rest, and you need some immediate attention." The nurse shepherded him away.

Paul winced as they worked on his mangled nose. In the blackness behind his shut eyes, he relived the battle with Nick. In his last look at him, he thought he saw one of Nick's eyes open, and hoped that it truly was over.

***

Nick returned to consciousness. He felt battered. Blood had dried around his nose and down his face. He slowly raised himself to his feet and went down to the river to drink.

Not far upstream, a bulky male grizzly rose on his hind legs and sniffed the air. The fresh smell of blood filled its nostrils. It was hungry, preparing for its winter's rest. It was well over a thousand pounds of muscle. Armed with wide, six-inch claws, it was capable of taking down a full-grown moose.

Unaware of this potential threat, Nick glared at the jet boat tied up across the rushing river from him. So close, yet so far; he didn't feel up to attempting its churning waters. Instead, he started to walk upstream, back to the cabin, where he hoped to lie down to recover more. He turned a bend and stopped dead in his tracks. A bear almost twice his size was coming down the sandbank toward him. He slowly walked backward, glancing over his shoulder for an avenue of escape.

The bear, for its part, sniffed again when it spotted Nick's silhouette. It had no fear of men: the valley had been unoccupied for generations. Although its normal habitat was up one of the many very small creeks, the salmon had tempted it to come to the main river. The bear increased its pace, easily catching up to the retreating Nick.

Nick bent down and picked up the large broken branch Paul had hit him with. With enough of a show of force, he could bluff the stupid creature into backing off. He kept retreating until his back was against the Big Fir. He screamed wordlessly at the shaggy monster, waving the branch at it.

But the bear only came faster, close enough for him to see its dark eyes. It curled its lip, and he shuddered when he saw its massive fangs. Its tongue tasted the air.

"Go away!" Nick shouted at the top of his lungs.

The bear stopped, but only for a moment. It circled to his left and Nick faced it. It stopped, and he heard it give a low growl. It paced to his right, inching ever closer to its unmoving target.

Nick screamed as loud as he could, but the bear didn't seem to care; it just stood there, swaying its massive head back and forth.

Nick hardly felt the dampness down his pant legs as his bladder let go. He knew he wouldn't be able to outrun it, but he also knew that grizzlies couldn't climb trees, unlike their smaller cousins.

So, when the bear turned to pace again, he made a break for the log jam. The massive trees in the grove didn't have any branches low enough for him to climb, but the log jam had some smaller nursery trees growing out of it. He scrambled up the nearest small tree, not daring to look back.

He managed to get up about 10 feet when he felt something catch his dangling foot. The bear was on two legs, and had easily reached up to swipe his foot with its clawed front leg.

Nick felt the sharp, burning pain of its claws raking his lower leg. He tried to climb further, but another blow held him fast. A claw had sunk deep into his flesh. He started to lose his grip to the powerful downward pull exerted by the creature below him.

One moment he was clinging to the branch, and the next he was falling. He rolled over, but the bear was on him immediately. He lifted his arm up to defend himself just as the bear bit down. The bones in his forearm cracked like twigs in the massive teeth.

The bear let go, and Nick rolled onto his stomach. The bear bit his back in an excruciating grip and lifted him up. It shook Nick like a rag doll and let him drop.

Nick cried out in fear and pain. The bear backed off a bit, but slowly circled him. Blood and saliva dripped from its mouth. Nick started to cry, mumbling incoherently. He rose and tried to run, but the bear was faster. It swiped him across his side and he was flung five feet across the sand, now stunned.

He lay still, the breath knocked out of him. He thought of the old tales that said if you pretended to be dead, a bear may leave you alone. So, he rested his head on the sand and held his breath as the heavy thump of its approaching footpads bore down on him.

The bear lowered its head close to Nick's face and opened its huge jaws, easily wide enough to fit Nick's head. Nick screamed as the bear bit down hard. He heard his own skull crack like a nut under the immense pressure.

The bear shifted its grip, and the last thing Nick Barrett saw was its mouth closing over his face.

Once the man lay still, the grizzly picked up its prize and walked back upstream to find a quiet place to eat. It passed the Big Fir, its wide, spreading branches wavering in the wind as it stood sentinel over the valley, as it ever had.